The Ring of Carnac

Brian G. Michaud

This is a work of fiction. All of the characters, organizations, and events
portrayed in this novel are products of the author's imagination.

Cover art by Clare Letendre.

The Ring of Carnac

© 2016 by Brian G. Michaud

ISBN: 1502986205
ISBN 13: 9781502986207

For my daughter.

My favorite little adventurer.

Acknowledgments

I owe the completion of this second book in *The Tales of Gaspar* series to all those who supported me through the release of *The Road to Nyn*. Though the first book took twenty years to bring to completion, *The Ring of Carnac* rolled off the pen (or keyboard) in less than a year.

Thank you to my wife, Kim, for your loving support and patience. I am lucky and proud to be your husband! Thank you to my mother, Doris, and my mother-in-law, Roberta, for being the initial proofreaders. I owe my gratitude to the beta readers, who were not afraid to tell me what parts needed fixing, tweaking, or all-out deleting. And, not least of all, thank you to the fans, who have made this journey of becoming a writer an exciting and enjoyable voyage.

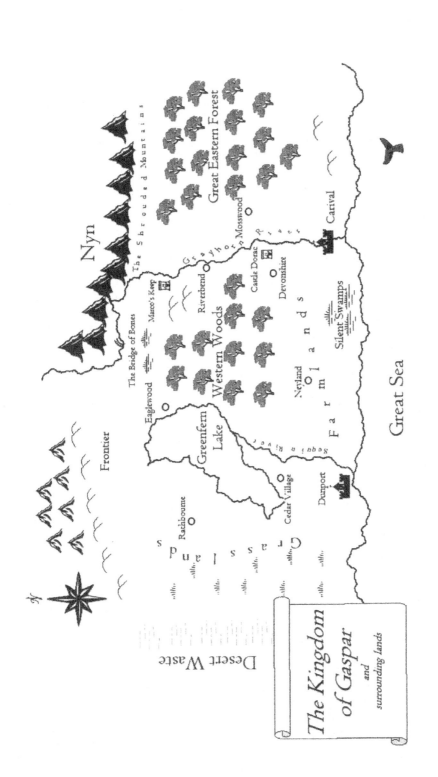

Chapter 1

Aplayful wind flew up the length of the Grayhorn River. It skimmed over the churning water that flowed swiftly past rocky shores and vast forests. The wind had encountered many travelers on its northward journey along the river's banks, but they were becoming fewer and farther between.

Fewer people. More danger, mused the wind.

A large castle came into view. The wind picked up speed and darted toward it. The fortress was unadorned except for two large flags that fluttered above its highest tower. The gray stone walls stood resolute as the wind buffeted against them.

A place of safety, thought the wind.

The wind continued on its way, slightly weakened from its battle with the stones and mortar. Not far to the north, the smells of decay and standing water told of the existence of a vast swamp. The wind headed for this new curiosity and danced among the ferns and quagmires until it came upon two unlikely companions. One was of the fairy folk, and the other was a young boy who seemed vaguely familiar...

***

"You've got to be kidding me!" Kay exclaimed while the murky waters of the Jirambe Swamp licked at his waist.

"Nope, not kidding," Felix retorted with a shrug of his shoulders and a flutter of his tiny wings. "His Wizardness says that he wants you back right away and to forget about the root."

Alamin had sent Kay to the Jirambe Swamp to search for a wildfire root. Why the wizard needed that specific root and what he was going to do with it, he of course never mentioned.

Kay pulled a leech off his arm and grunted with a mix of pain and frustration. "Easy for you to say. If I had wings like yours, I could be back in no time." Kay was sometimes jealous of his small friend's ability to fly his way out of sticky situations. Felix was a sprite and, although less than six inches tall, had an enormous appetite for pointing out humans' deficiencies.

Felix smirked. "If you had a *brain* like mine, you wouldn't be out here in the first place."

Kay shook his head and sighed. The past year had been the most grueling of his young life. He'd been bouncing back and forth between his magical studies with Alamin and his training as a squire with Lord Marco VI. When he wasn't being pummeled with a sword, his brain was swimming with the words to various incantations.

Every day was an adventure living on the frontiers of Gaspar. Marco's Keep was the most remote of all the kingdom's castles. Patrols went out daily to the nearby villages to deter attacks from bandits and goblins. Kay had seen his share of fighting in the last couple of seasons, and there was no promise of it stopping anytime soon.

A day of foraging for plants was a welcome respite until he learned that the root Alamin needed was only found growing in three feet of stagnant water. And now, just when he was in the heart of the swamp, Alamin wanted him back.

"Did he say what for?" Kay asked.

"Does he ever?" Felix answered with a question of his own.

Kay slapped a mosquito that had been feasting on the back of his hand. He brushed away the remains of the bug and watched a tiny welt form on his skin. It joined the dozens of other insect bites that he had received since the beginning of the day. Though he had searched diligently, Kay hadn't found any signs of a wildfire root and, at that moment, didn't care if he ever did.

What could be so important that Alamin wants me back right away? Kay pondered this question as he trudged back through the Jirambe, occasionally having to yank a stuck foot out of the muck. He grumbled and complained about the swamp with every step.

"You're a barrel of laughs today," Felix chided.

"Oh, sorry," Kay said sincerely. "I just feel like I'm being pulled in ten different directions at once."

"That's the hard part about making history. You're the first wizard-knight that Gaspar has had in centuries."

"Not yet," Kay corrected. "I'm still in training."

"That's right. You're a *squapprentice*," Felix said.

Kay shook his head in bewilderment. "A what?"

"It's a little name I made up for you. You're a squire and an apprentice. A *squapprentice*," Felix explained. "It rolls off the tongue much easier than *apprensquire*. Anyway, Mr. Squapprentice, you had enough training to defeat the Lord of Nyn. He's dead as a doornail. Kaput. Or should I say...kaboom? What other tests do you have to pass?"

Kay slipped on a tree root and sprawled headlong into the dark waters. He came up sputtering and choking on the vile water.

"See, you've done another amazing deed!" Felix commented.

"What's that?" Kay asked as he wiped the slime from his brow.

"You've found a way to smell even worse than you usually do."

Before Kay could react, Felix darted through the trees and disappeared from sight.

***

The imposing stone walls of Marco's Keep rose like a storm cloud on the horizon. The wind whipped Kay's hair, and the distant Grayhorn River seemed especially turbulent. As Kay rounded the top of the last grassy knoll before the castle, he was surprised to see the gate was closed, barring the entrance.

Kay picked up his pace. *Maybe they're expecting trouble*, he reasoned.

After hours of travel through the swamps, the timbers of the drawbridge felt welcomingly solid beneath his feet. Kay marched across the wooden planks and hailed the gatekeeper to allow him entry.

Nothing but silence and the increasing howl of the wind answered his summons.

Kay called out again, louder this time. A wooden door creaked open, and Alamin stepped out of the gatehouse with his long white beard blowing in the breeze. The wizard strode slowly across the sandy courtyard and stood behind the strong iron bars of the portcullis.

Unlike wizards who wore long pointed hats and robes covered with moons and stars, Alamin wore brown britches, a plain white tunic, and a leather vest. A person could have mistaken him for a blacksmith or a farmer. And that was the way Alamin liked it. No staring eyes. No unnecessary doting or questions. Plus, it didn't hurt to hide the fact that he was a wizard in a land where magic was outlawed.

Well, at least on the surface, Kay thought. Alamin was the official—although secret—Grand Wizard of Gaspar. Magic use in the kingdom was controlled, rather than forbidden. When those with magical talents were discovered, Alamin brought them to remote locations to teach them how to use their powers.

"Why is the gate closed?" Kay asked upon reaching his friend and teacher.

Alamin's eyes glinted from behind the bars in a mischievous grin. "Lift it."

"What? Are you crazy?" Kay was able to levitate, but levitating oneself was easier than sending magic into something else and then trying to control its movements. His latest accomplishment was to lift Strapper, Alamin's faithful dog, up to the parapets from the courtyard grounds—much to the canine's displeasure. But the castle gate? It was so huge! Alamin couldn't possibly expect him to move anything that heavy. *Could he?*

Alamin stood behind the portcullis with his arms folded and an "I'm waiting" expression etched on his face.

Kay shook his head and reached for the magic. The flows came around him, brushing his consciousness and body like soft breezes. He raised his hands toward the gate and chanted, "*Jymphilay, jymphilay, jymphilay...*"

It was like trying to move a boulder. Kay could feel the portcullis as if he was grasping it with his hands. Its size and weight were vividly apparent in his mind. Though he strained with all his might, Kay couldn't budge the giant gate in the least.

He released the magic and collapsed on the drawbridge. Kay sat up and ran a hand across his brow. "It's too big...there's no way I can lift it," he panted.

Alamin shook his head, "*Tsk, tsk, tsk.* Think, Kay. Simple men lift this gate every day without the aid of magic, and they don't look half as tired as you when they're done."

Kay stared at the thick iron bars that protected the entrance to Marco's Keep. *Sure, the guards lift it every day, but they use...*

Kay's eyes opened wide. Of course! Why was he trying to do it the hard way? He stood up with a renewed vigor and recalled the magic to him. He closed his eyes and pictured the scene in his mind's eye. Scrying—seeing another place without actually being there—was another of the latest spells that he had been practicing. Alamin could scry almost anywhere in the kingdom, but Kay could only see things that were close by or in places where he was very familiar.

His sight traveled through the iron bars and into the gatehouse. He could visualize the guardroom as if he were actually inside; the only difference was that there was a haziness around the perimeter of his vision. Like a fish swimming through a pond, Kay's consciousness floated through the room until he found what he was looking for. The winch for the portcullis was in the corner closest to the outside wall. Large chains wrapped around the gigantic spool and extended up through an opening in the ceiling.

Now came the tricky part—two spells at once. Kay stared intently at the winch's handle. Outside on the drawbridge, Kay whispered, "*Movarah.*"

The handle creaked as it turned, and the portcullis groaned. Kay rejoiced at his efforts, but his vision immediately blurred. Both the gate and handle stopped moving.

Concentrate, he admonished himself.

Kay refocused his sight inside the gatehouse and blocked out all other thoughts but the desire to move the handle on the winch before him. Once again, he whispered, "*Movarah.*"

This time the portcullis shuddered and smoothly rose to its zenith, allowing Kay to enter Marco's Keep.

Chapter 2

ALAMIN led the way up a winding set of stone stairs to the private study of Lord Marco VI. Upon reaching the landing, he stepped up to an oaken door and gave it three solid knocks.

"Come in. It's open," a hearty voice hailed from the other side.

Alamin entered first, and Kay followed with a mix of tentativeness and curiosity. Even though he was Lord Marco's squire, it was a rare event to be called to the knight's private chambers.

Despite the keep's stark outward appearance, the inside of the stronghold was ornate and well furnished—and Lord Marco's study was no exception. Colorful tapestries and fine paintings adorned the walls, depicting important personages or battles from long-forgotten times. On the far side of the room, a series of dark wooden bookshelves dominated the wall, bursting with tomes, scrolls, and stray pieces of parchment; some were decrepit with age, while the ink on others was barely dry.

A half-dozen high-backed chairs faced an imposing stone fireplace. A small fire crackled within, more for want of light than for warmth; outside the keep, the leaves were beginning to change color, but the summer heat still lingered stubbornly upon the land. Above the fireplace, the entire scene was presided over by Lord Marco's family coat of arms—an exceptionally large shield emblazoned with a war hammer on a background of red and yellow.

The lord of the castle rested his bulky frame in a plush, cushioned chair. Lord Marco matched his surroundings well; he always dressed as if the king were coming for a visit. He wore black pantaloons, polished boots, and a purple silk shirt, while his fingers glittered with rings of gold. Judging by his outward appearance, some people assumed that he was soft and had lost his warrior's edge, but they were gravely mistaken. Lord Marco was one of the fiercest and most powerful knights in all of Gaspar. He and his family had defended the kingdom's dangerous northern frontier for generations, fighting marauders and goblins on almost a daily basis.

"Come, Master Thatcher, join us," he beckoned to Kay while gesturing to the seats around the fire. Except for Alamin, Lord Marco always referred to people by their last names.

Us? Kay thought. There didn't appear to be anybody else in the room. Three of the chairs faced away from Kay, but there were no signs of anyone sitting in any of them. No legs dangled. No swirls of pipe smoke.

Did he mean Strapper? Alamin's dog was lying comfortably on his side near the grate of the fireplace with his eyes closed, apparently sleeping and enjoying the warmth. The dog looked like a miniature version of the wizard in some ways. His fur was all black except for a white patch that resembled a beard; it ran around his snout and down his belly.

"What took you so long?" a familiar voice called.

Kay should have known. Felix fluttered up above the crest of one of the chairs. His hummingbird-like wings fluttered so quickly they were just a blur in the firelight.

What's going on? Kay wondered. *Lord Marco could have met with us anytime. Why here? Why now?*

Kay's questions were answered when he stepped in front of the hearth and saw a figure covered from head to toe in thick, matted hair. It sat like a child, lost in one of the oversized chairs.

"Bibo!" Kay exclaimed happily. "What are you doing here?"

"Bibo bring news," the furry one said enthusiastically as he jumped from the chair and hugged Kay.

Kay bent down on one knee and returned his friend's affection. As usual, the telok's hair was tangled with leaves and twigs. Bibo probably traveled much of the way swinging through the forest rather than traversing its roads and pathways.

Kay stood up and tousled the hair on top of Bibo's head. "I was getting worried about you! It's been months since you checked in. Even Felix doesn't go away for that long."

"For once the furball seems smarter than me," Felix mused. "Stay away from Castle Boring for months at a time. Hmm…the idea has promise."

Three soft knocks sounded at the door.

Lord Marco seemed to be expecting yet another guest, and he beckoned the newcomer into his study.

"Sorry I'm late," Jerra apologized as she entered the room. "Someone decided that my test for the day would be to teleport all the dishes from the dining hall to the scullery…one at a time," she added with a sidelong glance at Alamin. Like Kay, Jerra was also an apprentice wizard.

"You obviously passed brilliantly," Alamin said with a smile.

"I didn't dare break a dish. Mistress Pomfret was watching me like a hawk," Jerra replied.

Mistress Pomfret was the head of the household staff at Marco's Keep. She always carried a large wooden spoon with her. Although Kay never saw her use it as a kitchen utensil, she did occasionally hit a lazy servant over the head with it.

Jerra's black, bobbed hair bounced as she walked, her step always seeming to have a natural spring. She was dressed in a clean, light-blue blouse with a bright-red silk scarf that she had received as a gift from some local gypsies after healing their leader of a life-threatening flu. In addition to being a wizard-in-training, Jerra was also a talented healer.

Kay suddenly became more than aware of his disheveled state. He glanced at his trousers that crackled with dried mud and self-consciously sniffed at his shirt.

"Hi, Kay. So what's the…Bibo!" Jerra ran over and hugged the telok, picking him up off the floor. "I missed you so much!"

"Now that the gang's all here, we should begin," Lord Marco suggested. "Please sit down and join us Miss Tully."

Everyone took a seat by the fire. Kay and Jerra cast curious glances at each other. It was obvious that neither knew any more than the other about what was going on.

"Should Bibo tell *now*?" Bibo asked.

"Are all teloks this impatient?" Alamin asked.

"I think he's been very patient," Lord Marco said. "He wanted to go to the Jirambe to meet Kay, but I talked him out of it." Turning to Bibo, Lord Marco suggested, "Now would be the perfect time."

Bibo's eyes widened, and he slid up to the edge of his seat. "Bibo gone long time. Go very far. You know, Felix and Bibo are Secret Scouts. Sometimes go on secret missions. This time Bibo go alone.

"Bibo travel toward setting sun. Always west. Walk, walk, walk. Bibo walk until no more trees, just grass and hills. Then Bibo walk until no more grass, just sand."

"The Desert Waste!" exclaimed Jerra with more than a little fear and concern in her voice.

Bibo nodded slowly and continued his story.

"Wizard Alamin give Bibo special potion so he can travel safely in big dry land. No heat, no thirst...even better, no see. Bibo invisible. But Bibo must work quickly. Potion only work for little while." Bibo reached into a worn leather satchel that he wore strapped across his chest and displayed an empty vial with a cork stopper.

"Bibo follow tracks left by goblins and goblin war machines. Bibo not have to travel far when rocky tower comes into sight. Old tower. Broken stones. Stand all alone in sandy desert.

"Goblins all around tower. Some go in. Many do not. Strange sounds come to Bibo's ears. Chanting, goblins' drums, screams. Go on for long, long time. Suddenly tower flash with light. So bright that Bibo had to cover eyes. Then all still, all quiet. Bibo tired, need rest. Potion wearing off, so Bibo must go back. Tell friends." Bibo said the last two words with a smile and open arms.

"Alamin, what does this all mean?" Kay asked.

Alamin gazed into the fire and took a ragged breath. "The Desert Waste still hides ancient magic. It's there for the taking if one knows the right places to look. The goblins are trying to unlock a destructive power that they don't understand nor will be able to control—a force that could destroy all of Gaspar!"

Chapter 3

A LAMIN leaned forward in his chair. "The Desert Waste was once called Celcia—the Land of Bountiful Harvests. It was a beautiful kingdom with peaceful rulers and powerful wizards. But there came a time when the leaders and magicians became corrupt and fought for more and more power over each other. It eventually ended with the destruction of the entire kingdom."

Kay wrinkled his nose. He had never really cared for the ancient histories. It seemed so pointless; it all happened so long ago. The Desert Waste was not important to Gaspar. Nobody lived there, and nobody went there—except for goblins, apparently.

Alamin seemed to be reading Kay's thoughts. "Don't dismiss the Desert Waste and its history so easily," the wizard reprimanded. "We study our past to learn more about ourselves and to avoid making the same mistakes in the future. The goblins have apparently been busy making dangerous plans of attack."

Lord Marco looked grim but skeptical. "We've had the goblins on the run and scattered since the defeat of the Lord of Nyn. What could they have possibly dug up out there that is so dangerous?"

Alamin hesitated. He pursed his lips and shifted in his seat, looking guardedly from one occupant of the room to the other. Finally, he spoke, staring into the fire as if he were telling his tale to the flames. "During the final battles of the Celcian War, a young prince and his wizard came up with a plan to end the fighting. They thought that if they could control the most powerful magical weapon, then they would be able to subjugate the other rulers and bring peace. The prince and his wizard decided to harness the power of a fire elemental—"

"What?" exclaimed Felix. "Were they crazy or just plain dumb?"

"They were trying to stop a devastating war," Alamin said sternly. Softening his expression, he sighed and added, "They were doing what they thought was best at the time."

"What's a fire elemental?" asked Kay.

Alamin leaned forward in his chair. "Our world is held in balance by four types of elementals: earth, air, water, and fire. All elementals are very powerful and potentially dangerous, but the first three are mostly benign. Though they are reclusive, we see the effects of their power in the world around us. Earth elementals lend their magic to help trees, flowers, and crops grow and flourish. Air elementals are the source of the movements of the winds, from the slightest breeze you feel on your cheek to the most devastating storms. Water elementals create the tides and care for the life that is under the rivers, ponds, and oceans."

"And fire elementals?" Jerra inquired.

"Fire elementals reside deep within our world," Alamin answered. "Their fury can be witnessed when volcanos erupt or when forest fires sweep across the land. But their essence remains underground."

"Like in the Goblin Realm?" asked Kay.

"No, Kay," Alamin corrected. "Deeper. Much deeper."

"So you were telling us about the prince and his wizard," Jerra jumped in, urging Alamin to continue his story.

"Yes," Alamin said. "The two of them thought that they would be able to control the fire elemental. They threatened the other rulers of Celcia with complete destruction, but they never truly intended on carrying out such a plan."

"You mean they were bluffing," stated Lord Marco.

"Exactly. But things went awry. They lost control of the fire elemental, and it began laying waste to all the land—turning everything in its path to ash. It was completely indiscriminate with whom or what it destroyed. The rulers and wizards of Celcia had no choice but to band together to fight this common threat. With their combined powers, the wizards were able to contain and imprison the fire elemental, but not before it left Celcia in ruins."

"Once they caught it, couldn't they have sent it back to where it had come from?" Kay asked.

"No," Alamin replied with a shake of his head. "That was a major oversight. They only knew how to summon the creature, not banish it. Not all spells are easily reversible." He leaned back in his chair and stared into the fire. "Unfortunately, by what Bibo described, the goblin shamans have already weakened the magical bonds. The elemental has surely detected that someone is tampering with its prison and will be attempting to break through from the other side."

"Wait," Kay interjected. "Goblin shamans? You mean there are goblin magic-users?"

"Yes," Alamin affirmed. "There are not many of them, but they are very dangerous. I suspected that they might have become active when we received reports of people disappearing on the frontier. That's why I sent Bibo on his mission."

"Are the goblins taking on slaves again?" Kay asked with a shiver. He remembered all too vividly his captivity in the Goblin Realm.

"No. It's much worse," Alamin replied.

"What's worse than being a slave to the goblins?" Felix asked. "Lousy food, the terrible smell...hey, it's almost like being here."

Alamin ignored the sprite and continued. "Goblin magic is different from the magic that we cast. It has an added requirement—a blood sacrifice."

"So you mean they're kidnapping the people to..." Jerra began but couldn't finish her thought.

"Our only hope is to reseal the prison before the fire elemental escapes," Alamin declared. "If we can renew the spell, the kingdom will be safe for another thousand years. At least from this particular threat."

"The only problem is..." muttered Felix under his breath.

"The only problem is that the final part of the spell that sealed the fire elemental's prison required a tear from a water elemental," Alamin explained. "Without that tear, the fire elemental will be able to break through any magical or non-magical bonds that we create. That tear still exists. We just have to find it."

"How do you know how they had cast the spell?" Jerra asked.

"I was there," Alamin replied simply.

"B-but, that was hundreds of years ago," Jerra stammered.

"Almost a thousand," Alamin clarified. "Remember, I'm older than I look."

"Oh, you don't look a day over six hundred," Felix quipped.

"The tear isn't nearby, I'm guessing," Kay said, eager to get the conversation back on track.

Alamin shook his head. "After sealing the elemental's prison, we all went our separate ways. One of my brother wizards encased the tear in a magic ring and took it with him. He wrote to me many years ago and said that he hid the ring for safekeeping."

"Did he tell you where the ring is?" Felix asked.

"Vaguely," Alamin replied. He stood up and strode over to a map on the wall. "Last I heard, he was living in the Southern Islands." The wizard pointed to a smattering of small islands many leagues south of Gaspar in the Great Sea.

At the mention of the Southern Islands, Bibo jumped up and did a cartwheel. "Bibo's home! Bibo's home! That where teloks live!" He waddled over to the map and tilted his head from side to side as he examined its features. "None of these look like Bibo's island," he said dejectedly. "Where are trees?"

Alamin chucked. "They usually don't show trees on maps. Let's see if you like this better." Alamin waved his hands and uttered, "*Abilar.*"

The water on the map began to ripple and shimmer while one particular island on the southwestern edge pulsed steadily. "This is your island, Bibo."

The island grew until it took up the entire map. Lush green vegetation and flowers of every color and size covered the ground. Trees, with gigantic leaves as big as a full-grown man, towered above the landscape. Upon closer look, Kay noticed that small thatch-roofed huts, connected by rope ladders and bridges, adorned the trees. Furry creatures, all which resembled Bibo, traveled in and out of the dwellings.

"Teloks!" Bibo cried. "Hello! Hi!"

"They can't see you," said Alamin. "This is only a vision of what I know about your island from what you have told me."

"Oh," moaned Bibo somewhat sadly while he continued to gaze longingly at the image. "We go to Bibo's island?"

"I'm not sure where our journey will take us," Alamin replied. "But once we complete our mission, maybe we can all take a trip there."

Bibo's face lit up, and he clapped his hands. "Bibo like very much!"

Alamin snapped his fingers, changing the map back to its original form.

Felix pushed past the wizard and flew to the lower part of the map where the Southern Islands were situated. "So you're saying that this ring is somewhere around here?" the sprite asked, waving his arms haphazardly. "Those islands are spread out hundreds of leagues in every direction. It could take years to search them all."

"You're right," Alamin admitted. "That's why we have to get help from Krellia."

Strapper had been lying quietly by the fireside, but his head snapped up at the mention of the witch's name. He issued forth a series of ferocious growls and grunts.

"Don't worry, Strap," Alamin said. "We're not making any more bargains with her."

Felix let out a snort. "Yeah, that didn't go so well last time," the sprite quipped. "If I remember correctly, she drained you of your magic and left you almost completely helpless."

Alamin huffed into his beard. "I believe that Krellia knows of the ring and is as eager to get her hands on it as we are. I've been scrying on her and her minions. They've been particularly busy in the Southern Islands. It didn't make any sense to me until now. She must be searching for the ring and has been at it for a while. We've got to find out what she knows about its location."

"I thought Krellia didn't care what happened to the kingdom," Lord Marco said.

"A fire elemental on the loose could mean just as much trouble for her as it does for anybody else," Jerra suggested.

"Yes, but if she got her hands on the only thing that could stop the fire elemental, that would put her in control," Alamin stated.

"Can't we just get another tear from a water elemental?" Kay asked.

Alamin shook his head. "That tear was shed when the fire elemental turned Celcia into the Desert Waste. We don't need another catastrophe like that."

"So I guess it's anchors away," Felix said with mock enthusiasm. "Off to the sunny Southern Islands. Who's working for Krellia down there? Goblins hate water almost as much as Strapper does."

Strapper eyed Felix sidelong but refused to debate with the sprite.

"Mostly pirates and mercenary soldiers," Alamin answered.

"Oh, joy!" Felix exclaimed sarcastically.

The door opened suddenly, and all conversation stopped.

A dark shape with frazzled hair stood in the doorway. It was huffing and puffing.

Stepping into the light of the room, Eudora grunted. "I'm always the last to know what's going on."

Eudora was the resident healer at Marco's Keep and Jerra's mentor in the healing arts. Eudora had been mending Lord Marco's soldiers' gashes and broken bones since the time of his grandfather, Lord Marco IV.

"I thought you were in Riverbend helping with the scarlet fever outbreak," Alamin said.

"I was, and I did," Eudora said. "Now what's going on? Have you been keeping my ward safe or filling her ears with every sort of foolishness that you boys can come up with?"

Eudora was very protective of Jerra. She felt it was her job to teach her protégé not only about the ways of healing but also how to deal with men—all of whom she considered nothing more than overgrown boys.

Alamin brought Eudora up to speed on what was going on.

"It will be good for Jerra to get away from here," Eudora said with a nod. "This is no place for a young girl."

"And so we're bringing her on a boat filled with sailors." Felix sighed. "That's a big improvement."

"I can take care of myself," Jerra interjected. "You don't have to worry about me."

Eudora smiled. "That's because I've taught you how to handle those pesky boys."

Felix stuck out his tongue and grimaced. "What would you know about it?"

"When I was young, I could really turn the boys' heads," Eudora said with a swagger and a hand on her hip.

"Oh, you still do," Felix said.

"Really?"

"Yep. They take one look at you, and then they turn their heads the other way."

Eudora aimed a swat at the sprite, but Felix flew out of her reach.

Alamin coughed. "Carnac may still have the ring. If he does, we need to get to him before Krellia does."

"And if he doesn't?" Kay asked.

"He may be able to tell us where to find it."

Jerra chimed in, "Why are you worried about Krellia getting there first? Do you think he would give her the ring?"

Alamin vehemently shook his long white locks. "No, but he is a little odd. His actions are somewhat haphazard."

Felix raised his eyebrows. "If Senior Senility thinks this guy is odd, I can't wait to meet him."

Alamin ignored the sprite's comment. "Meanwhile, we have to find out where Krellia's pirates have searched and where they haven't."

Felix rolled his eyes. "And how are we going to get information from them? Go up and ask, 'Found any rings lately?'"

"No. We're going to get captured by a crew of Krellia's pirates," Alamin said matter-of-factly. "Well, to be more specific, Kay and Jerra are going to get captured."

Chapter 4

"I still think this is nuts," Kay said for the umpteenth time as he walked with Alamin, Jerra, and Strapper through the crowded streets of Carival, the capital city of Gaspar. Having been a prisoner of both merfolk and goblins in the past, he was not exactly thrilled about adding pirates to that list.

Kay had racked his brain for a different strategy during the long journey on horseback from Marco's Keep down to Carival. Try as he did though, he could not come up with a better plan than the one Alamin had devised.

The wizard's plan was simple—dangerous, but simple. Kay and Jerra were to get captured by Krellia's pirates, find and take the ship's logbook, and then teleport back to Alamin by way of special magic charms that he would give them. Kay wished they could simply teleport onto the pirate ship and take the logbook in the dead of night, but teleportation into an unknown location was out of the question. Without being familiar with the surroundings, they could teleport into a wall or mast and become a permanent part of the ship for the rest of what would be very short lives. Or worse, they could teleport into another person. Those results were too gruesome to contemplate.

Jerra looked no happier with the idea than Kay did. "Isn't there a better way?" she asked.

"We're pressed for time, and neither Krellia nor her pirates will willingly give up their knowledge of the ring's whereabouts," Alamin explained, also for the umpteenth time. "She may not know where it is yet, but she knows where it isn't. We need to find out which islands her pirates have searched and which ones they're headed to next." Alamin stopped and looked around. "Now where are Felix and Bibo? They were supposed to have been here by now."

Bibo and Felix had entered the city gates separately so the group would not call attention to itself. Three humans, a fairy, and a telok all traveling together was not a common sight, even in the crowded and diversely populated capital. Felix used a shape-changing ring that he had once stolen from Alamin—or "permanently borrowed," as he liked to call it—to turn into a pigeon while Bibo entered through the livestock gate disguised as a beekeeper.

Kay's thoughts continued to drift as he took in the sights of the capital city. The streets were crowded and bustling with activity. In addition to the humans who dwelt in the city, dwarves, elves, and gnomes paraded down the streets of Carival in the distinctive and colorful garb of their races. Tall and slender, the elves strode stoically and confidently to their destinations. Their heads were adorned with delicate circlets of gold and silver, while their bright-green attire that camouflaged them in their forest homes made them a spectacle in the gray stone surroundings. The dwarves were short, stocky, and heavily bearded—both male and female alike. They wore gruff expressions that matched their dour orange and black clothing. The gnomes, pint-sized master jewelry makers, gleefully sold their wares to all passersby. Their threadbare outer garments belied their true wealth; a quick turn or a gust of wind revealed the rich and brilliantly colored satins and silks hidden underneath.

Carival's shops sold everything imaginable, from trinkets and toys to mechanical clocks and gold jewelry. Smells emitted from all around as street vendors cooked food in the open air and carts with fresh vegetables rolled by.

Kay stopped at a stall that sold fresh seafood. He stared at the baskets of clams, and memories of his time with the merfolk floated through his head.

"Hungry, young man?" asked the woman selling the seafood. She was dressed in grimy clothing and a simple straw hat. Her sunburnt and wrinkled skin bespoke a hard life at sea. "Only one raal a bushel. They're delicious. Ever try one?" she said, offering him a raw clam.

"Um, yes. Once...ooff!" Kay lost his balance as a miniature beekeeper bumped into him.

"Sorry, Bibo no watch where he going. Hard to see in costume," the telok said apologetically from behind the beekeeper's mask. He tilted his head back to look up at the high, blue-capped stone turrets of Castle Lleeds. "Buildings even taller than trees on Bibo's island."

A pigeon flew down from the top of a shop's awning and landed on Kay's shoulder. "Bibo's going to wind up falling into the sewers if he doesn't watch where he's going," Felix scolded. Turning to Kay, the pigeon-sprite asked, "How much longer do we have to stay here? There are so many of you smelly humans. Yuck!"

"Not long at all," Kay answered. "As soon as we get to the docks, we're going to board the ship."

A sparkle of sunlight caught Kay's attention. Felix was apparently enjoying his time in the city a little too much; a ruby bracelet adorned his neck, and silver rings encircled his legs. "It doesn't look like you're in a hurry to leave," Kay said, noting the trinkets that the sprite had collected.

"How do you like my new bling? They're fake but shiny," the sprite said as he lifted a clawed foot displaying his latest acquisition.

"Hey! Is that your bird?" a shopkeeper called out, pushing his way through the crowd.

"Oops! Gotta go!" Felix yelped as he took to the air. "Meet you at the docks!"

The shopkeeper leapt into the air in an unsuccessful attempt to capture the tiny kleptomaniac. He watched in dismay as the pigeon flew out of sight.

Kay searched the crowd and found that he had fallen behind Alamin and Jerra. He grabbed Bibo by the hand and pulled him through the crowd to catch up with the others.

"Where did you go?" Alamin asked. "We thought we lost you...oh, I see that you've found Bibo. Is Felix nearby?"

"He said that he'll meet us at the docks. He's busy adding to his collection," Kay added wryly.

Strapper barked.

"You're right. He's going to get himself into real trouble one of these days," Jerra commented.

"Not nice to take other people's things," Bibo said.

"The docks are not far from here," Alamin noted, changing the subject. "We're to meet one of King Roland's agents aboard a ship called the *Albatross*."

"Wait a minute," exclaimed Kay. "I thought this was a secret mission."

"Of course it's a secret mission," Alamin confirmed. "But you didn't think we were keeping it a secret from the king, did you?"

"No. I guess not," Kay replied with a shrug of his shoulders. Then a hopeful and exciting idea popped into his head. "Maybe the king's agent is bringing the amulet with him," he whispered excitedly. "The magic one that contains—"

"Are you talking to me?" Jerra asked.

"Oh no. Sorry," Kay answered evasively and continued walking with a renewed spring in his step.

As they approached the waterfront, the streets became more crowded, and the smells of salt and fish mingled in the air. Up ahead, opulent mansions lined the streets; their brick and marble facades soared four or five stories above the sidewalks. Kay marveled at the buildings' vivid colors and the gilded carvings on the gables.

"Big, big buildings!" Bibo exclaimed.

"If you look carefully, you can see that each gable is adorned with a different design," Alamin explained. "Those are the crests of the various shipowners and merchant families in Carival."

"They look like palaces," Jerra remarked, looking admiringly at the ornate facades. "I would love to see inside one of those houses."

"Maybe someday you will, my dear," Alamin said warmly. "But right now we've got a date with a ship's captain."

The street opened up to the docks on the western bank of the Grayhorn River. The dockside was even busier than the other parts of the city. Carts pulled by horses, donkeys, and oxen rattled along the cobblestone thoroughfares. Sailing ships lined the waterfront with sailors and dockworkers loading and unloading goods from all over Gaspar and beyond. The crates were labeled with big block letters boasting of their contents: SPICES, SUGAR,

COTTON, SILK, and more. In addition to the names of the goods, a family name and crest was stamped on each crate. Kay recognized some of the crests from the merchants' houses they had passed.

"Look out, kid!" one cart driver called out.

Kay leapt back just in time to avoid being trampled by a pair of horses straining under the burden of a wagon overloaded with barrels.

"Be careful, Kay," Alamin admonished. "Everybody here is in a rush. Some would just as soon run you over than be late for a delivery."

Alamin explained the geography of Carival as they traveled. "The Grayhorn River passes through the center of the city. This is the western bank. The eastern bank is where the poorer side of Carival resides."

Looking across the river, Kay could see what Alamin meant. The houses and shops on the opposite side were much smaller and made of wood. Many were dilapidated and in need of repair.

"I wouldn't want to get caught there alone at night," Kay commented.

"Really?" asked Alamin with raised eyebrows. "Because *this* side is much more dangerous."

Alamin continued to lead the way along the waterfront with Strapper at his heels. As they passed boats of various designs and sizes, Kay wondered which one they would be on. *If we're meeting a representative from King Roland, I'll bet we're in a grand ship*, Kay thought hopefully.

Bibo looked about nervously. He grabbed Jerra's hand and huddled close to her.

"What's the matter, Bibo?" Jerra asked.

"That boat like the one that evil men had when they took Bibo to bad place," Bibo said, pointing to a ship with red sails. His wide eyes quivered behind the mesh of his beekeeper's mask.

Bibo had not come to Gaspar of his own free will. A group of slave traders had captured him and sold him to the Lord of Nyn. Kay, Jerra, and Felix met him after the telok had escaped from the Land of Nyn—what Bibo always referred to as the "bad place."

"That's an Island Federation ship," Alamin noted. "Years ago, some of the more populous islands banded together to fight piracy."

"Seems to me, they're as bad as the pirates," Jerra said, putting a consoling hand on Bibo's shoulder.

They pressed on, and soon a particularly large galleon came into view. The ship had three tall masts with half of its white sails furled on the yards. Military officers in bright-colored uniforms shouted commands to the sailors who were lowering the sails, while other members of the crew diligently swabbed the deck and polished the railings. The bow was emblazoned with the name *Excelsior*, and the flag of the Kingdom of Gaspar, which bore a golden eagle on a bold-blue field, flapped in the wind at the mighty ship's stern.

"Here we are," declared Alamin.

Kay's heart leapt. *Now this is traveling in style.*

Kay's hopes, however, were immediately dashed when Alamin motioned to the schooner moored in the shadows of the *Excelsior*. The schooner stood in stark contrast to the grand warship. It had two masts that were, like the rest of the ship, weathered with age. A small cabin adorned the stern of the ship, out of which stepped a disheveled sailor. A wrinkled jacket hung on his shoulders, and an old, rust-colored knit hat sat crookedly upon his head.

Alamin led the way across a rickety gangplank.

"Welcome aboard the *Albatross*," the sailor called out as he approached and smiled warmly. Grabbing Alamin's hand, he said, "It's been a long time, my friend."

Alamin nodded. "Yes, Errohd, it has. What happened to you? You look terrible."

"Hard work will do that to you," the sailor said, running a hand through his greasy, steel-gray hair. "Working for the king isn't as profitable as smuggling, but it keeps a sailor out of the brig."

"You're a smuggler?" Kay asked in surprise.

"Former," Errohd corrected. "Your friend set me on the straight and narrow twenty years ago," the sailor said with a nod toward Alamin.

"So where's the captain?" Jerra asked, looking around. "Are you the only one on the ship right now?"

Errohd laughed and then looked around hesitantly. Leaning in close, he lowered his voice. "The captain? He's as dirty a scalawag as you're ever going to meet. And you'd better do what he says right away, or you'll be fed to the sharks before you know what hit you."

Jerra gulped, and Kay began to reconsider the wisdom of the adventure they were on.

"What's his name?" Kay asked.

The sailor pulled Kay and Jerra closer to him and whispered, "Captain Errohd."

"But that's…" Kay began.

Errohd slapped Kay and Jerra hard on their backs, knocking them off balance. "Oh, this is going to be fun!" Captain Errohd said with a hearty guffaw. "Have either of you been aboard an ocean-going vessel before?"

Both apprentices shook their heads.

"You, fuzzy one," Errohd said to Bibo who had by now scrambled out of his beekeeper disguise. "They're going to need some buckets," he said, motioning to Kay and Jerra. "See if you can fetch some from down below."

"His name is Bibo," Jerra said sternly. "You don't even know our names yet, and you want us to get buckets. For what? Cleaning the deck?"

The captain broke into new peals of laughter. "No, Miss…er…"

"Jerra. Jerra Tully."

"Miss Tully, I do not expect you to swab the deck. You'll find the need for the buckets when we hit the open seas."

Once the introductions were finished, the *Albatross's* crew began to return from their shore leave. They took to readying the ship for sea and paid almost no attention to the newcomers. None, that is, except for Jerra. The seamen were obviously not accustomed to having a female aboard ship. They went out of their way to accommodate her every need.

"Does the lady need water to quench her thirst?"

"Excuse me, miss. Can I help you with your backpack?"

Kay rolled his eyes and tried to ignore when the sailors flexed their muscles or called extra attention to themselves as they strained to hoist the sails and prepare the rigging for departure.

One especially young sailor, maybe only a year or two older than Kay, kept looking in Jerra's direction. Jerra would occasionally glance his way but would coyly turn her head if she saw him looking at the same time. A couple of the older sailors noticed this and teased their young comrade.

Kay grunted in frustration. *We've got an important mission to accomplish. Jerra doesn't need some dumb sailor boy distracting her.*

Although Eudora always gave him the evil eye, Kay suddenly wished the healer had come along on the mission. *She'd be slapping the sailors on the backs of their heads and telling them to mind their own business.*

Someone shoved Kay from behind.

"Outta the way, kid," a rough-shaven sailor snarled and then began barking orders to the crew. He called over to a pair of sailors mending one of the sails. "Keep those stitches tight." Looking over the side of the hull, he yelled to someone unseen. "You missed a spot. If you don't know how to caulk a ship correctly, I'll get someone else to do the job."

Kay begrudgingly stepped aside to avoid more roughhousing. It was then that he noticed a solitary man casually board the ship. The newcomer was dressed in common clothing and carried no baggage aside from a sword, which hung in its scabbard by his side. Captain Errohd hurried to greet the man and ushered him and Alamin into his cabin.

A few moments later, Alamin poked his head out of the door and beckoned to Kay. "Gather Jerra and Bibo, and meet us in here."

Kay did as commanded. He was soon standing with his friends in a corner of a tiny, cramped cabin. Two small windows on the port and starboard walls let in the only light. In the center of the room, the mysterious man sat at a rickety wooden table along with Alamin and Captain Errohd.

"Now, Errohd—" the man began but was interrupted by a knock at the cabin door.

"This better be good," Errohd called out.

"You wanted to see me, sir?" the rough-shaven man asked from the doorway.

Oh no! Not him again, Kay thought irritably.

"Yes, Asok. As first mate, I want you to sit in on this council," Errohd requested.

Asok scanned the room and looked uncomfortably at Alamin. Glancing over to Kay and Jerra, his expression changed to a scowl.

"I don't think there's room in your cabin for one more," Asok said. With that, he stepped out the door and was gone.

The king's agent raised a questioning eyebrow at Errohd.

"Sorry about that," Errohd said. "My first mate is from the Southern Islands and is a little skittish around magic-users." Shaking his head, he added, "He's also the worst man with a sword that I've ever seen, but he knows the waters of the Great Sea like the back of his hand."

Kay gasped and looked anxiously at Jerra. If the stranger alerted the authorities that there were wizards aboard the ship, Alamin, Jerra, and he would be dragged away in irons. Granted, King Roland would pardon them, but the delay could cost them precious time.

Alamin noticed Kay and Jerra's fearful looks. "Don't worry," he said, smiling as he gestured to the stranger at the table. "This is the king's agent. He knows who and what we are."

"Oh," Kay said with a sigh of relief.

King Roland's agent cleared his throat. "I'm here to make sure you embark safely and to communicate to the king that the operation is underway." He reached into his cloak, "I also have this for you. Without it, I'm afraid your mission will fail."

This is it! Kay thought excitedly. *He brought the amulet that contains the Sword of the Dragon's Flame and Gauntlets of Might. Those pirates won't stand a chance against us when I have them again.* With the power of the sword and gauntlets at his disposal, Kay had been able to organize a slave revolt and defeat the Lord of Nyn's minions. Upon escaping from Nyn, Kay had to hand over the artifacts to Alamin. Since then, they had been locked away in King Roland's armory, magically housed in a blue sapphire amulet.

Kay's reverie immediately dispelled when the agent drew froth not the magic amulet but rather a scroll bound with a thin red ribbon. The man placed it on the table and slid it to Captain Errohd. "This document identifies you as a registered Gasparian merchant ship and should see you safely through any port in the Island Federation."

Errohd took the parchment and untied the ribbon. His eyes darted back and forth over the writing. "It says that we're not supposed to be subject to search and seizure. Will they abide by that? I only ask because our collection of passengers is a bit unusual."

The agent gave a sly chuckle. "No, they will still search the vessel. Although, *without* that document, the Federation would subject you to search, seize what they wanted, and then set fire to what remained."

Captain Errohd nodded gravely.

"Oh, and there's one more thing you should know." The agent leaned in closer to Alamin and whispered loud enough for all to hear but quiet enough to protect from eavesdroppers. "The Island Federation has stepped up their no-tolerance policies on magic. If they discover that there are wizards aboard this ship, neither that document nor any pleadings from King Roland will protect you. They will sink this ship and send everyone in it to the bottom of the ocean."

"Well, that sounds pleasant," a high-pitched voice commented from the window behind Kay.

All heads snapped in the direction of the sound. The king's agent put his hand to the hilt of his sword.

Alamin signaled for him to stand down. "It's all right. He's with us."

Felix had opened one of the small, hinged windows and was struggling to lift something. "Can someone help me with this?" he asked, back in his original form.

Kay walked over to the window and saw that the sprite had a gold raal in his clutches. "Felix, where did you get this?" he asked, taking the especially large coin from his friend.

"It was just lying around," the sprite said innocently.

"Something's lying all right," Jerra said with a disapproving frown.

Kay dropped the coin in his pocket. "I'm going to return this to its rightful owner when we get back."

"Hmm…not sure who that is," Felix said while scratching his head.

"Then we'll put it in the poor box."

"You're no fun," Felix huffed. He crossed his arms and flopped down disgruntledly in the open window frame.

The king's agent rose from the table and shook Captain Errohd's hand. "Good luck on your mission," he stated simply then turned and walked out the door.

"He wasn't exactly the friendly type," Jerra commented. "He didn't even say his name."

"Secret agent," Bibo said.

"You're right," Alamin agreed. "This mission is not officially sanctioned by the kingdom. We have to remember that if we're discovered snooping about the Island Federation's territories, and they find out that there are wizards aboard, King Roland will deny any involvement in our voyage."

"So there's no safety net," Jerra noted.

"She's a sharp one," Errohd said with admiration. "And brave too, I'll wager."

Kay had not stopped staring at the closed door since the agent departed. "That's it?" he asked. "He only came here to bring a piece of paper?" Kay's voice rose to a shriek, and everyone stared at him like he was a blithering idiot.

"Were you expecting a present?" Alamin asked with a raised eyebrow.

"Y-yes...well, no...not a present," Kay stammered.

Alamin put a hand on Kay's shoulder. "You were hoping that he would bring a particular collection of magical items," the wizard said with a melancholy look in his eye. "I was expecting them too. I guess the king feels that we can make do without them."

Kay's shoulders sagged. "Why all the secrecy? Why can't King Roland let the Island Federation know about the ring? Maybe they can help us find it."

Alamin shook his head. "You heard the agent. The islanders fear all magic. If they discover the ring before us, they will toss it into the depths of the ocean. The elemental's tear would be lost forever."

"Then bad guys win," said Bibo.

"My men will be ready to set sail at first light," Errohd announced. "Where should we start looking?" he asked as he unrolled a chart of the Southern Islands.

"We need to get Kay and Jerra on Krellia's pirate ship as soon as possible. Then we should head to the island that Carnac chose

27

for his sanctuary," Alamin stated. "If he's still in possession of the ring, this may be a quick and easy voyage."

"Oh, I'm sure that's not going to be the case," Felix commented from his perch on Kay's shoulder.

"Where is this wizard's island?" Captain Errohd asked.

"His island is right about...here," Alamin said. His gnarled finger pointed to a patch of empty water in the southwestern corner of the map.

"That's open water. There's no island there," Errohd said, shaking his head.

"There is," Alamin said simply.

"I've sailed that region, and I can tell you that there's no island there," the captain replied with assurance.

"My brother wizard does not like visitors," Alamin insisted. "We will find his island right where I said it is."

Captain Errohd threw up his hands. "Whatever you say, wizard. I'm getting paid either way."

"What if Carnac doesn't have the ring?" Kay inquired.

Alamin shrugged. "If he hid it somewhere else, I'm hoping that I can convince him to disclose its location."

"And if you can't?" Felix asked.

"Then we turn to plan B," Alamin answered, motioning to Kay and Jerra. "We'll use the information found in the pirates' logbook and start searching."

Concern and doubt were etched on Jerra's face. "How can we find something as small as a ring on one of those islands?" she asked.

"The tear of an elemental is a very powerful force of nature," Alamin explained. "It will probably have some sort of magical effect on the surrounding area. What kind of effect, I cannot say."

"I haven't heard any stories of any mystical places from any of the inhabited islands," Errohd said ruefully. "The people of the Southern Islands would avoid such places, considering them bewitched."

"So that means that we should probably focus on the uninhabited islands," Kay suggested. "It's probably in an out-of-the-way place, or else someone would have found it by now."

Alamin nodded his head in approval.

"And if we can't find Carnac or the pirates' logbook?" Felix prodded.

"Then we turn to plan C," Alamin answered.

"And that would be…?" Felix asked.

"I haven't quite thought of that yet," Alamin admitted, tapping his fingers together.

Felix groaned and buried his face in his tiny hands.

Chapter 5

ONCE Kay and Jerra had finished settling into their respective cabins, they spent the rest of the afternoon investigating every nook and cranny of the ship. After the sun set, they relaxed on the bow of the *Albatross* with Felix and Bibo. The moon shone brightly in the night sky, and the lights of Carival danced on the waters of the Grayhorn River like thousands of stars.

"I'd love to explore the city," Jerra said, gazing out longingly at the variety of shops by the waterfront. Every once in a while, little bells rang as people entered and exited the stores that sold everything from cheap souvenirs to fine jewelry.

"Me too, but Alamin gave us strict orders not to leave the ship," Kay said with a sigh.

Bibo shook his head. "Dangerous. No go."

"Maybe for some, but we've got Felix to keep an eye out for trouble," Jerra said with a hopeful sidelong glance at the sprite.

"Hmm...I could be tempted," Felix mused. "It would be a shame to waste a night in the capital city sitting aboard this collection of broken timbers. What did you have in mind?"

Kay didn't like where the conversation was going. "Jerra, I don't think—"

"Of course, you don't think," Felix interrupted. "Let the young lady tell us her idea...uh-oh."

"What is it?" Kay asked.

"Don't look now, but someone has the same plan we do." Felix gazed in the direction of the gangplank. "And he looks like he's also afraid of getting into trouble. He's wearing a hooded cloak, so I can't see his face."

Kay slowly glanced over his shoulder and saw a cloaked figure walk off the end of the gangplank and into the shadows of the *Excelsior*. "We should follow him!" he whispered excitedly.

"Oh, look who's ready for an adventure now," chided Felix.

"Bibo don't think this good idea," the telok said, tittering nervously from side to side.

"Bibo, stay here," Jerra suggested. "We shouldn't all go anyway."

Kay vaulted over the ship's railing and grabbed hold of one of the mooring lines. He nimbly scrambled hand over hand down the rope and hopped onto the dock. Jerra climbed down behind him and was soon standing by his side.

"Felix, did you see where he went?" Kay asked.

"Yep, he's up ahead by the stern of the *Excelsior*. I don't think he sees us."

"Look!" Jerra said pointing. "He's crossing the street and going into that tavern."

"Maybe he's just thirsty," Felix suggested.

"Sneaking off the ship under the cover of darkness? No, he's up to something," Kay asserted. "We can't follow him in there though. We're not old enough to go inside."

"Can you scry on him?" Jerra asked hopefully.

Kay shook his head. "I've never been in there."

"We could follow him if we were invisible," Jerra suggested.

"I still can't get that spell right," Kay grumbled. "Last time I tried, I turned poor Strapper into a flowerpot."

"Well, maybe *you* can't, but *I* can," Jerra said with a smile. "And Alamin showed me a way that I can take you with me."

Kay felt a pang of jealousy flow through him. He was further along in his training than Jerra, but occasionally she could learn a spell that had escaped his grasp. That was the way with magic; wizards all had their strengths and weaknesses. Spells that came easy for one wizard may forever be a challenge for another. Alamin, for example, was terrible at full transformations—such as changing oneself into an animal. That was the reason he had forged the shape-changing ring that now had its home on Felix's finger.

Without waiting for an answer, Jerra began moving—first her fingers and then her arms. She whispered a single word, *malachai*, and bent down while weaving her hands over and around her legs. Her feet disappeared and then her shins. As her hands rose, the rest of her body followed suit until she was completely gone.

"Take my hand," Jerra commanded.

"Where is it?" Kay reached out to where Jerra had been. He felt her take his hand and was surprised at how soft it was. He could sense her waving her other hand over his arm and watched in amazement as it faded and then vanished from sight.

"Wow! You're good! When did you learn this?" Kay asked.

"Shhh! I have to concentrate." Jerra flickered into view but then disappeared again as she regained her concentration.

Soon, both Kay and Jerra were nowhere to be seen on the docks of Carival. Even Felix had disappeared, but the casual observer may have noticed a small seabird with an eye for gold take flight from the vicinity of the *Albatross* and head to a small tavern called the Happy Wanderer.

Chapter 6

THE Happy Wanderer was one of the oldest establishments on the waterfront. Its thick stone walls were marked with only a few windows to let in the light during the daytime and to hide most of the proceedings that went on after dark. The weather-beaten sign bearing the tavern's name hung from a beam that jutted out above the doorway and creaked as it swung in the wind. It was carved with a relief of a shabbily dressed gentleman carrying a walking stick in his hand. Most of the paint had chipped and worn away over the years with only a few random splashes of color remaining.

"Don't let go of my hand," Jerra reminded Kay as they filtered in behind a group of rowdy patrons entering the tavern.

"Don't talk. Every time you do, I can see you fade back into sight," Kay noted.

Jerra nodded and winked out again.

The first thing that hit Kay upon entering the tavern was the foul stench of tobacco. Gentlemen lined the bar and gnawed on pipes of all shapes and sizes with rings of smoke curling above their heads. A fiddler played in the corner, surrounded by revelers dancing and stomping their feet to the beat of the music. Men and women alike were engaged in boisterous conversations throughout the tavern; some were yelling just to be heard above all the commotion.

Kay wanted to ask Jerra if she saw the sailor they were following, but he knew that he couldn't disturb her. They picked their path carefully through the maze of people, being especially vigilant not to bump into anyone. Kay felt a sudden squeeze of his hand and a gentle tug as Jerra led him into an adjoining room.

A bard sat by a fireplace surrounded by a small group of interested faces. Kay wished he could stop and listen. Bards always told the best stories. And the way they told them…Kay could imagine he was right there and part of the tale.

The bard leaned in close to his listeners and continued his story with wide eyes. "The knights spurred their steeds across the plains, giving chase to the goblins. The creatures' dark banners of war fluttered on the edge of the horizon, mocking their pursuers. Faster and faster the knights traveled. And, with each stride of their horses, they took one step closer to their doom."

Uh, I've had enough of goblins for one lifetime, Kay thought. He was thankful for the tug on his hand, leading him down a dark, narrow hallway and deeper into the Happy Wanderer's maze of rooms.

They stopped at the entrance of a dimly lit chamber. Rather than the raucous banter and flurry of activity that greeted them upon entering the tavern, this room was almost completely quiet. Two men occupied a small round table and were holding a hushed conversation.

Kay and Jerra's quarry sat with his back to the entrance and leaned forward, listening intently to the man across from him. The speaker had short-cropped hair and a beard that was such a light blond it almost looked white. He was dressed in the finery of some of the upper-class merchants of Carival.

The din from the main room filtered in, along with occasional cheers from those listening to the bard, and drowned out the men's conversation. Kay was only able to pick out bits and pieces, but the words he did hear filled him with dread.

"…Krellia…"

"…pirates are close…"

"…gets what she wants…"

"…fire elemental…"

"…destroy everything…"

Jerra squeezed Kay's hand tightly.

"…Alamin's apprentices…"

"…it's them or us…"

"…destroy the kingdom…"

Another squeeze. This time much tighter.

Kay felt Jerra lean close to his ear. "I can't keep up the spell much longer," she whispered.

"You've got to," Kay responded.

Wanting to hear more of the men's conversation, Kay took a careful step into the room.

A floorboard creaked beneath his feet.

"What was that?" the sailor asked. He leapt out of his seat and stood in a fighting stance, dagger in hand.

Kay tried to get a look at his face, but the hood from the man's cloak hung low. All Kay could make out was that he was clean-shaven, and the hint of a gold tooth shone in his mouth. *Well, that at least eliminates some of the crew,* he mused. He thought that he recognized the voice, but he couldn't quite place it.

"Nobody is there. Put that dagger away before you hurt yourself," the other man scolded. "These old buildings make all sorts of creaks and groans."

"I can't help it. I don't like this business," the other answered, sheathing his blade awkwardly. Their conversation had risen to a normal volume and became easily discernable.

Kay felt Jerra trying to pull him back down the hallway, but he resisted.

"What else have you found out?" the bearded man asked. His icy-blue eyes stared piercingly at his companion.

"Not much yet," the sailor said with a shake of his head. "But I didn't expect Alamin to bring an entourage along. This complicates matters. He knows—"

"He doesn't know you," the other snapped. "That's why you're doing this rather than me."

Jerra tugged again. Much harder this time.

"I'm telling you, Zelok. If I could get Errohd to—"

"No!" the bearded man interrupted. "Remember the directive."

Zelok, Kay mused excitedly. *At least we've got a name. Maybe Alamin will know who he is.*

Zelok stood up, indicating that their conversation was over.

Jerra's grip on Kay's hand loosened, and she popped into view.

Kay looked back at Zelok.

The man was staring directly at them.

"Run!" Kay shouted, thrusting Jerra ahead of him.

No longer hidden by the invisibility spell, they bolted down the hallway to the room where the bard was entertaining. Kay and Jerra pushed past the audience, causing a stir as chairs toppled over and people spilled the contents of their mugs all over each other. The storyteller stopped his tale and cursed the interruption.

"Sorry!" Kay called over his shoulder as Jerra and he dashed into the main room of the inn, shoving and ducking their way past the crowd of patrons. Jerra led the way out of the tavern with Kay close behind.

Just as Kay exited the Happy Wanderer, he felt a pair of strong hands wrap around his legs.

"Gotcha!" Zelok cried.

Kay crashed to the cobblestones of the dockside street. The force of the impact knocked the wind out of him.

"Tell me what you heard!" the man demanded, flipping Kay over and pinning him to the ground.

Kay refused to answer.

"Tell me what you heard!" Zelok yelled while shaking Kay by the shoulders.

"None of your business!" a high-pitched voice squeaked.

Kay heard a loud crack and felt the man's hands go limp.

Kay staggered to his feet. Zelok was knocked out cold by the tavern's sign, which lay broken in half on the street beside him.

Felix hovered where the Happy Wanderer's sign had once hung. The sprite brandished his tiny sword and bore a wide smirk. "Bull's-eye!" he exclaimed.

Jerra ran to Kay's side. The two apprentices stood poised and ready for the sailor to exit the building. People came and went, but no sailor.

The bartender stuck his head out the door. "Hey, what were you kids doing in here? This is no place for you. Get outta here!" He looked to the unconscious form of Zelok on the street, mopped his bald head with a dirty rag, and ducked back in the tavern.

Jerra slapped Kay on the shoulder. "What part of me trying to pull you out of that room didn't you understand?" she asked in a huff. "I can't cast that spell again. I'm exhausted!" She threw her arms up in the air. "Eudora was right. Men and boys are as stubborn and pigheaded as the day is long."

Staring at the prone form of the man on the ground, Kay suggested, "Let's go back to the ship and get Alamin. He'll know what to do."

Jerra nodded. "We're going to be in big trouble for leaving the ship though."

Kay winced. "I know." He looked up at Felix. "Felix, make sure this guy doesn't go anywhere."

Felix performed a mock salute. "Yes, sir! Captain, sir! Whatever you say, sir. Got another sign that I could drop on him in case he gets up?"

"Let's hope he doesn't," Kay said, and then he and Jerra ran back toward the *Albatross* with all haste.

***

After relaying a very quick version of the evening's events, Kay and Jerra led Alamin back to the Happy Wanderer.

"He was right here!" Kay said, looking up and down the street in frustration.

"Felix, where did he go?" Jerra asked. "Felix? Felix?" She clasped a hand over her mouth and pointed above the doorway. "Oh no!"

The Happy Wanderer's sign was hanging in its place above the tavern's entrance as if it had never been broken. However, instead of the carved figure of a man, the wooden sign now bore the image of Felix on it—his face frozen in shock!

Chapter 7

JERRA'S eyes welled up with tears. "We shouldn't have left him here," she said, shaking her head.

"Who could have done such a thing?" Kay asked with his fists clenched in rage. "Whoever did this is going to pay."

Alamin, however, did not seem to be very upset. The wizard called to someone on the inside of the tavern. "Excuse me, but I need to borrow your sign for a moment." He began whistling a tune and snapped his fingers. The sign floated down into his hands. He tucked it under one arm and headed in the direction of the ship.

Alamin looked over his shoulder and asked, "Well, aren't you coming with me?"

***

Alamin laid the wooden sign on a small table in Captain Errohd's private quarters. He waved his arms and quietly chanted a songlike spell. Kay, Jerra, and Bibo looked on with much concern while Strapper slept quietly in a corner of the room.

"There, that ought to do it," the wizard said and tapped the carved image of Felix.

A yellow glow emitted from the sign, and thousands of tiny sparkles rose from the table. They shimmered in the dim light of the room, growing brighter and closer together until they finally coalesced into the familiar form of Felix.

"Okay, that was *not* fun!" the sprite said as he shook and stretched his tiny frame.

Bibo clapped his furry hands, "Felix! Bibo so glad you're back!"

"What happened?" Jerra asked.

The sprite began to speak but then hesitated. "It's all kind of fuzzy." He scrunched up his face in thought. "After you left, the man started to get up...and I told him to stay put."

"I'm guessing he didn't listen," Kay commented.

"Thanks for pointing out the obvious," Felix grumbled and then continued his story. "He looked up at me and said, 'Why don't *you* stay put?' He just stared at me, and the next thing I knew I was part of the Happy Wanderer's decor."

"Another wizard!" Kay exclaimed.

"What color were his eyes?" Alamin asked.

"Um...I don't know," Felix answered in a perplexed tone. "What does that matter?"

"They were blue," Jerra interjected. "An icy-blue. I remember because I've never seen eyes that color before."

"Hmm..." mused Alamin. Turning to Felix, he asked, "Did he blink?"

Felix looked exasperated. "I don't know. What does that matter..." The sprite trailed off, and a look of thoughtfulness crossed his face. "Wait a minute. Now that you mention it, right after he told me to stay put, he closed his eyes. I remember thinking for a split second that he was going to pass out again."

"Why does it matter how he cast the spell?" Kay asked in exasperation. "They must be working for Krellia. Jerra and I heard them. They want to stop us from finding the ring."

Alamin began pacing the room. Kay noticed that the wizard looked more thoughtful than concerned. Every once in a while, Alamin would stop and hold up his finger as though he were going to say something, but then he would let out a big "hmm" and resume pacing.

***

Early the next morning, Captain Errohd gave the order to weigh anchor. He personally manned the helm to ensure that his ship was navigated safely through the crowded, busy harbor.

Kay and Jerra tried their best to keep out of the sailors' way. They found an open spot of railing that they could lean against and watch the moored ships they passed. The military and merchant ships that they had seen the previous day lined the western bank of the Grayhorn River. The *Excelsior* also looked ready to depart. Sailors hoisted its mighty sails—some of which looked big enough to cover the *Albatross* like a blanket.

On the eastern bank, smaller fishing vessels lined the waterfront. Boys pulled carts loaded with fish, occasionally stopping to pick one up that managed to flop out. Fishermen industriously readied their sails and nets for their next journey down the Grayhorn River to the open sea.

Ahead of the *Albatross*, two large stone towers flanked each side of the river, rising out of the water like enormous sentinels. The towers were so tall that Kay had to crane his neck to see their tops. Far above, guards marched along the battlements, watching everything that was taking place in Carival's harbor. Thick stone walls extended from each tower, cradling the river and the waterfront.

"Like two giant arms with fists," Kay thought aloud.

"The towers are connected by heavy chains that run underwater," a cheery voice explained.

Kay spun around to see the young sailor who had captured Jerra's attention. A pang of jealousy washed over Kay, but he was curious to find out what the boy was talking about. "Chains?"

"Yep, in case of attack," the young sailor responded excitedly. "There are winches in each tower to tighten and raise the chains out of the water, creating a type of gate to block the river and stop any ships from entering the city."

"Couldn't an enemy just cut the chains?" Kay asked with a shrug.

A terse laugh interrupted their conversation.

Asok, the first mate, was passing by; he stopped and pointed at the towers. "Look at those cannons up there," he directed. "A ship sitting between them wouldn't stand a chance. They'd sink a dozen ships before anyone could cut through those chains. It's much more efficient to attack the towers first. Actually, concentrating your fire on one would get you in the city the fastest. Once a tower collapses, the chains will drop into the water, and you're in."

Without waiting for a response, Asok sauntered away and called to a pair of sailors working the rigging on the bow. "Loosen up those ropes! We need to sail, not fly, out of the harbor!"

Kay had hardly heard a word that Asok had said. His attention had been focused on the first mate's freshly shaved face and the gold tooth that flashed in the bright sunlight. *Asok is the one! I've got to tell Alamin! I wonder if Jerra noticed.*

"The name's Seamus, by the way," the young sailor said as he extended his hand, breaking in on Kay's thoughts.

"Oh...I'm Kay," he said distractedly. Kay shook Seamus's hand but continued to look off in Asok's direction.

"And my name's Jerra." She offered her hand to shake as Kay had done, but Seamus gently took her hand and kissed it.

Kay silently fumed as Jerra giggled and blushed.

"Jerra, can I talk to you for a second? *Alone,*" Kay added with emphasis.

"Why? Not now. You're being so rude." Turning to Seamus, she asked, "How long have you been a sailor?"

Kay stopped paying attention to their conversation for a moment. *I guess it can wait until later, but...ugh...*he thought in frustration.

As the *Albatross* passed between the towers, Kay saw the chains Seamus had described. Two great iron chains, with links each as big as a man, extended out of openings in the towers. Kay thought of the test Alamin had given him with the portcullis at Marco's Keep. *An attacking ship with a wizard aboard wouldn't be hampered by any chains.*

"How far to the ocean?" Jerra asked.

"Not far," Seamus answered. "See how the river widens up ahead?"

Jerra and Kay both craned their necks. Unfortunately, the mass of ships ahead of them blocked most of their view downriver.

"Yeah, kind of," Jerra said uncertainly.

Seamus's eyes opened wide as though he'd just had an idea. He smiled and asked, "Are you afraid of heights?"

"No," they both answered in unison.

"Come on then. Let's go up to the crow's nest to get a better look."

"I'd love to!" exclaimed Jerra.

"I'd rather not," Kay said. "You two go ahead."

"Suit yourself," said Seamus good-naturedly. He took Jerra's hand and guided her to the ladder that led up to the crow's nest.

Kay watched them climb until they reached the small basket at the top of the main mast. There wasn't much room up there, so Seamus and Jerra huddled side by side.

Kay slumped glumly on the railing. "Ugh! I hate sailors," he complained.

"Don't say that too loud around here," Felix said in his ear.

"Where did you come from?" Kay asked.

"Oh, I was hanging out under the railing listening to that sailor boy put the moves on Jerra."

"He wasn't putting moves on her," Kay said sulkily.

"Oh, really?" Felix chided with a smirk. "It looks like she's having a nice time in the crow's nest."

Kay looked up and saw Jerra and Seamus. The sailor had his hand on her shoulder as he pointed off in the distance. They were talking and laughing. Jerra threw her head back, and her hair fluttered in the wind.

"Who cares? I'm going down to my cabin," Kay announced and marched across the deck to the hatchway and down the ladder. "I *really* hate sailors," he grumbled.

***

The Grayhorn River opened wider and wider until it finally spilled out into the Great Sea. By midafternoon of the first day, nothing but open water was visible in all directions.

At first, Kay found it eerie to be beyond the sight of land, but he soon became accustomed to the vastness of the open ocean and began to understand what sailors meant when they talked of the "freedom of the seas." The young apprentice—or "squapprentice," as Felix had dubbed him—enjoyed getting up early each morning to the smell of the pure salty air and to greet the sun as it rose over the horizon. Sometimes Kay would enjoy this morning time alone, and sometimes Alamin would join him.

Alamin was like a little kid aboard the sailing vessel. He climbed to the top of every mast and was often seen swinging from the rigging, all the while shouting out pirate clichés like "Shiver me timbers!" or "Avast, ye mateys!" Captain Errohd commented more than once that "the old bugger was going to hurt himself," but the seaman didn't dare rebuke the wizard's peculiar antics. Kay chalked it up to one of the many behaviors that Alamin displayed that he just didn't understand.

Strapper, on the other hand, was scarcely seen above deck. On the rare occasions when he made an appearance, it was usually to find a new place to sleep. One afternoon, Strapper had taken a nap in a coil of rope that the sailors needed. Rather than waking his pooch, Alamin levitated Strapper down to the berths below. The wizard explained that Strapper suffered from seasickness, but the situation was a little too much for Felix, who spent the rest of the day commenting on how Alamin "spoiled that mangy mutt."

While the weather was pleasant, Kay's favorite pastime aboard ship was practicing his swordsmanship with Captain Errohd. He learned a lot from the former smuggler, and the captain appreciated the opportunity to keep his skills sharp.

One evening, they were sparring on the main deck with a crowd of sailors cheering on one combatant or the other. Kay danced around the captain while unleashing an onslaught of slashes and thrusts. Errohd usually bested him, but this time Kay had the upper hand and was wearing the captain down.

"You're pretty good, kid," the captain panted as he weakly parried Kay's blade. "You've just got one flaw in your technique."

"What's that?" Kay asked, readying for a fresh series of strokes.

Errohd reached into his pocket and tossed a large glass marble into the air. Kay followed the trajectory of the shiny object then heard the scrape of steel upon steel as his sword was ripped out of his hand. He looked down to see the tip of Errohd's sword pressed against his chest.

"You don't cheat enough," Errohd answered with a self-satisfied smile and then withdrew his sword.

The sailors laughed and cheered for their captain. Then, with the entertainment being over, the crowd disbursed and shuffled back to their posts.

Kay shook his head in embarrassment and frustration.

"Always expect the unexpected," the captain warned. "Not everybody fights according to form or by the same rules."

"Thanks for the advice," Kay sighed. He wanted so badly to have another go at the captain. That last move was dirty, but Kay had to admit that the sailor had taught him a valuable lesson: it didn't matter how you won a swordfight—only that you won.

The marble rolled lazily across the deck and settled at Kay's boot.

"Hey, do you want this back?" Kay beckoned to the captain.

"It's yours," Errohd said over his shoulder. The captain slid his sword into his scabbard as he walked away. "Keep it as a reminder."

***

The first four days were mild and sunny with just enough breeze to fill the sails, but the fifth day brought a change in the weather. The clouds darkened and the wind picked up. Kay and Jerra soon learned the use for the buckets that Captain Errohd had Bibo fetch for them on the day they boarded the *Albatross*. They could hardly keep an ounce of food in their stomachs once the seas began to churn.

"When will we get there?" Jerra asked from her bunk with her head between her knees.

"Captain Errohd said that we should be within sight of some of the Southern Islands later today," Kay answered, quickly clamping his mouth shut for fear of getting sick again. He sat on a wooden shelf that doubled as a stool in a corner of Jerra's cramped cabin.

"Ugh! I don't think...I can take this...for much longer," Jerra choked out.

"Stop your bellyaching," Felix chided as he flew through the open door of the cabin.

"We wish we could," Kay said with a wry grin.

A pop sounded off in the distance.

"Did you hear that?" asked Jerra.

Before Kay could answer, a loud splash roared just outside the walls of the cabin, and shouts from the sailors on deck echoed overhead.

"This can't be good," Kay said, rising shakily to his feet.

Jerra stood up slowly and followed Kay out of the cabin. They gingerly climbed up a nearby ladder and onto the deck.

The *Albatross* was abuzz with activity. Captain Errohd barked orders from the quarterdeck, and sailors ran to and fro. Kay and Jerra made their way to the rear of the ship in time to hear an exchange between Errohd and Asok.

"Should we fire back?" the first mate inquired.

"Asok, are you a fool? We have one forward cannon. That's an Island Federation warship. They'd sink us before we could dent her hull. Send up the signal flag."

"What should I signal? Surrender or parlay?" the first mate asked.

"Surrender? You want to hand over our ship to them?" Errohd seethed. "Parlay!"

Asok ran to the bow and hoisted a tricolored flag up the rigging. The bright yellow, orange, and white banner stood out like a beacon among the sails.

Kay looked worriedly at Jerra. The night after their departure from Carival, he had told the companions about his conviction that the first mate was the one who had met with Zelok in the Happy Wanderer. All but Alamin thought that they should alert Captain Errohd of the first mate's treachery. The wizard suggested that they watch and see what comes to pass. Kay had pleaded his case until he was blue in the face, but it was to no avail.

Off the starboard bow, a large vessel with red sails approached from a short distance away. Someone aboard that ship raised a similar tricolored flag.

"They must have seen our signal," Jerra noted.

Bibo appeared out of nowhere and rushed by them. "Oh no! Oh no!" he cried. "Bad boat! Red sails! Oh no!"

Asok called over to Kay. "They're going to search for live cargo. Your telok friend is a liability. Hide him."

"But he's not cargo," Kay protested. "He's one of us."

"They won't see it that way," Asok answered and strode over to Captain Errohd.

Kay braced himself against the nausea that plagued him and chased after Bibo. He caught the furry creature by the arm and ushered him below deck. "I won't let them hurt you. Stay down here and don't make a sound."

Bibo nodded and slunk down the ladder.

Kay joined Jerra at the railing to get a better look at the approaching ship. Its sailors wore uniforms of black with red sashes tied around their waists and red caps on their heads. From a distance they looked like dozens of industrious ants, moving purposefully across the deck and up and down the rigging and masts. As the red-sailed ship loomed closer to the *Albatross*, Kay was amazed to see that it was even bigger than the *Excelsior*. Two rows of gun decks flanked each side, while the forecastle and stern were also heavily armed with cannons and small catapults. The red sails billowed in the strong winds as the ship pulled dangerously close to the *Albatross*.

Seamus appeared beside Kay and Jerra. "That's the *Scimitar*. It's one of the biggest ships in the Federation's fleet."

"I'm glad it's not one of the smallest," Felix gulped.

A small troop of sailors from the *Scimitar* boarded a skiff that lowered into the churning seas. Four of the men manned the oars, while the other sat in the bow. Kay guessed that the one sitting was probably an officer due to his silver sash and extremely large hat with decorative plumage.

Captain Errohd ordered a rope ladder to be thrown over the side of the *Albatross* to accommodate boarding. The crew of the *Albatross* gathered in formation on the main deck, standing silently with their hands behind their backs. Errohd motioned for Kay and Jerra to fall into place behind the sailors. They obeyed his command and waited for the Islanders to board.

The sound of the wind and the flapping of the sails were the only sounds to be heard. Soon, red caps popped over the ship's rails, and the boarding party assembled in a straight line, facing the crew of the *Albatross*. The sailors from the *Scimitar* were each armed with a dirk and short sword. Their skin shone bronze from continual exposure to the warm southern sun, and they all wore short, thin mustaches.

The officer with the silver sash stood in front of his men and addressed Captain Errohd. "I am first officer Pike of the Island Federation ship, *Scimitar*. You have entered our waters. What is your business?"

"We are a simple trading vessel," Captain Errohd answered. "I have traveled this route many times. Is the Federation now stopping all ships that enter its waters?"

"Piracy is on the rise," the officer explained. "We are searching all vessels that we come across."

Kay and Jerra exchanged worried looks. *If they find Bibo, what will they do with him?* But the telok was not his only worry. Looking at the line of sailors before him, Kay spied Asok. All the first mate needed to do was step forward and announce that there were wizards aboard, and that would be the end of their mission.

Officer Pike ordered the sailors to begin the search. Turning back to Errohd, he asked, "How many aboard the ship?"

"My crew numbers fifteen sailors, and we have three passengers."

"Any live cargo?"

"Just the old man's dog."

"Ahem…you mean dogs." Alamin corrected, appearing out of nowhere. Sitting on either side of him were two identical black dogs with white fur that ran around their muzzles and down their chests.

"Ah…yes…ahem…dogs," Errohd said, clearing his throat. "I very rarely see them together, and they look so much alike that I forget he's got two of them."

Officer Pike took out a pad of parchment and a quill. "Two dogs," he said as he wrote on the pad. "Any other animals?"

"No," Errohd replied. "All the other cargo doesn't bark. Just textiles and pottery mainly."

Pike nodded. Apparently assuaged after the initial formalities, he engaged in banter with Captain Errohd about the state of the seas while waiting for his men to finish combing the ship.

After a thorough search, Pike's sailors reported that all cargo in the ship's manifest was accounted for, and there was no illegal contraband aboard the vessel. Pike thanked Captain Errohd and bid him and the rest of the crew a safe voyage.

Kay kept his eyes on Asok, but the sailor stayed in line like the rest of the crew as the *Scimitar's* sailors descended the rope ladder to their skiff. *What game is he playing at?* Kay wondered. *He could have turned us in. Maybe he's waiting until we find the ring, and then he'll steal it for Krellia.*

Alamin leaned over to Kay and asked in a conspiratorial whisper, "Still think he's working for Krellia?"

"Yes," Kay answered without hesitation.

Captain Errohd ordered the crew back to their posts. They immediately obeyed, many wearing expressions of relief while keeping a wary eye on the heavily armed vessel that hovered nearby.

With Asok out of earshot, Kay addressed Alamin. "Why aren't you worried about him? It's obvious that he's working for Krellia."

"Is it? It would be an easy life if everything could be right or wrong—black or white. But there's a lot of gray in this world."

"And there's a lot of gray in your beard," Felix quipped from above, flittering down and alighting on a coil of rope. He held out his hand and addressed one of the Strappers at Alamin's feet. "I'll have that back now, if you please."

One of the dogs grew and transformed into the familiar form of Bibo. The telok twisted a gold ring off his finger and handed it to Felix. As it fell into the sprite's palm, the ring shrunk to an incredibly small size.

Felix slipped the ring on his finger and then spoke directly to Alamin. "Now that you're done lecturing us, what's the next step?"

Alamin stroked his beard. "I have to divine the whereabouts of Krellia's pirates. Once I do, we will have several preparations to make." Alamin motioned for Strapper to follow and headed below deck to his cabin.

Kay and Jerra looked at each other and gulped. They had tried their best to forget about this part of the mission. Neither was eager to be at the mercy of Krellia's pirates, but they both were determined to see this through to the end.

Chapter 8

KAY sat in his bunk and scratched his head while eying the playing cards in his hand. Felix stood at the other end of the bed with his set of cards floating in front of him. Kay had cast a levitation spell on the cards so the sprite didn't have to struggle to hold the objects that were more than half his height. Bibo sat on the berth across from them with his legs crossed and watched in wide-eyed silence.

"Hmm…" Felix uttered for about the fourth time as he went to remove a card from his hand, hesitated, and then began fidgeting with another card.

"Will you take your turn already," Kay said in an exasperated tone.

"I'm thinking."

"I know. I can smell the smoke."

"Hey, that's not nice," Felix said with a fake pout. Then his expression changed to a proud smile. "I see that I'm finally rubbing off on you." He swiftly slid a card into the discard pile.

Their conversation was interrupted by a knock on the cabin door.

"Come in," Kay called out.

Alamin stepped into the room. "I hope I'm not interrupting anything important."

"Nope," Felix responded. "I'm just giving this kid a lesson on how to lose at jacks."

Alamin chuckled and looked at Kay. "Oh, Kay, there are two things you never challenge a sprite to—insults and cards. They always cheat."

Felix puffed with indignation. "I never cheat...well, okay...sometimes. But Kay is so bad at cards that I can actually beat him fair and square."

"Gee, thanks," Kay said as he put down his hand. "Jacks and eights?"

"Heh! I don't even have to take my last turn." Felix flipped his cards around. "Jacks and queens! I win again!" the sprite exclaimed in triumph.

Kay sighed and looked at Alamin. "So what brings you by? Have you discovered where Krellia's pirates are?"

"Yes," Alamin answered. "But I'd like to talk to you all at once. Where's Jerra?"

"She said that she needed some fresh air," Kay replied.

"More like some fresh sailor," Felix quipped. "She's been chatting with that boy, Seamus, every chance she gets."

"Seamus nice sailor," Bibo chimed in. "Bibo like. He give me this." The telok proudly displayed a small golden compass. He hopped off the bunk and pointed in the various cardinal directions. "North. East. South. West."

Kay couldn't take any more talk of how nice Seamus was. He ended the levitation spell on Felix's cards, causing them to fall haphazardly on the bed, and abruptly stood up and left the room, slamming the door behind him. "I hate sailors!" he fumed while climbing the ladder leading up to the main deck.

The *Albatross* was much quieter at night than it was during the daytime. The moon shone brightly just above the horizon and shed enough light for Kay to see easily about the ship. The sailors manned their posts stoically and diligently to allow their brethren to get a good night's rest. Asok was at the helm, but he neither acknowledged nor seemed to notice Kay's presence.

Scanning the ship, Kay's eyes finally rested on two figures standing close together at the forecastle. Jerra and Seamus were locked in a hushed conversation with their heads almost touching. Kay thought of calling out Jerra's name, but the stillness of the ship made him refrain from doing so. He wasn't sure why he didn't want to disturb them, but he walked quietly across the ship to the forecastle.

As Kay mounted the stairs that led to the upper deck, one of the steps creaked loudly. Jerra quickly pulled away from Seamus and turned to face the unknown intruder.

"It's only me—" Kay began.

"What are you doing sneaking up on us?" Jerra demanded in a huff as she stomped toward Kay.

"Alamin wants to see us. Right now," Kay barked, trying to assume an air of authority.

If Jerra had been a balloon, Kay would have sworn that she was about to pop. Her fists clenched, and her face became beet red with frustration.

"Tell him I'll be right there," she said sharply.

"Don't take too long." Kay turned and descended the steps to the main deck.

When Kay was about halfway across the ship, an old sailor beckoned to him. "Psst. Come here, kid."

The man was sitting on a stool and whittling away at a piece of wood. Kay recognized him as Martin, one of the older and more respected members of the crew. He was gruff but fair with the other sailors and passengers.

Kay walked warily over to the sailor. "What is it?" he asked shortly.

"Don't give me any attitude, kid," the grizzled sea dog remonstrated. "I was going to give you some advice, but you seem too full of yourself to need it."

"Advice about what?" Kay asked.

"I overheard your conversation up there," Martin said, motioning to the forecastle.

Kay followed the man's gaze to where Jerra and Seamus sat. His shoulders sank in defeat. "What's your advice?"

"Don't just let things happen around you," Martin said, giving Kay's chest a hard poke with his forefinger. "If there's something that you want, sometimes you've got to fight for it."

"I don't want to fight Seamus..." Kay began.

The sailor shook his head. "I don't mean literally, son. I mean that you can't just sit on your hands and watch the world go by you."

"You have no idea what I've been through," Kay said defensively. "I don't just sit idly by—"

"Well, in this case you are," Martin interrupted. Without another word, Martin looked down and returned to his whittling, indicating that their conversation was over.

Kay shook his head and strode off in the direction of the hatchway. As he put his foot on the first step, he looked to see if Jerra had finally decided to follow.

A lump formed in his throat, and a pit opened in his stomach.

Jerra and Seamus were holding each other, and Seamus bent down to kiss her.

Kay all but fell down the ladder to the lower decks. He kicked open the door to his cabin and ignored the astonished faces of Alamin and Bibo as he flopped down on his bed.

"What's this all about?" Alamin asked. "Where's Jerra?"

"I bet I know," Felix said in an excited tone. "Jerra and Seamus, sitting in a tree, k-i-s—"

"Shut up, Felix!" Kay growled.

"Hey, I didn't get to finish my song," Felix whined.

Alamin sighed. "This is what I get for having two teenagers as apprentices."

Shortly after, footsteps creaked on the ladder. Kay hastily sat up and ran his fingers through his unkempt hair.

Jerra opened the door and stiffly entered the room. "You wanted to see me, Alamin."

"Yes, I wanted to see all of you," Alamin answered with a forced smile that indicated he was happy to change the subject. "Krellia's pirates are just over two days' journey to the southwest. She cast charms of concealment on their ship that were difficult to break through."

"What are we going to do when we reach them?" Jerra asked.

"Something that will require the bravery of everyone aboard this ship," Alamin announced solemnly.

Chapter 9

KAY and Jerra moped about the main deck of the *Albatross*. Over the past two days, they had sailed by numerous tropical islands. If they were in another time or place, they might have marveled at how each was unique in its beauty. Gigantic palm trees swayed gently in the warm breezes that caressed the Southern Islands. Against a backdrop of lush vegetation, brilliantly colored flowers dotted the jungles, and the waters of the lagoons glowed a sparkling turquoise. Some islands were sparsely populated; wood and grass structures blended into the thick green foliage. Other islands loomed large and mountainous, possessing stone castles that rivaled the great spires of Carival.

Neither Kay nor Jerra had exchanged more than a couple of short words, partly due to their encounter on the forecastle and partly due to the anxiousness that they both felt about what was to come. The wind was fair and the seas were calm, but that didn't help the churning in their stomachs.

A rope ladder hung over the rails and led down to a crude raft; it looked like a broken section of a ship's deck. Alamin's plan was to set Kay and Jerra adrift on the makeshift raft when they were close to the pirate ship. The young apprentices were to tell the pirates that their ship crashed against a reef and they were the sole survivors. Pirates were usually willing to impress new recruits—especially children, so they could mold them to their ways and ideals. The problem was getting the *Albatross* close enough to the pirate ship without being spotted—that's where Alamin's magic was to come in.

Kay looked about the *Albatross*. None of the sailors stirred from their posts, not because they didn't want to, but because they couldn't. All were lashed around their waists with short ropes that led to a mast, post, or the rigging.

Alamin had explained his plan to all in a meeting with the crew. "I will cast an invisibility spell on the *Albatross*. Though it will make us invisible to the pirates, you will not see the ship either—or your own bodies, for that matter."

Captain Errohd had chimed in and continued the briefing. "The most difficult part will be the handling of the *Albatross*. I will be at the helm, but you will still have to man the sails and the rigging entirely by feel."

The seasoned sailors of the crew had looked on with grim understanding of the difficulty of the task, while some of the younger sailors had appeared eager and excited at the chance to become invisible.

Now it was time for the plan to be put into action. Alamin strode across the main deck with a small bag in his hand and called to all those aboard. "The pirates are just beyond the horizon. Everyone make sure you are securely lashed in place." After scanning the ship and apparently satisfied with what he saw, Alamin called out to Captain Errohd. "Ready? This is going to be a whopper!"

"Ready," the Captain answered with much uncertainty in his voice.

Alamin placed the bag down on the deck and proceeded to empty it of its contents. Very powerful spells sometimes required special components. Most wizards used things like eye of newt, bats' wings, and dead frogs—but not Alamin. Alamin's bag of spell components consisted of things that could have been found in an abandoned house, such as a shoe with a hole in the sole, pieces of glass, and a moldy tomato. He also had some bizarre items such as something he called a "by sickle horn." Kay could only guess that it was for calling farmers back in from the field when they were out harvesting wheat. Alamin meticulously arranged the jumble of curiosities as if in celebration of some bizarre holiday.

Once he was satisfied that all the components were in the correct places, Alamin closed his eyes and began the incantation.

He spoke in the ancient tongue of Celcia and wove his arms in intricate patterns. Soon his whole body seemed to be incorporated in the casting. With a final lithe movement, Alamin bent down and placed his palms on the surface of the ship's deck.

Though Kay had heard the explanation of how the spell was to take effect, the young apprentice still gasped when he saw the upper deck start to fade into nothingness. Radiating from Alamin's hands, a hole appeared with the wizard floating in the center. The lower deck, which contained the passengers' and crew's cabins, came into view as more and more of the upper deck disappeared. The invisibility spell crept its way up the masts, and soon the sails seemed to float in the air of their own volition.

Kay gripped the rail tighter as the boards beneath his feet disappeared and the spell wove its way up his legs. Looking about, he saw expressions that ranged from excitement to absolute fear on the faces of the crew. It was not long until only the very bottom of the hull and the uppermost sails were visible.

When the spell was complete, nothing remained of the *Albatross*. Kay took a deep breath and looked down. He swallowed hard at the view of the sea far below him. The only evidence that the ship still existed was the indentation in the water made by the hull.

Felix gave a low whistle from his perch on Kay's shoulder.

"This is spooky," Kay gulped.

"You're telling me," Felix answered.

"Jerra, are you there?" Kay asked.

"Yep, I'm here," Jerra said with a deep intake of breath. "But you should start calling me Ari."

Alamin had instructed Kay and Jerra to use fake names in case Krellia had communicated their identities to the pirates. They were to be Thomas and Ari—siblings who were the lone survivors of a wreck at sea. They had spent part of the morning making rips and tears in their clothes and staining their shirts and pants by rubbing them on the well-traversed deck of the *Albatross*. Kay had never seen Jerra so disheveled, and he imagined that he struck a pretty sore sight as well.

All that could be heard aboard the *Albatross* were the light splashing of waves and the creaking of the ship's timbers. Kay fingered the rope bracelet that Alamin had given him. Jerra also wore a similar one around her wrist. The wizard had placed a powerful charm on the unassuming trinkets. When the time came for Kay and Jerra to leave the pirate ship, or if their lives were in danger, they had to simply think of Alamin and touch their bracelets. The charms would teleport them safely back to the wizard, no matter where he was. Kay and Jerra had both practiced teleportation spells, but only on inanimate objects; neither had ever tried to teleport themselves or any other living being. Luckily, the bracelets would do the magic for them.

Kay groped for the rope ladder that led down to the raft. The raft was invisible too, but Alamin had explained that the raft, along with Kay and Jerra, would become visible as soon as they untethered from the ship.

Captain Errohd's voice suddenly broke through the tranquil sounds of the ocean. "Steady as she goes! Hold tight to your posts!"

A chorus of sailors answered in a jumbled exclamation, "Aye, aye, Captain!"

"Well, here goes," Kay said. He cautiously climbed over the railing and felt his way down the rope ladder. When he reached the raft, he called to Jerra to follow. The ladder wiggled in Kay's hands as Jerra descended.

"Ow! That's my finger!" exclaimed Kay.

"Sorry, but I couldn't exactly see it," Jerra snapped.

Felix groaned. "Oh, this is going to be a pleasant trip."

***

Kay and Jerra drifted farther and farther away from the *Albatross* and were soon alone in the wide expanse of the Great Sea. Felix transformed into a seagull and flew high above to make sure they were still heading toward the pirates.

"Thar she blows!" Felix squawked. "Off the starboard bow!"

"That was quick," Kay said. "I was beginning to enjoy my time away from the ship. Now we have to deal with more of *them*."

"Them who?" Jerra asked pointedly.

"Sailors. I hate sailors."

"Really? Why?" Jerra pressed.

"Because…just because. That's why." Kay lay flat on the raft and paddled with his arms in the direction Felix had indicated.

"That's what I thought," Jerra retorted and dipped her arm into the water to help propel the raft.

They paddled on in silence from that point on.

Felix looked down from overhead and sighed. "Yep, definitely a pleasant trip."

Chapter 10

THE pirates had apparently spotted the two castaways; their ship veered from its course and headed directly toward Kay and Jerra's raft.

The two apprentices hailed the approaching ship, waving their arms wildly and shouting for help.

"Um, Kay, do they seem to be coming at us a little too fast?" Jerra asked.

"You're imagining things," Kay said dismissively.

"I don't think so. They're coming straight for us," Jerra insisted.

Kay huffed impatiently and flopped down on the raft. "Just paddle a little more to the left."

"You mean port."

"Ugh! Whatever."

They turned the raft and headed on a new course. When they looked up, the pirate ship appeared to have changed its heading also and was bearing down on them!

"They're going to ram us!" Kay realized in horror. "Felix! Where are you?"

A fish poked its head out of the water. "What's all the commotion about up here?"

"The pirate ship is aiming for us!" Jerra said anxiously.

"Isn't that what we want?" the fish-sprite asked.

"Not like this. Look!"

Felix turned in the direction of Jerra's outstretched arm. The pirate ship was just a stone's throw away. "I'd suggest you jump ship. Now!"

Kay and Jerra dove into the water just in time. Seconds later, the prow of the pirate ship crashed into the raft, reducing it to splinters. Hearty laughter sounded from above while the two apprentices bobbed in the salty sea. The pirate ship pulled alongside them, and a collection of bedraggled mariners leaned over the rails to jeer at the ocean's newest flotsam.

"Arr, bull's-eye!"

"Did you see the looks on their faces? Too bad we can't do it again."

"Throw some raw meat in the water. The sharks will come, and we'll have a good show."

"I bet they eat the girl first."

"Was this part of the master plan?" Felix whispered as he surfaced behind Kay and Jerra.

Ignoring the sprite, Kay called out to the pirates. "Mind giving us a lift? We seem to have broken our raft."

The pirates broke out into peals of laughter.

"He's got spunk."

"Either brave or stupid."

A bearded pirate in a long black-and-red coat pushed past the others and stood on the railing. Kay guessed that he was probably the captain by the speed at which the other pirates got out of his way.

"Who are you? And what are you doing in the middle of nowhere?" the captain bellowed.

"Our ship was wrecked on a reef last night," Kay answered, trying to sound innocent and desperate. "We've been drifting ever since. Can you help us?"

The pirates erupted into another chorus of laughter.

The captain motioned for his sailors to settle down. "Of course we can help. Send the girl up first."

"I don't trust them," Jerra whispered.

"Neither do I," Kay agreed. "I'll follow close behind."

The pirates lowered a knotted rope over the side of the ship. Kay and Jerra swam doggedly toward it, their waterlogged clothing weighing them down. Kay reached the rope first and held it tight for Jerra, who nimbly pulled herself up hand over hand.

"Oh, she's a tough one! Look at her climb!" chided a bald pirate with a pockmarked face.

"Watch out for that vixen. I bet she bites!" another jeered.

Kay followed close behind while keeping his eyes on Jerra and the pirate crew. When Jerra neared the railing of the ship, a pirate grabbed her roughly by the arm and hauled her onto the ship's deck.

A bad feeling seized Kay. He attempted to scramble up the few remaining feet.

A scruffy face with missing teeth and an eye patch leered at him. Kay saw the sunlight gleam on the man's dagger as it cut cleanly through the rope!

Chapter 11

THE rope went slack, and Kay began to freefall. Instantly, he spoke the word for levitate—*jymphilay*—and made it look like he succeeded in making a last desperate grab for one of the balusters of the ship's railing. Kay hung for a moment by one hand and then climbed over the rail and onto the deck.

The pirate who tried to cut him down spun around in surprise when his companions pointed out that he failed to get rid of "the boy."

"You're lucky, kid," the pirate said with a sneer. "But your luck has just run out." He spun a curved, single-edged dagger in his hand and lunged for Kay.

Kay nimbly leapt aside and avoided the man's attack. Again and again, the pirate thrust and jabbed at Kay, but the squire remained unscathed.

Facing off against his foe, Kay prepared for the pirate's next move.

The other pirates taunted their fellow buccaneer.

"The boy's getting the best of you, Deets!"

"Why is this taking so long? I think you're getting slow in your old age."

This infuriated the one-eyed pirate, and he redoubled his efforts. He reached for a second knife that he had in his boot and lunged at Kay with both deadly blades.

Kay ducked and dodged the best he could, but he knew that it was just a matter of time before he made a fatal slip. He was unarmed and had to avoid using magic unless absolutely necessary.

If he used even a minor spell their cover would be blown, and they would have to abort their mission.

"Stand still, will ya!" the pirate commanded. He was flush with anger, and sweat beaded down his face.

"I'll stand still if you give me a weapon to defend myself with," Kay said staunchly.

To Kay's surprise, Deets paused and smiled. "Oh, this is going to be fun." Turning to his fellow pirates, he called out, "Give me a sword and give one to the boy. We'll settle this nice and quick."

A sword slid across the deck and skidded to a halt at Kay's feet. He picked it up and squared off with Deets. The pirate wasted no time and unleashed a furious attack that pushed Kay back against the ship's railing. Kay jumped out the way just in time to avoid an overhand blow that would have cloven him in two.

Before Kay could regain his balance, Deets swung his sword again and grazed Kay's left arm. Kay felt the sting of steel and then a warm wetness as blood flowed out and stained his shirt.

Deets smiled. "Ah, first blood. Get ready for more."

The other pirates began to jeer.

"It won't be long now, boy."

"We'll feed you to the fishes once Deets is done with ya."

"If there's much left."

Kay steadied his nerves. "*In a sword fight, always keep calm,*" Lord Marco had advised him. "*When your emotions take over, you lose control. If possible, force your opponent to lose control of his emotions. He will become sloppy, and you will find your opening.*"

Kay glanced at his arm and shrugged his shoulders, doing his best to mask the pain. "It's just a scratch. You're not very good at this for a pirate," he taunted. "I thought you said that this was going to be quick."

The other pirates laughed, and Deets's face turned beet-red.

"Why...I'll...arrrgh!" Deets sputtered. He ran toward Kay with his sword extended in an attempt to skewer the young squire.

This was the moment Kay was waiting for. He nimbly sidestepped the attack and tripped the pirate. Deets went sprawling across the deck, his sword flying from his hand. The pirate lay groaning and was not making any attempt to get up.

Kay walked confidently toward his fallen opponent. "Have you had enough?" he asked boldly.

Without warning, Deets flipped over and swung his legs in an arc, knocking Kay's feet out from under him. Kay landed on the deck with a hard crash, and pain shot through his wounded arm. With his head spinning, Kay struggled to get up, but he immediately stopped when he felt the cold steel of a blade against his throat.

Deets knelt on his chest and sneered. "It's all over," the pirate spat. "Nice knowing you, boy."

"Drop the sword and get off him," a harsh and commanding voice ordered. The pirate captain stood behind Deets and held a scimitar pressed against his crew member's back.

Deets glowered and answered his captain without taking his eyes off Kay. "He's mine."

The captain edged closer, and Deets grimaced in pain as the sword dug into his back.

Deets growled in frustration, but he reluctantly obeyed his captain's order. Kay felt a flood of relief when the sword left his throat.

"Next time you won't be so lucky," Deets said. He threw his sword to the ground and stormed off.

"You fight well for someone so young," the captain said, changing his tone to one of admiration. He helped Kay to his feet and gave him a friendly slap on the back. "We could use someone like you aboard the *Black Dagger*. I'm Captain Gallard. And you are?"

Before answering the captain, Kay wanted to make sure that Jerra was safe. He looked among the pirates, but she was nowhere to be found. "Where's Ari?"

"The girl is safe," Captain Gallard assured.

"Where is she?" Kay pressed.

"Do you doubt my word?"

"No, but you haven't answered my question."

Captain Gallard took a deep breath and then let out a hearty laugh. "I like your spunk…and your loyalty. You'll make a good pirate."

"Pirate?" Kay asked, feigning surprise. "This is a pirate ship?"

"If we were a merchant ship, would we have greeted you with jeers, attempted to feed you to sharks, and then challenge you to a sword fight?" Gallard asked.

Kay looked at the unsavory faces that leered at him. "No, I guess not." Then, realizing that he had still not answered the captain's initial question, he extended his hand. "My name is Thomas. I come from the city of Dunport."

Captain Gallard gave Kay a firm handshake and put an arm around his shoulder. "Well met, Thomas. I'll show you to where your girlfriend is."

"She's my sister," Kay said defensively.

"Ah," nodded the pirate. "I could see the look in your eye. It was either love or family." The captain turned and led Kay to the forecastle. "Where are your parents?"

"They went down with the ship," Kay answered, trying to look upset.

Gallard nodded. "That happens at sea." Arriving at a wooden door with a padlock, the pirate grabbed a key off his belt and inserted it in the lock. "A pirate ship is no place for a girl. I had her placed in here for safety."

Captain Gallard opened the door and ushered Kay in. Jerra was pacing back and forth in front of a row of barrels. She rushed up to greet him but stopped abruptly. She eyed his arm. "You're hurt."

"Yeah, just a little," Kay said, extending his arm displaying a sleeve that was almost completely red with blood.

The sound of a door slamming interrupted their conversation. It was followed by a quiet *click*.

"Hey! What are you doing?" Kay cried out. He ran to the door and pounded on it with his good arm.

"A pirate ship is no place for a young boy either," came Captain Gallard's voice from the other side. "I'm keeping you in there until I can figure out what to do with you."

"Let us out!" Kay yelled, beating and kicking the door with greater intensity.

Jerra grabbed Kay by the shoulders. "Calm down. I need to take a look at your wound. You're losing a lot of blood."

"I'm fine," Kay said, pulling away and staggering backward. His head spun, and his vision was getting blurry.

"Really? You're fine?" Jerra interrogated with folded arms.

"Yes…" Kay said and then slumped to the floor.

Chapter 12

THE gentle rocking of the boat was in stark contrast to the turmoil that was raging inside Jerra. She fingered the rope bracelet around her wrist and wished that she could activate it right then and there. Kay was still unconscious and lay with his head resting in her lap.

For some reason, which she couldn't fathom, she wasn't able heal Kay's wound. Something went wrong each time she tried. There would be an interruption in her mind, like somebody was trying to force their way in. It frightened her to the core. She had to settle with binding Kay's arm with a strip of cloth ripped from his shirt. The salt water had washed off some of the grime, but it was still the dirtiest bandage that she had ever used.

Jerra looked down at Kay's sleeping form and sighed. She felt like she was facing this all alone and fervently wished he would wake up. Stories of pirates and buried treasure were far from the reality of an actual ship full of thieves and cutthroats. The men of the crew had made it a point to walk by the door of the cabin and threaten her and Kay with unspeakable violence.

"Have you ever heard of keelhauling, miss?" one pirate had asked as he *pressed his eye to a knothole in the door.*

Jerra refused to answer.

The pirate spoke slowly and venomously. "Well, it's when we tie a rope around your hands and another around your feet. Then we throw you overboard and pull you across the bottom of the ship. The barnacles on the hull usually cut you up nicely. If you can hold your breath long enough and don't drown, the sharks arrive to finish off the job."

Jerra found herself unconsciously running her hand through Kay's hair and abruptly stopped, shaking her head. *Oh, Kay, why can't you look at me the way Seamus does?*

Because that would be wrong, a voice echoed inside her head. She and Kay were friends. They were training to be wizards together. It would just mess everything up. She carefully moved his head off her legs and stood up to stretch her aching muscles.

We've got to get the logbook and get off this ship, Jerra thought, trying to focus on the mission at hand. *Captain Gallard must have it in his private quarters. It shouldn't be too hard to get ahold of it and then activate the bracelets.*

A moan interrupted her thoughts. Kay was beginning to come to.

Jerra rushed to his side. "How are you feeling? You lost a lot of blood."

Kay opened his eyes groggily. "Um, okay, I guess." He sat up and winced. "Except for my arm. Can't you heal it?"

Jerra shook her head. "I'm sorry. I couldn't. I...I don't understand, but something kept stopping me. Something or someone was breaking into my thoughts. I had to settle for bandaging it with part of your shirt."

Kay looked down at his shirt. It was frayed at the bottom and quite shorter than it had been. "Don't be sorry. I'll be fine." Then he added with a grin, "You just owe me a new shirt."

"How about I just let you bleed out next time?" Jerra taunted back.

"Fine, you win," Kay said and tried to stand, but then he slumped back down. "Maybe I should just sit here for a bit. How long have I been out?"

"At least a couple of hours," Jerra replied. "Kay, we've got to—"

A pounding at the door cut off Jerra's words.

"Is that lazy scallywag awake yet?"

"It's Gallard," Jerra whispered.

The door swung open, and the pirate captain entered the room. "Ah, finally," Gallard said as he grabbed Kay by the shoulder and lifted him to his feet. "Time to put you to work."

"He still needs to rest," Jerra protested.

Gallard ignored her request and pushed Kay out the door, leaving Jerra alone with her thoughts once again.

***

Kay squinted at the bright sunlight that invaded his eyes.

"Grab a mop and swab the deck," Gallard ordered. "Just because we're pirates doesn't mean we have to live in filth."

The captain walked away, and Kay looked around for a mop and bucket. Unfortunately, the first thing he found was Deets.

"I'm not finished with you, kid," Deets said, giving Kay a rough shove. "When you least expect it…" The pirate made a slashing motion across his neck.

"I'll remember that," Kay replied.

"Aye, that you will," Deets said with a malicious grin and walked off.

Kay found a mop and an empty wooden bucket near the forecastle. He grabbed a nearby rope and tied it to the handle of the bucket. Lowering it over the side, he filled it with seawater.

Kay hauled the bucket up slowly, trying to ignore the throbbing in his arm. With each tug on the rope, he felt the gash open anew and saw blood begin to seep through the bandage.

I wonder why Jerra couldn't heal this. Maybe she just needs to try again later, he thought.

When the bucket was within reach, Kay grabbed the handle with his good arm and lifted it onto the deck. Deciding to use his injured arm as little as possible, he gripped the mop in his right hand and scrubbed the grime off the deck as best he could.

Kay used the opportunity to get a better look and feel for the layout of the ship. The galleon was well armed with cannons on the upper and lower decks and a catapult on the bow. The *Black Dagger* wouldn't stand a chance against a warship like the *Scimitar*, but it could easily overpower most merchant ships and the smaller Island Federation patrol schooners.

The pirates were making a leisurely afternoon of fishing, card playing, and knife throwing. Captain Gallard stepped out of his cabin and started bantering with a couple members of the crew.

Kay smiled as an idea formed in his mind. He knew how they were going to get the logbook and get off the ship. Putting a little more vigor into his mopping, Kay began to whistle a tune. *This will be like taking candy from a baby.*

Chapter 13

WHEN the pirate ship passed beyond the horizon, Alamin ended the invisibility spell. Sighs of relief echoed throughout the *Albatross*; the sailors were brave, but this was something that was way beyond anything that they had ever experienced.

Captain Errohd walked over to Alamin and Strapper. The wizard was crawling about the deck, collecting his spell components and stowing them in his bag.

"I hope they're going to be okay," the captain said.

"They can take care of themselves surprisingly well," Alamin said while twirling a rusty doorknob. "Plus, Felix is there. He'll be an extra set of eyes and ears that the pirates won't expect."

Strapper bent his head down and picked up a chicken bone. The dog pretended to put it in the bag and then skulked off toward the stern of the ship.

"Oh, no you don't," Alamin scolded. "I may need that later."

Strapper looked innocently at the wizard and then spit the bone into the bag. He sat on the deck and barked apologetically.

"Sure, you didn't know that it was mine," Alamin scoffed. "Just like the time you ate that piece of ham right before I had to dispel a hurricane. It's a good thing there was a pig farm nearby."

Strapper barked again.

"These *are* normal spell components," Alamin said defensively.

Captain Errohd cleared his throat. "So now we're off to that island that doesn't exist," he joked.

"You'll see," Alamin huffed.

"Care to make a wager?"

"Sure. Your ship against my bag of spell components," Alamin said, waving the bag enticingly in front of the captain's face. "I've always wanted a boat."

Errohd looked disdainfully at Alamin's collection of oddities. "No deal," he said and turned stiffly in the direction of the helm.

Alamin shrugged his shoulders and called out after the captain, "It's your loss!" Huffing into his beard, he added, "Hmmph! No respect for magic. Now, where's my broken coffee cup handle? Oh, there it is!"

***

As they sailed farther south, the *Albatross* passed many more tropical islands. The sailors grumbled with each missed opportunity to set their feet on dry land and entertain themselves at the local ports.

Alamin noticed that there was another aboard ship who was looking forward to stopping at an island, but for a different reason. Each morning, Bibo would climb to the top of the main mast and spend most of the day in the crow's nest looking wistfully toward the horizon. Whenever an island came into view, he would perk up and stare at it intently. Those sailors working in the rigging nearby reported that they could hear him mutter, "Home? Home?" None of the islands they passed were Bibo's home, and the telok grew sadder with each false alarm.

One evening, Alamin happened to be on deck when Bibo descended from the crow's nest. The telok hung his head and walked morosely across the deck.

"Bibo, come here for a minute," Alamin called. "Are you all right?"

"Hi, friend Alamin," Bibo said with a sigh. "Bibo miss home. Bibo miss trees."

"I know," Alamin said, patting him on the head. "We're not close enough to see your island from here, but it's not far away."

"Can we go to Bibo's island?" the telok asked hopefully.

Alamin smiled sadly. "I wish that was why we were here. But I promised you before, and I'll promise you again—we *will* visit your island when this is all over."

Bibo perked up but then looked at Alamin curiously. "Is Alamin all right?"

The comment caught Alamin off guard. *Is it becoming obvious?*

"Alamin walk differently," Bibo said with a cock of his furry head. "Slower. More tired?"

Alamin shifted uncomfortably. "Y-yes. Just tired from the journey. These old bones were not meant for the sea." With a smile and a tousle of Bibo's head, he added, "I'm fine, my friend. You should head below deck. It's almost time to eat."

Bibo smiled back at Alamin, apparently satisfied with the explanation, and trotted down the ladder to grab his evening meal.

Leaning heavily on the ship's rail, Alamin watched the last rays of daylight dance on the waves and felt a strange kinship with the setting sun.

***

The next morning, Alamin was rudely awoken and tossed out of bed. The *Albatross* rocked violently from side to side. Cries rang out from the deck above, and footsteps pounded on the ceiling of Alamin's cabin.

Captain Errohd's voice cut through the tumult. "Hard to port! Full sail! Don't panic! We'll get around it!"

Strapper barked hysterically and ran in circles around the cabin. The dog had never been overly fond of water, and being on a ship in the middle of the sea had already tested his fortitude to its limits.

"Don't worry, Strap," Alamin said as he picked up his frightened pet. "There's magic in the air…and I think I recognize it. Wait here. I'm going above deck."

Alamin placed Strapper on his bunk and quickly threw on a shirt and trousers. He left his cabin and headed up the ladder to the main deck. When Alamin opened the hatch, he was greeted by a spray of water from a heavy rain that pelted the *Albatross*. He struggled to gain his footing as the ship tilted precariously.

"Get back to your quarters!" Errohd yelled when he saw Alamin stumbling across the deck.

"What's going on?" Alamin asked, ignoring the captain's order.

"You want to know? Look!" Captain Errohd exclaimed and pointed to the raging sea. "That's what's going on!"

Alamin followed Errohd's gaze through the salty spray. A gigantic whirlpool loomed just off the starboard bow!

The *Albatross* leaned heavily to port as the sailors made all efforts to steer the ship away from the deadly vortex.

"Hmm…I see," said Alamin with wide eyes. "Well, there's only one thing to do: head straight for it."

"What? Are you nuts?" Errohd screamed. "That's a maelstrom—the granddaddy of all whirlpools. It'll drag us to the bottom of the sea!" His words were barely audible over the wailing of the wind and the ship's creaking timbers and flapping sails.

Alamin gripped a nearby bollard to steady himself against the wind. "We'll be fine. Tell your men to steer straight for its center."

"No!"

"Trust me, Errohd. I give you my word that you and your crew will be safe," Alamin pleaded.

Errohd's gray hair was plastered to his face from the barrage of rain. He looked desperately from the whirlpool, to Alamin, and back to the whirlpool. He shook his head as if to clear his indecision and then called to the helmsman.

"Hard to starboard!"

The sailor did not seem to notice or hear the captain's request.

Captain Errohd marched up the stairs to the helm while waving his arms emphatically. "Jack! Hard to starboard!"

The helmsman finally appeared to notice the captain's request, and a look of surprise and fear crossed his face. Alamin could not hear the sailor's words over the wind and rain, but it was obvious that he was refusing the captain's orders. Errohd rushed forward and attempted to force Jack to give up the helm. The men's four hands were entangled on the wheel—Errohd trying to steer the ship to starboard, and Jack to port.

Alamin decided it was time to intervene when the two men began to shove and pummel each other. He mounted the stairs and pointed his index finger at the two combatants. Both froze in place and immediately ceased their fighting.

"Now, boys, stop all this pushing and shoving and tell me how to steer this thing." Alamin took control of the wheel and gave it a hard clockwise spin.

The *Albatross* lurched hard to port. Sailors in the masts called out profanities as they clung to the riggings for dear life.

"Go easy on her," Errohd mumbled from nearby. "Let me go before you send us all to the bottom of the sea."

"Just a minute. I think I've got it," Alamin said as he gave the wheel a sharp turn to the left.

The *Albatross* tilted in the opposite direction, and the sailors redoubled their cussing.

Alamin stared at the wheel and then at Errohd. "Okay, have it your way. You can drive."

Alamin snapped his fingers, and Errohd immediately sprang forward and took the helm.

"Captain, don't," Jack pleaded, still frozen in place.

"Don't worry. If Alamin says we're going to be safe…well, then I believe him." Errohd steadied the ship and slowly turned it in the direction of the whirlpool. Then to Alamin, he grunted, "I hope you're right about this."

Chapter 14

THE *Albatross*'s sails flapped violently in the gale-force winds that attacked the ship. Sweat beaded across Captain Errohd's brow as he held the wheel with a look of mixed determination and fear. Up ahead, the massive whirlpool swirled, threatening to swallow anything that came within its reach.

"Steady, Errohd. It will all be over soon," Alamin said above the shriek of the wind and put a hand on his old friend's shoulder.

"That's what I'm afraid of," the captain replied wryly.

Sailors shouted warnings and exclamations of confusion and fear.

"What are you doing?"

"Captain, are you mad?"

"We're doomed!"

"We're going to have a mutiny on our hands," Errohd warned. His knuckles were turning white from his grip on the wheel.

"Not so," Alamin said with a shake of his head. "Watch."

"Easier said than done," Errohd gulped.

The *Albatross* approached the edge of the whirlpool. Some sailors appeared ready to jump ship and take their chances in the water.

Alamin magically enhanced his voice and shouted so that all would hear. "Man your posts! Do not leave this ship!"

Maybe it was the sheer unexpectedness of the command or maybe it was the way that it was intoned, but every sailor obeyed the order and remained steadfast at their posts. They stared with wide eyes at what many of them probably expected to be the last thing they ever saw. The maelstrom was like a gigantic beast, opening its jaws to swallow the ship whole.

What happened next surprised even the most experienced of sailors, who later admitted that they had thought they had seen everything possible on the open seas.

The wind, rain, and whirlpool suddenly vanished as if they had never existed. The *Albatross* floated on a calm, sun-warmed sea off the coast of a tiny tropical island.

Alamin took a deep breath, let it out, and clapped his hands. "Well, we're here."

"Where's that?" Errohd asked.

"Oh, just that island that you said didn't exist on the part of your map where you said there wasn't an island," Alamin retorted.

Errohd looked out at the island in amazement. "I'm glad I didn't make that bet with you."

"Can you let me go now?" a muffled voice sounded from over the wizard's shoulder.

"Oh, certainly. Sorry, but it had to be done." Alamin said as he snapped his fingers.

Jack took a step back and steadied himself on the ship's rail. "Don't ever cast your magic on me again, wizard," he seethed. Once he regained his composure, the helmsman stormed down the ladder to the main deck and headed to his cabin below.

"He'll get over it," Errohd shrugged. "So what's next?"

"Bibo, Strapper, and I will take the skiff over to the island. Carnac is not fond of company, so the fewer that go the better."

***

From a perch on one of the island's tallest trees, a pair of prying eyes watched as a smaller craft lowered into the water from the larger ship.

The eyes' owner fidgeted to and fro. This was not good. They ignored the illusion. Now company was coming.

"Don't like company. Don't want company. Go away," he mumbled.

It had been years, eons maybe, since anyone had come to his island. They always came wanting something. Never to give. Always to take.

Time to prepare.

Chapter 15

STRAPPER pawed nervously at the bottom of the small wooden rowboat. To say that he did not like water was an understatement, and his master's antics were not helping matters in the least. Fascinated with the colorful fish that inhabited the warm waters, Alamin leaned over the side of the rowboat causing the small craft to lean precariously. Old and wise as he was, the wizard often emulated the behavior of a young child—to Strapper's great annoyance.

"Look at that bright yellow fish, Bibo," Alamin said excitedly. The wizard leaned over the left side of the boat until his nose almost touched the water. "What's it called?" the wizard asked.

"Bibo's people call that yellow fish," the telok replied.

Alamin shifted his position as he followed the path of a fish that swam underneath the hull. "Oh, and this one's blue!"

The boat tilted to the right.

"What's that one called?" Alamin asked.

"That one called blue fish," Bibo answered.

As they neared the island, Strapper gratefully felt the waves propel the rowboat toward the beach. The sailor who had been rowing the skiff stepped out of the boat and pulled it ashore. As soon as Strapper heard the boat hit bottom, he leapt out and danced around on the dry, sandy beach.

Strapper had never been on a tropical island before, and he marveled at the different smells that floated through the air. The trees had a different fragrance, and the sweet scent of flowers invaded his nostrils. As he padded through the soft sand and continued to sniff, a new and unfamiliar smell came to him.

Strapper scanned the dense jungle flora where it met the beach and saw some movement in the undergrowth. He let out a bark of warning, issued a low growl, and bared his teeth.

"Something seems to be bothering your dog," the sailor said to Alamin.

Strapper could smell fear coming from the seaman.

Alamin walked over to Strapper and patted him on the head. "What is it, Strap?"

Strapper grunted and nodded toward a path that led into the jungle. Something was definitely there, watching their every move. He sniffed the air. It was some sort of animal, but one that he'd never encountered before.

Strapper didn't like this at all. The more he sniffed, the more different animal scents he detected—all heading their way!

***

Alamin squinted in the bright sunlight at the stretch of jungle before him. Strapper's growling intensified, and his hackles were raised. A footpath emptied out onto the beach, and the wizard soon saw the object of his dog's consternation. A small primate hobbled out onto the beach and stopped when it saw the wizard and his companions.

"Monkey!" exclaimed Bibo excitedly. "We have monkeys on Bibo's island. No see monkey for long time. Hi, monkey!"

Bibo took a step toward the monkey, but Alamin put a restraining hand on the telok's shoulder. "Wait, Bibo. Let's watch and see what it does."

The monkey paced back and forth, as if it were guarding the entrance to the path. Every once in a while, it would stop and make shooing gestures toward the group on the beach, indicating that it wanted them to go away.

Strapper woofed at Alamin.

"You're right. It doesn't seem like we're welcome here," Alamin agreed. "But we can't stay on this beach all day." He started walking toward the path.

Strapper barked a warning.

"More?" Alamin stopped short. "More what?" he asked with raised eyebrows.

As if in answer to his question, the foliage along the beach rippled and swayed, and an army of animals stepped out from the undergrowth! First came the smaller beasts; the front line consisted of mice, squirrels, moles, voles, and many other burrowing and tree-dwelling creatures. Behind them were aardvarks, badgers, raccoons, skunks, and lemurs. Tigers, giraffes, lions, ostriches, gorillas, and other larger creatures filled in behind them, completing the ranks.

The monkey ambled over to the front of the pack. It repeated the shooing gestures and then stood on its hind legs and folded its hairy arms.

Alamin sighed. "Well, this makes things a little more difficult."

Chapter 16

A LAMIN blinked at the array of animals before him. *Some things never change. Carnac was always fond of his pets.* He motioned to Bibo and Strapper to stay where they were.

Rolling up his sleeves, Alamin took a step forward.

The lion stepped forward.

Alamin took another step.

The tiger joined the lion.

"Nice kitties," Alamin said. He wanted to do this without having to cast any spells. Harming Carnac's animals would not aid their quest in any way.

"Hmm…I wonder," Alamin mused aloud. He was thinking back to when he and Carnac were friends in their younger days. His brother wizard had a way with animals. All he would do to gain their trust was…

Alamin began to whistle a tune from long ago.

The animals looked to Alamin with interest. The lion and tiger stepped back to join the others.

"Animals like your music!" Bibo whispered.

Alamin nodded and motioned for Bibo and Strapper to follow him. They did as requested, and the wizard continued to whistle.

The three companions stepped forward, and the animals remained in their places. When they were within a couple of paces of Carnac's furry honor guard, the monkey broke ranks and hobbled over to Alamin. It reached up and gently took the wizard by the hand with a benign and docile expression on its face.

Alamin allowed the animal to lead him and his companions down the jungle path. As they stepped into the welcome shade of the trees, the sounds of many feet stomping through the sand followed in their wake.

Alamin had only journeyed to the Southern Islands one other time, but he could easily understand why Carnac would make his home in such a remote place. The weather was always beautiful—well, except for the occasional hurricane, but those were few and far between. No worries, quarrels between nobles, or the snows of winter.

His musings made him realize how old and weary he actually was. *Someday, others will need to take over from where I left off, but there is still some life left in these old bones.*

Bibo was examining everything around him with wide, excited eyes. He leaned over and sniffed a plant with narrow green leaves and then proceeded to pull it out of the ground and eat the root.

"Oh, yummy!" the telok said with a mouth full of white mush. "Bibo no have this in long time."

Strapper snorted and stuck out his tongue in disgust. If it wasn't meat, Strapper wouldn't eat it.

The monkey suddenly began jumping excitedly and pointed to an area up ahead. It issued a series of screeches and tugged Alamin's hand to make him move faster.

Alamin carefully stopped whistling and asked the creature, "What is it, my little friend?"

The monkey gestured for the companions to keep following.

"It looks like we're getting close," Alamin said to the others. "I've never spoken with one of his kind, but I believe the monkey is saying that Carnac's home is just up ahead."

A rich, black soil replaced the white sand of the beach and promoted the growth of bigger and bigger flora. The plants encroached upon the trail until it was almost impassable, but the monkey pushed back a pair of enormous palm fronds that blocked the path and led the group into a small clearing. The vegetation in the area was much sparser, as if it had been trampled by frequent travel. The lion, tiger, badger, and other animals gathered in a wide circle around Alamin and his companions. They bowed their heads and then receded into the undergrowth, leaving only the monkey.

Alamin was about to speak, when the sound of whistling drifted to their ears from overhead.

Chapter 17

THE whistling continued, and the monkey performed a slow, mesmerizing dance to the music. Alamin was captivated by the monkey's lithe movements and the swaying of its tail as it swished back and forth, over and under, twisting like a snake. It seemed like there were two dancers, with each step perfectly synchronized to the accompanying whistling. The entire world sank into the background; there was only the motion and the music. On and on it went until—

The music stopped abruptly.

Alamin shook his head and looked around. "Well, that was odd. Don't you think so, Bibo?"

No response.

"Bibo?" Alamin looked around, but the telok was nowhere to be found. Strapper was gone too. *Now where did they wander off to?* "Strapper! Bibo! This is no time for playing games!"

Still no response.

Panic began to set in. Alamin rushed through the undergrowth of the island jungle calling out their names. The vegetation became thicker and thicker. Soon it was as if he was swimming through a never-ending sea of ferns and leaves. All around was nothing but a deep, dense green.

He pushed past an especially large set of leaves and stopped short. He found himself standing in a long, high-ceilinged corridor. A series of doors stretched down the hallway to his left, and to his right stood a row of tall, oblong windows. Sunlight streamed in, lighting up the area—all traces of the jungle were completely gone.

"I know this place…" Alamin mused while gently tracing his hand across a finely wrought wall tapestry.

He continued down the hall. *There should be a spiral staircase just around the next corner.* Sure enough, it was as he remembered. "This can't be…"

Alamin gulped and took the first step that led up to the Wizards' Tower. As he crested the top of the staircase, he stepped out onto a small balcony and was greeted by a view that neither he nor anyone else had seen in over a millennium—the great city of Ton stretched out in all directions. An uncountable array of buildings of all shapes and sizes clustered together in a neat checkerboard pattern as far as the eye could see. Palaces of brilliant white stood out from the smaller structures of houses and shops, while the Veda River ribboned its way through the city.

Part of his mind refused to believe what he was seeing, but the rest of it yearned for it to be true. He left the balcony behind and quickened his pace down a wide hallway. Passing the large double doors that led to the Masters' Chambers, Alamin walked until he found a short, unassuming side passage. His legs faltered as he approached the wooden door to the acolytes' quarters. Acolytes were wizards that were too old to be considered apprentices but were not yet masters.

Alamin lifted the latch, and the door swung smoothly open. He stepped inside the common room of the acolytes' apartments. A small mirror adorned the wall next to the door, and the image that Alamin saw made him stop short. Staring back at him was a very young man who just recently traded the blue robes of the acolyte for the red robes of the master wizard. He was looking at his own eyes, but the eyes from another time and place. A time before the Desert Waste was created through the greed of princes and wizards of Celcia hungering for more and more power. A time when he was about to be called "Great" for his discovery. A place where he was happier than he had ever been in his whole life. At least before that day—

"Ceremon, is that you?" a musical female voice called.

A young woman bounded into the room, her short blond hair swishing in the breeze. She ran up and hugged him. Alamin's breath caught in his throat, and every muscle in his body froze.

No, it can't be…

"Where have you been? Off on another secret mission for the prince? I was getting worried." She finished with a playful pout.

"I...I..." Alamin stammered.

"I know. You can't tell me. It's for my own good. Blah, blah, blah. I've heard it all before." She cocked her head and rolled her eyes as she always did when she was exasperated with him. It was a trait that sometimes irritated Alamin, but, at that moment, it was the most wonderful expression in the world.

"Greta, I'm sorry it's been so long," Alamin found the words coming out just as he remembered.

She suddenly grabbed his hand. "Come here. I want to show you something." Greta rushed him down the narrow hallway to the door of her room. She was smiling and virtually overflowing with excitement.

"Ready?" she asked as she lifted the latch.

Alamin nodded.

Greta swung open the door. The fragrance of spring blossoms floated out into the hallway. The room beyond was a small, typical acolyte's cell. A cool breeze blew through the only window in the room, fluttering its thin curtains. Sunlight shone on a narrow bed and an old, wooden writing desk. A trunk bearing Greta's belongings adorned the foot of the bed. It was just as he remembered—every detail in its place.

His attention was drawn to a small furry object rolling around in the middle of the floor.

"Isn't he cute?" she exclaimed, rushing into the room and scooping up a tiny black puppy in her arms. "See? He's even got a long white beard like Master Talamar." She traced an area of white fur that wrapped around the dog's mouth and extended down his chest.

Alamin was locked in his memories. He was not thinking of himself as Alamin anymore but rather the young Ceremon. His words were the words of the conversation he and Greta had long ago.

"Greta, you can't have a familiar yet. They're only for master wizards," Ceremon said in exasperation and fear for Greta. "If anyone catches you trying to bond with that animal, you'll be banished...or worse. You could be sentenced to death for dabbling in magic before your time. You've got to get rid of it."

She simply giggled and put a finger to his lips in order to shush him. "First, the puppy is a 'he,' not an 'it.' Second, he's for you, silly." She handed the wriggling dog to Ceremon. "You're going to need to choose a familiar soon. Every wizard—"

"Yes, yes, I know," Ceremon interrupted. "Once we don the robes of a master, we need to bond with a familiar—an animal of our choosing that will share in our magical essence. Without a familiar, our use of magic will eventually cause us to shrivel up and die a horrible death. Don't you think I know all this?"

Ceremon picked up the puppy and held him in front of his face. *A dog? I was thinking of a firedrake or maybe an imp. Oh well.* "And what's your name, little friend?" he asked apathetically.

"I named him Strapper," Greta said.

"Now that's the dumbest name for a dog that I've ever heard," Ceremon answered, crinkling up his nose. "Where did you come up with that?"

Greta shrugged. "His favorite toy is the strap of my spell-component satchel. Watch. Put him down."

Ceremon did as requested.

Greta jiggled the strap of her bag, and the puppy immediately sunk his teeth into the leather and shook his head from side to side. A one-sided wrestling match commenced, and soon Strapper was entangled in the strap. He spun his way out and started the process all over again.

Ceremon chuckled. "He *is* cute. I have to admit it."

"I have another present for you, but you can't tell anybody about this," Greta said secretively and walked over to her writing desk. She tapped the side in a rhythmic pattern. A small flap opened up on one of the legs, revealing a secret compartment. She reached in and took out a slender silver vial with a crystal top.

"What's that?" Ceremon asked.

Greta's eyes lit up with excitement. "It's a longevity potion. It's been my project in the lab."

Ceremon shook his head dismissively. "Master Decan has everybody try to create that in Potions class. It's meant to show you that there are things magic can't do. And it's a good thing that we can't live longer than anybody else. Imagine how powerful some wizards might get and how they could misuse their abilities.

Look what's happening now. We're on the brink of war. Each prince is trying to get the upper hand on every other one."

Greta ignored his speech and held up the vial in her hands. "Ceremon, I got a fly to live for half a year. They usually die in a month."

"A fly? You're experimenting with bugs? What happened to the mice?"

"Mice can live for a couple of years. We never know if our longevity potions work because the mice would be alive at the end of the class anyway. I decided to try the potion on something that lives only a short while."

"Well, just because it works on a fly doesn't mean that it will work on a human," Ceremon lectured.

"And just because you're a master wizard doesn't mean that you know everything," Greta snapped back.

Ceremon felt his temper beginning to flare, so he took a deep breath. This was not the time or place to have an argument, especially since it may be the last time they see each other. Prince Falco's plan to bring the other rulers of Celcia under his submission was bold and dangerous.

"Let me see it," he said, holding out his hand.

Greta handed him the vial. Ceremon could feel the flows of very strong magic radiate from the tiny container. He opened the crystal stopper and immediately pulled his head back. "Ugh, it stinks!"

"That's because it's made from wildfire root, found in only the smelliest of swamps."

"Have you tried it on anything other than flies?"

"Not yet. I was hoping to try it out on you," Greta said with a sly smile.

"Not funny." Ceremon shook his head and placed the stopper back on the vial. "You have the strangest sense of humor."

"And you need to find one. You're always too serious."

Ceremon huffed. He reached out to hand the vial back to Greta, but she shook her head.

"No. It's yours. You may need it someday," she insisted.

"If it works." Ceremon furrowed his brow. "Did you tell anyone else about this?"

"Only my lab partner, Laserrure," Greta answered. "He won't tell anybody. I promise," she added quickly.

"Laserrure? The blinker?" Ceremon asked disdainfully. "Will he ever learn to cast a spell with his eyes open?" Ceremon shook his head and placed the silver vial in a pocket of his robe. As he did so, it brushed against the small scroll that was already in there. He rubbed his finger along the length of parchment and felt its power flow through his hand. The feeling was exhilarating. He quickly let it go and tried to concentrate on the conversation at hand, but a voice seemed to be calling to him from the back of his mind.

Don't do it. Take Greta and leave Ton.

Ceremon took a deep breath to clear his thoughts. He listened. The voice was gone.

"Are you okay?" Greta asked, taking him by the arm. "Do you need to sit down?"

"No, I'm all right," Ceremon answered. "I thought—"

Don't let her go. Destroy the scroll and leave now!

Ceremon staggered. "Where is that voice coming from?"

"What voice?" Greta asked. She gripped his shoulders and stared straight in his face. "You're not well. You look so pale." She led him to the bed and forced him to sit down.

Do not summon the fire elemental.

Ceremon bolted up off the bed and looked around the room. "Who are you? How did you know about that?"

Greta's eyes were wide with fear and concern. "Ceremon, you're scaring me. There is no voice. Please sit down."

He ignored Greta's pleas and began frantically pacing the room.

It will fool you. The elemental will never truly be under your control.

"You're wrong!" Ceremon screamed. "I can do it. I *will* control it."

"I'm going to get Master Talamar to help," Greta said with tear-filled eyes and ran from the room.

The fire elemental will grow stronger with every battle. Its hunger for destruction will never be sated.

"I will control its every move."

It will destroy everything you love.

"Get out of my head!" Ceremon screamed.

Burn the scroll.

"Go away!"

Burn the scroll!

Ceremon heard rushing footsteps enter the acolytes' apartments and then Greta's voice. "He's in my room. I don't know what's wrong. Please help him."

Ceremon turned to see Master Talamar standing in the doorway. The wizard whispered a single word and waved his hand.

Ceremon immediately crumpled to the floor.

Chapter 18

STRAPPER watched as first Bibo and then Alamin closed their eyes and collapsed to the ground. The whistling stopped, and the monkey slipped into the underbrush and out of sight.

He padded over to his master and nudged the wizard's face with his wet nose. Whoever lived on this island knew how to deal with a wizard: hypnotize him and then cast a sleep spell. Simple, but effective. Luckily for Strapper, hypnosis did not work on dogs. Strapper had never met Carnac, but he heard the stories. *Crazy* and *eccentric* were the most common words used to describe the wizard. And coming from Alamin...that meant something.

Strapper's ears perked up at a sound coming his way. Footsteps. Slow and steady. Most likely human. He positioned himself in front Alamin and Bibo.

A gnarled and wrinkly hand appeared and pushed aside a large fern.

Strapper issued forth a low growl.

The hand hesitated and withdrew.

An ancient face with the largest nose and the bushiest eyebrows Strapper had ever seen poked out from the underbrush. "Nice doggie," the old man said in a frail voice. "Now, time to go to dreamland. Like the others, go to the place you most want to be. And like a good dog...stay!"

The old man finished with a flick of his hand.

Strapper felt his eyes droop and his body go limp as he slumped to the ground.

Chapter 19

CEREMON tossed and turned in his sleep. Fitful dreams filled with a strange presence invaded his mind. He was supposed to go to the Great Volcano with Master Talamar to summon the fire elemental, but the presence tantalized him with the promise of a peaceful life with Greta and warned of a catastrophe beyond imagination.

Find Greta and escape from the city of Ton, the voice insisted. Ceremon tried to block it out, but it assailed him relentlessly.

Destroy the scroll.

Find Greta.

Escape from Ton.

Destroy the scroll.

Ceremon's eyes snapped open, and he sat bolt upright. "Where am I?" His breath came in gasps, and sweat ran down his face.

Master Talamar's voice answered sternly, "You're back in your chambers, and here you'll stay until I return from the Great Volcano with the fire elemental."

Master Talamar sat in a chair by a small fireplace. The elder wizard rose, his red robes flowing behind him; the ornate gold trim on the hems and cuffs marked him as the Grand Wizard of Ton. In his right hand, he held the scroll that had formerly been in Ceremon's pocket.

"Master Talamar," Ceremon said with a bow of his head, acknowledging his superior. "But what do you mean? I thought we were going together. The spell was *my* discovery. I inscribed it on the scroll."

Get the scroll. Destroy it before it's too late!

Ceremon shook his head. There it was again. *Who are you?* he thought.

"And you will forever be given credit for the discovery of how to summon an elemental. I will make sure that nobody steals that glory from you," Talamar said gravely, staring into the fire and not noticing Ceremon's pained expression. "But something happened to you back there in the acolytes' apartments. You're not stable. I can't risk anything going wrong with this mission. It's too important and too dangerous."

I need to get that scroll, Ceremon thought. "Master Talamar, this is a mistake. We shouldn't try to summon the elemental. It's not going to do our bidding. It's going to destroy us!"

Why did I just say that? Ceremon thought frantically. *Am I truly going mad?* Then he felt the presence again, only this time it was overpowering. It pushed on his consciousness, and Ceremon knew that it was trying to take him over. He fought back, but it was no use; the presence burst forth with incredible power and a single word—*Alamin.* Only it was more than just a word; it was an identity. An identity that Ceremon could not combat. Ceremon fell into the dark recesses of his mind, and Alamin took control.

"Nonsense," Talamar said with a frown. "I've examined every part of the spell, and it will work perfectly. The fire elemental will be under our control."

"We will only *think* it's doing our bidding," Alamin argued as he rose from the bed and put on his red robes. "It will grow stronger and stronger until we can no longer hold its bonds."

"This crazy talk only convinces me of my decision," Talamar asserted, brandishing the scroll like a schoolmaster's stick. "You will remain here. Don't make me put you under house arrest."

"You will not go!" Alamin exclaimed and cast a spell to freeze Talamar in place.

The other master countered Alamin's spell and unleashed a spray of fiery darts aimed at Alamin's chest.

"*Mithandril!*" A shield appeared in front of Alamin. The darts deflected off its glowing surface.

Talamar dove out of the way as a stray missile nearly singed his head. He dropped the scroll, and it skidded across the floor.

Alamin reacted quickly and sent a fiery dart of his own, disintegrating the parchment.

"You fool!" Talamar shrieked. "You have doomed us all!" The master wizard's head drooped in defeat, and his voice dropped to a whisper. "This was our chance to make the other princes succumb to our will. We could have brought peace to the land," he said despondently, staring at the small pile of ashes at his feet.

"We would have only brought about our own doom," Alamin said.

"How do you know?" Talamar asked.

"Because I have seen it," Alamin answered simply and walked out of the room, leaving Talamar staring forlornly after him.

Alamin headed down the hall toward the acolytes' apartments with a confident stride. This was what he should have done a millennium ago. Destroy the scroll. Save Greta. Save them all from his youthful folly and ambition.

Stopping in the common room, he looked in the mirror. Ceremon glanced back at him. For a moment, Alamin's head reeled. He felt the old desires for glory and power begin to surge back. He created the spell. He could rewrite the scroll. He could control—

No! You can't, and you won't!

Alamin regained his composure and marched straight to Greta's door. He gave a single knock and opened it wide.

Greta sat at her writing desk with Strapper on her lap. She was stroking the tiny puppy's head with her index finger. Without looking up, she asked, "How is he?"

"Better than he ever was before," Alamin proclaimed.

Greta looked up in amazement. Tears streaked her face, but her mouth beamed with a radiant smile. Placing Strapper on the bed, she ran to Alamin and wrapped her arms around him.

"Gather your belongings," Alamin said. "We're leaving."

"W-where are we going?" Greta asked.

"You'll see," Alamin answered with a grin.

In no time, Greta had assembled her small collection of clothes, spell components, and personal items. All the while, she had been asking for hints to where they were going, but Alamin had remained silent.

"Ceremon, why won't you tell me where we're going?"

"Don't call me Ceremon anymore. It's time for new beginnings. Call me Alamin."

Greta looked puzzled. "That means something in the Old Tongue." She furrowed her brow. "Oh, I was never good with languages. Um...servant...no..."

"Repentant," Alamin answered to help her along.

"What are you repentant about? You didn't do anything wrong."

"I almost made the biggest mistake of my life. I never want to forget this feeling I have right now." Scooping Strapper off the bed, he asked, "Do you have everything?"

Greta nodded.

"Then take my hand," Alamin said, reaching out for Greta.

She took his hand, and Alamin reached into his bag of spell components. He drew out a feather and traced it in the air while chanting in the magical language of Celcia.

The room began to spin around them until it was only a blur of swirling colors. When the landscape came back into focus, they were no longer inside the Wizard's Tower in the city of Ton but rather in a cheerful clearing surrounded by tall oak and elm trees. The sun warmed their faces. Birds chirped from all around, and the wind gently blew their hair.

"What is this place?" Greta asked. "It's beautiful!"

"Where did you say you always wanted to live?"

"Far, far away," Greta laughed, and then a look of understanding crossed her face along with a smile that spread from ear to ear. She continued breathlessly, "In a cabin...in the forest...surrounded by nothing but nature."

"Stay here," Alamin said, handing Strapper to Greta. He reached into his spell-component bag and produced an array of odds and ends. As he walked toward the other side of the clearing, he dropped various items on the ground. A root here. A piece of string there. A small rubber ball went rolling across the grass.

After he was satisfied that all the items were in their correct places, Alamin began the incantation that would bring Greta's dream to reality. He chanted louder and louder, and then clapped his hands together. Hedgerows and flowerbeds sprouted out of the ground where only grass had been moments before. Trees, arbors, and gravel pathways created a picturesque backdrop for what was to come.

The ground shook, and Greta looked a little nervous. Alamin smiled to reassure her and pointed to the far end of the clearing. The air shimmered in an assortment of colors that would make a rainbow pale in comparison. Soon, a quaint cottage appeared as the centerpiece of Alamin's creation.

Alamin returned to Greta, who was nuzzling Strapper happily.

"Where are we?" she asked.

"Far to the east of Celcia. Away from princes. Away from wars. Away from trouble." Alamin felt a sensation of peace like he had never known coupled with a desire to stay in that place forever and ever. He led Greta to the cottage and closed the door behind them.

Chapter 20

"Yo, ho, ho, and a bottle of boring," Felix sang as he swam around the hull of the pirate ship. Over the past few days, the sprite had transformed from fish to bird and fish again in order to keep watch on Kay and Jerra.

I don't know why they need me for this, he thought, taking to the air in the form of a small gull. He circled high above the pirate ship to get a look at their surroundings. *Hmm, water…water…more water. Oh, land ho!*

In the distance, silhouetted by the setting sun, a small island dotted the otherwise unbroken expanse of ocean. It wasn't too far away, so Felix decided it couldn't hurt to go investigate. *Anyway, it seems that the pirates are heading straight for it. If there's anything troublesome on the island, I can warn Jerra and Kay.*

Felix made it to the island in short order and was extremely disappointed to find it completely deserted except for a couple of trees, some scrub brush, and various small animals and seabirds. He changed back to his natural form and landed in the bough of a palm tree.

"Yo, ho, ho…" he sang and drifted off to sleep.

***

The warm breeze that blew through the trees gave Felix a feeling of such peace and contentment that he was reluctant to open his eyes. The wide palm leaf had become contoured to his body during his extended nap, making him very comfortable indeed.

"Well, I'd better check on them," Felix mumbled groggily. He rose from his perch and took to the air. The moon floated high in the night sky, illuminating the pirate ship anchored in the island's lagoon. "Oops. Must have slept a little longer than I thought. Oh well, how much trouble could they have gotten into?"

Needing some variety in his life, Felix changed into a plover and flew toward the *Black Dagger*. The ship was strangely devoid of any activity. The few pirates that he could see were sleeping at their posts.

As he approached, he spied Kay and Jerra exiting the storage chamber that they had been kept in. They tiptoed across the main deck toward the captain's cabin.

Oh, just in time for the show! Felix thought excitedly as he flew higher and landed on the topmost yard of the main mast.

He watched them enter the cabin and waited. All was quiet until a voice from nearby shattered the silence.

"Whatcha doin', sprite?"

Felix turned toward the sound. A pirate was leaning over the edge of the crow's nest, glaring straight at him.

*How does he know I'm...*Felix's thought trailed off as he looked down at himself. He was back in his original form!

But that can't be. I didn't change back.

"I asked you a question," the pirate pressed and then reached out to grab him.

Luckily, Felix was much quicker than the pirate. He took to the air, easily avoiding the buccaneer's grasp. As he did so, he realized that he had changed back into a bird.

This is odd, Felix thought. He flew to a yard on the mizzenmast. As soon as he touched the beam, he immediately became himself again. "Magic must not work aboard the ship," Felix reasoned. "This isn't good. I've got to warn Kay and Jerra."

Felix leapt from the yard and swooped down toward the main deck. That was when he heard the captain shout from below.

Oh no! I'm too late, Felix despaired.

Chapter 21

"HERE goes nothing," Kay said, taking hold of the latch. Since arriving on the *Black Dagger*, Kay and Jerra had spent their time working and learning the flow of the pirates' routines. Kay did his best to fit in with the crew; he didn't let anyone bully or push him around, and he got into more than his share of scuffles. As time went by, the pirates gave him grudging respect, and both he and Jerra were allowed more freedom. The pirates hadn't even bothered to lock them inside their cabin anymore; Kay and Jerra were able to roam about the ship at will. And that was exactly the way Kay had hoped his plan would go.

As they stepped out into the night, they found the deck deserted. No one was at the helm, and the sails were furled. The ship lay anchored in the shallows near a small deserted island.

"This is almost too perfect," Jerra whispered.

Kay nodded, smiling. "Let's get the logbook and teleport back to Alamin."

They tiptoed across the deck to Captain Gallard's cabin. Kay was prepared to cast an open portal spell if the door was locked. To his surprise, the latch lifted easily, and the door swung open. He looked at Jerra. She shrugged and then motioned for him to lead the way.

The room was quiet except for the steady sound of the captain's snoring. Moonlight streamed in through windows that lined the back of the cabin. A large wooden desk adorned the center of Gallard's private quarters. The captain was sleeping in the far left corner in a small berth recessed into a wall with an ornately carved wooden frame. His boots lay at the side of the bed, and his sword and scabbard were in close reach.

Although the captain was sleeping, Kay decided that he would cast a sleep spell for good measure. He drew a quick pattern in the air and whispered the ancient word for sleep, "*Liate.*"

Kay felt the magic dissipate into nothingness.

Jerra must have noticed the expression on his face. "What's wrong?" she mouthed, trying not to make a sound.

Kay didn't want to admit that he failed to cast the spell. "Nothing. Let's just get the ship's log and get out of here," he whispered.

"Shhh!" Jerra hushed and motioned for Kay to follow her to the desk.

Kay obeyed but took a furtive glance back at the pirate captain. Gallard's chest rose and fell heavily with the steady breathing of a deep sleep. *I didn't need to cast the spell anyway*, he thought dismissively.

The captain's desk was almost completely clear except for a single, large, leather-bound book. Kay opened the book and poured over the pages. This was it!

A red ribbon marked the last completed page. Kay read:

Continuing to sail westward toward our next destination. We came very close to the wizard's ship, but oddly it never came into sight. Maybe this device that Krellia gave me doesn't work.

Thought it was going to be one more day of visiting one more deserted island until we picked up two children who were adrift at sea. They said that they were shipwrecked, but something about their story is suspicious. They didn't seem overly distraught about the loss of their parents, and the boy is a much better fighter than would be expected of a typical merchant's son. I plan on keeping my eye on them. There is more to their story; I'm sure of it. Could they have a connection with the wizard? Krellia said that a wizard, Alamin, could be sending his agents in search of the ring, but the witch never mentioned children.

Jerra gave Kay an urgent look and motioned for him to close the book. Kay was about to comply when something caught his eye. A loose page dangled out of the logbook. He pulled it out and opened it.

It was a map of the Southern Islands. Many of the islands on the eastern side were crossed out with red Xs.

"They're making their way west," Kay whispered excitedly. "And it seems like they're only exploring deserted islands," he added, noting that the crossed-out islands were the smaller ones not marked with villages or seaports.

Alamin was right! Kay thought.

"Examine it later," Jerra hissed. "Close the book, and let's get out of here."

Kay reluctantly folded the map and returned it to its place between the pages. Tucking the logbook under his arm, he took one step and stopped dead in his tracks.

Captain Gallard stood in front of the door. He was dressed only in his long nightshirt, but the moonlight gleamed off the cutlass in his hand.

"How dare you intrude on my cabin! Put that logbook down!" Gallard let out a shrill whistle. "Logan! Deets! Jay! Get in here right now, and bring some rope!"

Chapter 22

CAPTAIN Gallard walked toward Kay and Jerra with his hand extended, "I said give me that logbook!"

Heavy footsteps pounded on the deck outside the cabin. Soon the room would be crawling with pirates.

Kay handed the book to Jerra. "I don't think so, captain. So, sorry, but we'll just be going." He touched a finger to his bracelet and whispered the word to teleport him back to Alamin.

Nothing happened.

Jerra had a hand on her bracelet and a look of shock on her face.

The talismans didn't work!

The door to Gallard's cabin burst open, and a steady stream of pirates filled the room. In no time, Kay and Jerra were lying on the floor, bound hand and foot.

The captain stood over them with a look of triumph on his face. "I knew there was something fishy about the two of you. What do you want with my logbook? Who sent you?" Gallard demanded.

Kay and Jerra remained silent. Neither had expected this, so they didn't know what to say or do.

Gallard kicked Kay in the ribs. "I asked you a question!" he yelled.

Waves of pain shot through Kay. He wanted to scream, but he refused to give the captain the satisfaction. Instead, Kay remained stubbornly silent and only allowed a slight grunt to exit his lips.

"As tough as a pirate," Gallard said with a smile. "You want to act like a pirate? We'll treat you like a pirate." He turned to the other sailors in the room. "Boys, tomorrow we're going to have a keelhauling!"

The sailors erupted into cheers and peals of malicious laughter.

Kay looked questioningly at Jerra whose eyes were wide with fright. He took advantage of the din the pirates were making to whisper to her, "What's a keelhauling?"

Jerra's eyes began to fill with tears. She wore a grim expression and quietly answered, "You don't want to know."

***

Soaring high above the *Black Dagger*, Felix watched the pirates carry Kay and Jerra out of Gallard's cabin and back to the storage room. His mind raced with the few options that he seemed to have. He could fly to Alamin as quickly as possible, but he had no idea what the pirates had planned for the young captives.

"I think I have to run a little experiment," Felix reasoned. He flew a safe distance from the ship and took to the water in the form of a puffer fish. Swimming up to the hull, Felix gently touched the bottom of the boat with a fin. He immediately changed into his original form. As soon as he took his hand away, he transformed back into a puffer fish.

Felix swam to the surface and changed into a hummingbird. He carefully flew up the side of the *Black Dagger* and over the stern of the ship. No one was at the helm. He flew over and around the wheel and remained a hummingbird. As he landed on one of the handles of the wheel, Felix instantly became a sprite again.

Okay, test number three coming up, Felix thought, taking to the air and becoming a hummingbird once more. He flew to an open hatch on the main deck and dove into the interior of the pirate ship. To his relief, he remained in the form of a hummingbird. *It's only when I touch the ship*, Felix mused. *This may give them a chance.*

Chapter 23

"BREAKFAST is served," Alamin announced as he placed two steaming plates on the table.

"It smells delicious!" Greta exclaimed. "But you're forgetting someone." She lifted up the small black-and-white puppy. "Strapper's hungry too," she finished with a playful pout.

Alamin smiled. "I didn't forget our furry friend." He grabbed a smaller plate and placed it at the foot of the table. "Here you go, boy."

As soon as Greta put Strapper on the ground, the puppy ran to the dish and attacked his meal with happy slurping sounds. In a matter of seconds, the plate was licked clean.

"Nothing wrong with his appetite," Alamin commented as he took his chair across from Greta.

Greta grabbed her fork and was about to dig into an egg when she suddenly stopped. "Cer…uh…Alamin…will they be able to recreate your spell?"

"To summon the fire elemental? Hopefully not. I stumbled upon it by accident while I was trying to create something completely different. That's one of the reasons why no one has done it before."

They were interrupted by a knock on the door.

"Now who could that be?" Alamin wondered aloud. "I'm coming!" he called out and then rose from the table.

The knocking became louder and more insistent.

"Don't worry. I can hear you!"

Soon it sounded as if someone was trying to break down the door. Alamin readied himself to cast a defensive spell for whatever was outside the cabin. He rushed to the front entry.

The whole cabin began to shake. Books toppled from their shelves, and plaster fell from the ceiling. Alamin bounded to the door and swung it open wide. A blinding light shone into the room, and a tremendous wind whipped through the cabin. Alamin tried to cast a shield spell, but his magic wasn't working.

"Greta! Run!" he screamed as an unseen force pulled him toward the door. He grabbed a stout oaken table, but the wind was too strong. His fingernails dug channels in the wood, and he was dragged closer and closer to the light.

Chapter 24

THE table splintered apart in Alamin's hands. He flew through the air and caught himself in the doorframe. He revolted against the power that was pulling him away—away from where he most wanted to be in his deepest and most cherished desires.

Over the sound of the wind, a familiar voice sounded from beyond the light. *Alamin! Wake up!*

He closed his eyes and clung tighter to the doorframe. "No!" he shouted back.

"Alamin, what's happening?" Greta called frantically as she ran into the room. Her eyes were wide with fright and concern.

"Greta, help!" Alamin called, reaching out to grab her hand.

Greta tried to make her way across the room, but sliding furniture and falling debris slowed her progress. The same force that was pulling Alamin seemed to be pushing her back.

The voice continued to beckon, but Alamin resisted with all his might until the voice was joined by a soft, plaintive sound...

Woof.

Alamin's resolve left him. He looked back at Greta, thankful that he had this one last final moment with her. "Good-bye, Greta," Alamin said as he released the doorframe and flew into the light.

***

"I don't know what else to try," a man said with frustration.

"Maybe he wake up soon," the familiar voice of a telok answered.

Light footsteps padded through the sand, and then Alamin felt a wet nose touch his cheek. He opened his eyes to see Strapper looking down at him. The dog barked happily and licked his master's face.

"Okay, okay," Alamin said as he sat up. "I'm glad to see you, too."

"Alamin, you awake!" Bibo exclaimed. He teetered over to the wizard and gave him a big furry hug.

Looking around, Alamin discovered that they were surrounded by three of the sailors from the *Albatross*.

"Did you have a nice nap, old man?" one of the seamen chided. "Ooff!"

The sailor next to him had given him an elbow to the stomach. "Uh, not a good idea to tease a wizard, you moron."

The youngest sailor bent down and reached out his hand to assist Alamin to his feet. "Here, let me help you up." Alamin recognized him as Seamus. He seemed like a kind and gentle lad— a little out of place on a sailing vessel.

Seamus explained, "You were supposed to be back by sunset yesterday. Errohd sent us out at dawn to go look for you. What happened? Was some kind of sleep spell cast on you?"

Alamin took a deep breath. "Much more than that. Sleep spells usually wear off in a couple of hours. This one was intended to keep us asleep forever. If I'm guessing correctly, Bibo and Strapper were both in their own personal dreamlands."

Strapper barked in affirmation, and Bibo nodded vigorously.

"Bibo went home to teloks. Music and dance and celebration!" His face suddenly changed expression to one of sadness. "But not real."

Placing a consoling hand on Bibo's shoulder, the wizard smiled. "It will come true soon enough."

"What did wizard dream?" Bibo asked, wide-eyed with curiosity.

Alamin smiled sadly and shook his head. "Something that should have happened but is now long gone and never will be."

"Shhh," Seamus shushed. "Did you hear that?"

Everyone froze and listened. All around them, the leaves rustled. The group huddled in a defensive formation with their backs to each other. They looked out into the sea of waving fronds. From all around, the animals of the island stepped forward from out of the vegetation.

Bibo sighed. "Oh no. Not again."

One of the sailors took an involuntary step backward. "Billy, is that a lion?" the sailor whispered.

"I've never seen one before, Jonas, but I think you're right," the other answered with a gulp.

The animals stood like silent sentinels waiting for a cue. Only their fur moved from the occasional pleasant ocean breeze that meandered into the jungle.

"I don't think they will hurt us," Alamin announced to his companions. Then to the animals, he commanded, "Take us to Carnac. We have urgent business, and we need his help."

The howling of a monkey resounded from overhead, and the animal swung down from a vine. It landed in front of Alamin and then turned to face the other animals. The monkey made a couple of gestures accompanied by various sounds, and the other animals parted to reveal a very wide trail that had not been there a moment before. The monkey beckoned Alamin and the others to follow him.

Seeing no other alternative, the group followed the monkey through the break in the circle of animals. As they took to the trail, the other animals fell into file behind them. The sand that coated the jungle path eventually gave way to bricks arranged in staggered rows and geometric patterns.

"More than just animals live here," remarked Seamus, looking at the stonework.

Billy tapped Alamin on the shoulder. "Uh, Mr. Wizard, sir…Captain Errohd has only told us a little about why we're out here. Now that we're knee deep in this, can you tell us where we're going?"

Alamin stopped and turned to the sailor. He poised himself as if about to give a lecture. "We're going to ask an extremely powerful wizard of questionable mental capacity if he will hand over or tell us the location of a talisman of vast power that could ultimately save our world."

"Oh…" was all Billy managed to say.

"What if he says no?" Jonas asked, jumping in on the conversation.

Alamin considered answering but then resumed walking. "Let's not talk about that."

The companions continued down the paved pathway followed by the parade of animals until the road ended abruptly. They looked all around for a side path, but the jungle undergrowth was thick with heavy ferns and vines. There were no signs of passage by man or beast.

"Dead end," Bibo said.

As if hearing his words, the large palm leaves that blocked the path moved aside. Gasps of wonder echoed through the group at the sight before them.

Chapter 25

EVEN Alamin was impressed.

Houses of all shapes and sizes adorned the branches of the enormous trees. White walkways and bridges with lacework patterns connected the buildings and ran in complicated zigzag paths. Lights twinkled from every open window and doorway, and the trees and air shimmered and sparkled with countless fireflies.

"Oooooh, palace in trees!" remarked Bibo.

From above, the sound of a harp floated through the air. Its melody was angelic and beckoning. A glowing staircase magically extended its way down from one of the balconies and came to rest at the travelers' feet.

"Carnac always enjoyed his music," Alamin noted. "That was one thing we had in common. Maybe I'll get to play my lute tonight!"

Strapper groaned and snorted.

"Hmmph!" Alamin snorted back. "You just don't appreciate good music."

Strapper barked.

A big smile broke across the monkey's face, and he cackled shrilly.

Bibo giggled. "Why say wizard's music not music?"

Alamin rolled his eyes and looked to the treetop palace. "Are you going to chatter all day, or are you going to help me get what we came for?"

The harp abruptly stopped, and the staircase retracted up the tree. All the lights in the treetop palace winked out.

The enormous boughs and great buildings blocked most of the sunlight, leaving the jungle dimly lit even though it was the middle of the day.

"Well, that was unexpected," said Alamin, looking around at his companions.

They stood in silence for a moment until an irritated voice sounded from above.

"Always take! Never give! Go away!" This was followed by chattering similar to that of the monkey.

Alamin recognized the voice of his former friend. "Carnac, it's Alamin. I've come to ask you a question. We need your help."

The chattering stopped. "Alamin?"

Two of the stairs reappeared at the edge of the balcony.

"Yes. Do you remember me?" Alamin asked.

Two more steps appeared.

"I knew it was you by your music," Alamin continued. "Maybe we can play together tonight. I brought my lute."

Three of the steps disappeared.

"Um…or maybe not," Alamin corrected.

The three steps reappeared.

Alamin huffed into his beard. "The Kingdom of Gaspar is in great danger."

The stairs remained as they were.

"This has to do with the fire elemental."

One more stair appeared.

"There are those who are trying to free it from its prison," Alamin continued. "I need the ring."

The stairs remained as they were, but the sound of a door opening and closing came from above. The tip of a straw hat appeared just above the railing of the balcony and slowly made its way toward the stairway.

"This wizard is a little short," Seamus muttered to Alamin.

"Shhh," Alamin hushed. "He's a gnome and is sensitive about his height."

As the hat reached the opening at the top of the stairway, it floated in midair, and a stout bearded gnome in a floral shirt and short pants stepped out from the other side. The straw hat floated onto his head, and the little wizard folded his arms across his chest.

"The ring is gone. Didn't want it. Try somewhere else," Carnac called down.

Alamin had expected his old friend to be evasive. "How about if we just come up and play a game?" he asked.

The others looked around in confusion. More than one of them mouthed the word *game* with questioning looks.

The gnome's face brightened immeasurably. "Game! Game! Now why didn't you say so?" Carnac waved his hand, and the golden stairway extended to the ground at Alamin's feet.

"Just follow my lead," Alamin said. As his foot touched the first step, the sound of a harp string intoned the first note of a musical scale. The second step sounded the second note. Patting his leg, he called, "Come on, Strapper. This shouldn't be all that bad."

Upon reaching the top of the staircase, Alamin stepped out onto a wide veranda that afforded a beautiful view of the jungle and the ocean waters beyond.

The little wizard skipped around joyfully and clapped his hands. "Oh, game, game! It's been so long since I've gotten to play a game!"

"We will play a game, but first I need to talk to you about the ring," Alamin said.

The little gnome pouted. "Game first! Game first!"

"You've already played your first game today." Alamin snorted. "Or did you already forget about the sleeping spell?"

Carnac stopped skipping and shrugged his shoulders. "Sorry about that. But I didn't recognize you." The little gnome walked up to Alamin and tugged on his beard. "You look so old."

Alamin pulled his whiskers out of the other wizard's grasp. "I guess there are no mirrors on your island."

The gnome resumed his skipping. He encircled Alamin, all the while chanting, "Game! Game! Game!"

Sighing into his beard, Alamin asked, "What kind of game do you want to play?"

Carnac skidded to a halt and threw his hands in the air. "Oh, who *knows*?" he said with a mischievous grin and a wave of his hand.

"Well, if you don't know…" Alamin said, but he stopped short when something invaded his vision.

His nose was growing at an alarming rate!

The sailors, and even Bibo, began to chuckle.

Who knows...nose...oh no. Here we go. Alamin snapped his fingers and his nose returned to its original size.

"Oh, Alamin, you're no fun," the gnome chided. "It was becoming on you. Are you *sure* you don't like it?" He waved his hand.

Alamin saw his nose growing again. He snapped his fingers. "I'm sure I don't like it."

"Come on. Try it for just a little while." Carnac pleaded. He gave Alamin an imploring look and waved his hand.

"No." *Snap.*

"Please." *Wave.*

"No." *Snap.*

Wave.

Snap.

Wave.

Snap.

Snap.

The others broke out into laughter.

"What's so funny?" Alamin asked and was taken aback at how stuffed up his voice sounded. He touched his face and realized that his nose was gone!

"Gotcha!" Carnac said, pointing at Alamin and slapping his knee. "One too many snaps will get you every time."

Alamin huffed into his beard. He returned his nose to normal and looked down at the other wizard. "Carnac, we've come a long way. Can we talk about the ring?"

"Of course we can," the gnome replied with open arms. "But first, I'd like to hear about the adventure that brought you here. I'm sure it was an amazing *feat.*"

Did he just wave his hand again? Alamin wondered.

Seamus appeared to be stifling a laugh. "Um...Alamin," he said while pointing at Alamin's feet.

Alamin looked down and saw that his feet and boots had grown to about three times their normal size and were continuing to get larger and larger. He tried to turn around to face Carnac, but he lost his balance and toppled over.

Billy and Jonas both caught Alamin by the arms and righted him long enough for the wizard to give a quick snap and reverse the spell.

Carnac clapped his hands. "This is fun!"

"I'm guessing the game's not over yet," Alamin said with a grimace.

"Why now?" Carnac replied. "It's going so *perrrrfectly*." He waved his hand.

Uh-oh. Alamin did a quick inventory of his person and found nothing amiss.

"Meow."

Alamin looked down at a black-and-white cat rubbing his leg. "Oh no! Strapper! Now this has gone too far!" Alamin fumed at Carnac. "You know I'm not good at reversing full transformations. Change him back right this instant!"

"But, Alamin…" Carnac said beseechingly.

"No buts," Alamin replied.

"But…"

"I don't want to hear it. Just do it!"

"But…" Carnac broke into a big grin, and the sailors fell into raucous laughter.

"Now what?" Alamin asked irritably. He attempted to turn around, but it felt like there was an anchor tied to his waist. He looked behind him and saw that his backside had grown to enormous proportions and was sagging all the way down to the floor.

"Oh, you're hysterical," Alamin grumbled. He had to snap his fingers three times to get his body back to normal.

Carnac began skipping around the veranda again. The little gnome sang a tune.

Tra la la. Tra la la.
You came for the ring, but it isn't home.
Tra la la. Tra la la.
I sent it away long, long ago.
Ringinaring, ringinaring.
You need to find the ringinaring.
Ringinaring, ringinaring,
What you want is the ringinaring.

The strains of the harp and other stringed instruments joined in and accompanied the gnome's song. Soon, the sailors were stamping their feet and whistling along. Billy took out a small tin whistle that he always carried in his pocket and improvised a lively counter melody.

Tra la la. Tra la la.
On another island, it can be found.
Tra la la. Tra la la.
The ring stays hidden underground.
Ringinaring, ringinaring.
You need to find the ringinaring.
Ringinaring, ringinaring,
What you want is the ringinaring.

"Which island? We don't have a lot of time." Alamin tried to keep up with Carnac as the little wizard bounded from place to place all the while singing his tune. But the gnome did not give a straight answer and continued his song.

Tra la la. Tra la la.
I'm surprised that you don't know.
Tra la la. Tra la la.
Ask the furry one where to go.
Ringinaring, ringinaring.
You need to find the ringinaring.
Ringinaring, ringinaring,
What you want is the—

Carnac abruptly stopped singing and stared with saucer-like eyes at something directly behind Alamin.

"Ahhh!" The gnome screamed. "Invasion! Invasion!" He spun around and ran inside the closest room, slamming the door behind him.

Alamin turned to see a tattered form sprawled face down on the veranda—sopping wet, coughing, and sputtering incoherently.

Chapter 26

THE sun sailed to its zenith and presided over a cloudless sky and calm seas. The *Black Dagger* floated almost motionless off the coast of a small tropical island. Captain Gallard paced the deck, awaiting word from the search party that had gone out to the island just after the break of dawn. He wore a grim expression that made the other members of his crew keep a safe distance from their moody and ill-tempered captain.

Gallard had ordered the pirates to rise earlier than usual and make the *Black Dagger* ready for sail. If the search party didn't find anything on the island, they would be off again.

"One more deserted island, I'll wager," Gallard muttered. "One more fool's errand." He was beginning to doubt the existence of the legendary ring. "Either that, or that silly 'magical' divining rod Krellia gave me is just a useless twig."

Gallard's gaze strayed to the two children tied to the main mast, and he shook his head. They looked haggard and fearful. *Probably didn't sleep a wink all night. I know I wouldn't have.* These were the days when he regretted becoming a pirate. Justice had to be swift and severe; there was no time for debate. You either obeyed or were disposed of—otherwise there would be mutiny.

Why don't you talk? He wondered in frustration. *Thomas and Ari. I bet those aren't even your real names.* His mind wandered to other children who would now be just about their age. *Don't make me do this—*

A sudden voice interrupted his thoughts. "Captain, the search party is returning," Digger, the helmsman, announced.

"And?"

"They didn't give the signal. They found nothing."

Gallard nodded and motioned for Digger to go on his way. As the helmsman descended to the lower deck, Gallard heard a slight buzzing sound.

A large dragonfly circled overhead. It flew across the deck and landed on Thomas's shoulder. The boy looked thoughtfully at the dragonfly, and a slow smile crept across his face.

"The kid must like bugs," Captain Gallard reasoned.

***

The *Black Dagger* cut through the waves of the open ocean with a crew of pirates eager for the day's events. Keelhaulings were rare even on pirate ships, so the entire crew was on deck to watch the spectacle. Captain Gallard oversaw the proceedings with a face devoid of all expression.

The boy was stretched across the deck with his hands and feet lashed together. Members of the crew fastened additional ropes to his arms and legs. The rope attached to his legs went over the starboard railing, under the belly of the ship, and back up the portside, where a group of pirates zealously readied themselves to pull him across the razor-sharp barnacles that clung to the hull of the ship.

The girl had been released from the mast and was being marched to a plank that extended out from the main deck.

First the boy. Then the sharks will come with the smell of blood. They'll shred him to pieces until there is nothing left. Next, it will be time for the girl, so the beasts can continue their feast. My crew wants blood...they'll get their share of it today.

Gallard strode to where Thomas was bound and stood over the boy. "Last chance. What did you want with my logbook? Who sent you here? Tell me, and we'll let you go with a flogging."

Thomas remained stubbornly silent.

Gallard gritted his teeth. *Stupid, stupid boy. Why are you throwing your life away?*

Gallard walked to the plank were Ari was waiting to be shoved overboard. "And you, miss. Anything you would like to tell me?"

The girl shook her head.

"Your silence means your brother's death...and yours."

The girl turned her back on him and said nothing.

Frustration welled up inside the captain. Gallard walked briskly toward the helm. He looked at the other pirates and grunted, "They're all yours."

The pirates erupted into malevolent cheers and laughter, and then they began to chant. "Keelhaul! Keelhaul! Keelhaul!"

Gallard watched as they lifted Thomas and slung him over the side of the ship. The boy winced in pain as the ropes cut into his wrists. Blood dripped down his arms while he hung suspended over the water. The pirates holding the rope on the other side of the deck pulled on it until there was no more slack and the boy's body was stretched out like the figurehead that adorned the hull of the ship.

Some of the pirates sang a shanty about death at sea, while the echoes of "Keelhaul! Keelhaul!" provided a steady and macabre accompaniment. Those holding the ropes that suspended Thomas began a slow sawing motion to the beat of the music as if cutting down an enormous tree. With each pull, the boy inched closer to his doom.

The boy remained stubbornly silent throughout the ordeal to the disappointment of the pirate crew. No screams. That was one of the facets of keelhauling. The pain was delivered underwater where the victim's cries died in his throat. The commotion on the deck was made with the intent of making the one being keelhauled scream like a baby until the waves choked off his cries.

He's taking it as bravely as any pirate I've seen, Gallard noted with somber admiration.

The singing and chanting grew steadily louder until the captain could hardly hear himself think. Suddenly, the pirates holding the ropes fell backward, and each group slammed into the other, creating a tangled mass of pirates on the main deck. The shanty came to an abrupt halt. Cries of confusion rang throughout the *Black Dagger*.

"Who tied those ropes?" Captain Gallard called out vexedly. "Was tying a knot too much of a challenge for you scallywags? Haul him back up!"

A pirate looking into the waters below called out, "Captain, he's gone!"

"That can't be..." Gallard looked to the girl who was now creeping closer to the edge of the plank.

"Where do you think you're going?" he asked Ari as he approached the plank.

"Oh, just away," Ari said with a smile. Turning to the other pirates she called out coquettishly, "Good-bye, boys!"

The girl jumped into the air and, touching a bracelet on her wrist, winked out of existence.

Chapter 27

KAY coughed and sputtered as the last of the water spewed forth from his lungs. Taking a deep and thankful breath of fresh air, he opened his eyes. He lay face down on glistening white floorboards. *Where am I?*

Brisk footsteps reverberated through the wooden decking, and a familiar weathered voice called out, "Kay, you're back!"

Alamin rushed to his side and tried to help him up. "Tell me what happened. Where's Jerra?"

Kay pulled away roughly and stood up on his own. Pausing to examine his surroundings, he found that he was on a giant balcony outside some sort of treehouse palace far above the jungle floor. *Is this Carnac's island?* He turned to Alamin and spoke hotly. "Well, for starters it would have been nice to know ahead of time that magic wouldn't work on the ship. And…oh, hold on…" Kay reached inside his shirt and pulled out a wriggling fish.

The fish slipped out of his hands and flew into the air. Before it hit the ground, it sprouted wings and gracefully looped and fluttered nearby.

"Ugh! You need a bath!" exclaimed Felix. "Remind me not to travel that way ever again."

A sudden shriek, followed by a thud, announced Jerra's arrival. She had materialized next to Kay and collapsed on the veranda.

"Ouch!" she said, rubbing her knees. "Remind me never to teleport while falling."

Alamin smiled as he helped Jerra to her feet. "Welcome back. Are either of you hurt?"

"Kay is," Jerra said, nodding in his direction. "I couldn't heal him. There was something blocking any use of magic or healing aboard the pirate ship."

"Kay mentioned it too, although less eloquently," Alamin said with a look of deep concern. "I didn't anticipate that."

A nearby door burst open, and a gnome in a straw hat and strange attire began running about in circles while yelling at the top of his lungs.

"Invasion! Invasion! Commence Operation Ostrich!" the little fellow exclaimed.

Kay wondered if this was the brother wizard that they were supposed to meet. He definitely fit the bill of being stranger than Alamin—at least on first impression.

A deep rumbling echoed through the jungle, and the veranda shook violently. Leaves fell like rain, and the noise of cracking branches filled the air.

Uh-oh. Are we having an earthquake? Kay wondered.

The trees seemed to be growing taller right before his eyes. Kay grabbed the banister of the staircase and looked out on the surrounding jungle. *The trees aren't getting taller; this whole structure is sinking into the ground!*

"Everybody scatter!" Alamin shouted above the din.

Kay looked over the railing in morbid fascination; the palace and trees were being sucked into the sandy soil of the jungle as if it were quicksand. As the balcony touched the jungle floor, Kay and the others found their feet on the sandy soil and ran. From a safe distance, they watched the palace sink into the sand like a ship beneath the waves.

"Bye-bye, Alamin," the little wizard called out from the roof of a whitewashed hut.

Alamin called out in frustration. "Carnac! Come back! You didn't tell us where to find the ring!"

The last gable disappeared beneath the sand, leaving no trace of the amazing treetop palace. Even the army of exotic animals was gone.

"Can somebody fill us in on what just happened?" Kay asked no one in particular. "And who was that little gnome?"

Alamin appeared to be about to answer, but Jerra interrupted.

"First things first. You've got a nasty wound that needs to be taken care of."

"Is it bad?" Alamin asked in concern.

"Yes," Jerra said with pursed lips. "Kay decided to begin our voyage on the pirate ship by taking part in a sword fight."

"I almost won," Kay said defensively. "But he cheated."

"Pirate hurt bad, too?" Bibo inquired.

"Not a scratch," Jerra answered. She turned back to Kay. "Let's take a look at your arm."

Kay was getting more and more annoyed at the direction things were taking. "Why here? It can wait until we get back to the ship."

Jerra shook her head. "No, it can't. I've found that my healing powers are stronger when I'm in close proximity to life sources. This jungle is teeming with life. I can feel it. On the ocean, it's more spread out most of the time. Now would be better."

Kay rolled up his sleeve and tried not to wince as Jerra removed the bandage.

"Ew. That's a nasty one," Billy said, nodding.

"I like the green pus," Jonah commented. "Nice touch."

Kay looked down and immediately wished he hadn't. The wound had become badly infected. He felt his stomach begin to churn, so he quickly turned his head away.

"Lie down," Jerra commanded.

Kay reluctantly obeyed. He noticed that, in addition to the gash on his arm, his wrists were badly bruised and cut as well. Kay touched them gingerly. "Can you do anything about these, too?"

"I'm going to take care of the wound on your arm first. The flows of healing will also aid your wrists, but they will mostly heal on their own." She looked to where the sailors were standing and smiled.

Ugh, is she doing this just to show off for Seamus? Kay was annoyed to see that the young sailor was part of the group that had come ashore.

Jerra placed her hands over the gash on Kay's arm and closed her eyes.

Everything that happened next came in a sudden wave. Images, sounds, and smells blasted Kay's senses. At first he couldn't distinguish one from the other; bands of golden energy flowed into his body, making him feel exuberant and powerful. When he was finally able to sort out the sensory overload, he imagined that he was flying high above the island with the whole world stretched out before him. Nothing big or small escaped his senses. He could smell every flower, the salt of the ocean, and every leaf and fern. The sounds of birds chirping, jungle cats growling, and even the marching feet of troops of ants filled his ears. Kay felt that he could do anything. And then it all ended as abruptly as it began.

His breath came in heavy gasps. Kay opened his eyes and looked up at Jerra. "Wow! I've got to get hurt more often!"

Jerra gave him an exasperated look and helped him to his feet. "Don't make a habit of it," she scolded.

"Oh, I'm sure he will," Felix piped in. "Let's see. In addition to being stabbed, I've seen him fall off a cliff, get battered by a troll, and almost get eaten by a dragon. Guaranteed, he *will* hurt himself again."

Jerra ignored Felix and put her hands on her hips while looking around at the others. "So, can anybody tell us exactly what is going on?"

Alamin gestured to where the structures disappeared beneath the sand. "Well, that was Carnac, my brother wizard."

"He's not like I pictured him to be," Kay said dubiously.

"Looks can be deceiving. Carnac is very powerful, but very eccentric. Unfortunately, your arrival came at the most inopportune time. He didn't reveal the location of the ring. Please tell me that you were more successful, or else we're back where we started."

Kay's heart sank. He sighed and related their adventures aboard the *Black Dagger*. "So all we know is where not to look."

It was then that a voice from far off sang:

Ringinaring, ringinaring.
All you need is the ringinaring.
Ringinaring, ringinaring,
What you want is the ringinaring.

"That doesn't help us!" Alamin called out.

Bibo tottered over to Alamin and tugged on his arm. "Alamin, Bibo have question."

"Yes, Bibo," Alamin sighed.

"Why did funny little man sing about Bibo?"

"I don't know," Alamin said, shaking his head.

"Carnac sang about Bibo?" Jerra asked.

"Wait! Let me guess," Felix interrupted and then chanted, "*I dream of furball with the light-brown hair.*"

Alamin shook his head and snorted into his beard. To get Kay, Jerra, and Felix up to speed, he related all that had happened since they left the *Albatross*. Alamin ended by reciting the last verse of Carnac's song.

"Ask the furry one where to go…" Jerra repeated thoughtfully. She turned to Bibo. "He thinks you know where it is."

"Teloks no wear jewelry," Bibo said shrugging.

Kay sat down in the sand. "What a waste of time," he said dejectedly.

Jerra began pacing excitedly while repeating slower and slower, "Ringinaring… ringinaring…ring…in…a…ring." She turned to Bibo again. "Is there anything round on your island?"

Bibo looked surprised by the question. "Round like rock?" he asked, picking up a small stone.

Pursing her lips, Jerra answered, "Well, yes, but bigger." She bent down and drew a circle in the sand. "It doesn't have to be round like a stone, but maybe a circle. Is there any place like this on your island?"

Bibo's eyes opened as wide as saucers, and he drew in a deep breath. "On Bibo's island is sacred place. But no shiny rings are there. Just big stones." He bent down and drew squares at even intervals around the circumference of Jerra's circle.

The others stood in rapt attention as Jerra and Bibo continued their drawing and conversation.

"And how about here?" Jerra asked, pointing to the center of the ring. "Is there anything inside the ring of stones?"

Bibo nodded. "Yes, but no ring." He finished with a shake of his furry head. "Sacred place has healing spring. Water good. Healing powers. Make teloks better when sick."

Everyone exchanged expressions of excitement.

Placing a hand on Bibo's shoulder, Alamin smiled down at the telok. "Bibo, my friend. It looks like we'll be visiting your island much sooner than expected."

Felix fluttered down onto Kay's shoulder and put his head in his tiny hands. "Really? A whole island of Bibos? I think I'm going to miss the pirate ship."

"Meow!"

All eyes turned to the cat, who was plaintively clawing at Alamin's pant leg.

"Oh, I almost forgot," the wizard said sheepishly. "Felix, I'm going to need to borrow your ring."

Chapter 28

UPON the companions' return to the *Albatross*, Captain Errohd set a course for Bibo's island. It was at least three days' sail, providing the winds were fair. With the object of their quest so close at hand, the tension and excitement aboard the ship were palpable.

That night, Alamin and Strapper gathered in their cabin with Kay, Jerra, and Felix. The sprite was especially agitated about the voyage ahead.

"So let me get this straight," Felix began while fluttering about the room. "Once we retrieve the ring, we have a date with a goblin horde?"

A knock on the door interrupted the conversation, leaving Felix's question hovering in the air. The door opened, and Bibo tottered into the cabin.

"Sorry Bibo late," the telok apologized. "Sailors interested in Bibo's island. Bibo tell stories. Make sailors laugh. Seamus especially nice. Want to know more about teloks."

"They'll soon get a firsthand experience of your people," Alamin noted. "Will the teloks be fearful of strangers? Should a small group go over first?"

Bibo smiled wide and shook his head. "No. Teloks love company! Everybody welcome!"

"That's good to know," Alamin said. He took a deep breath and staggered suddenly.

Kay caught the wizard by the arm and steadied him.

Alamin's face had drained of color, and he didn't look well at all.

"What's wrong? Are you feeling all right?" Kay asked with great concern.

Alamin sat down in a chair and smiled. "I'm fine. It's just that the sea doesn't agree with me. I'll be better when we're on dry land again."

***

Jerra stared out at the dreary midmorning sky.

A driving rain soaked all those aboard the *Albatross*. The ship's timbers creaked in protest as the waves grew in size, and the vessel rocked dangerously from side to side.

Undeterred by the wind and rain, Bibo pranced about the deck in excitement for his first glance of his home in over a year. Jerra and Kay were huddled under a canvas sheet on the bow; they both wanted to share in their friend's homecoming celebration.

A dense, dark cloud of fog loomed up ahead. As the ship got closer to it, a smell drifted on the wind.

"Is that smoke?" Jerra asked, sniffing the air. A bad feeling settled in her stomach.

"I think so," Kay replied with his brow furrowed.

Others must have noticed it as well, because the nearby sailors started to echo their concerns.

Bibo stopped his joyful dance and looked over the rail. "What wrong? What wrong with Bibo's home?"

Kay stepped out from the protection of the canvas and put a hand on Bibo's shoulder. "I don't know. But it seems like there's a fire up ahead...and a big one at that."

"Where's Alamin?" Jerra asked. "We need to let him know."

"I think he's in his cabin. I'll go get him." Kay ran across the deck and practically jumped down the hatch.

Jerra waited anxiously. Moments later, Kay and Alamin resurfaced with Strapper at their heels. Alamin was still not looking well; he walked slowly, hunched beneath a heavy cloak while supporting himself with his staff.

Jerra had asked Alamin the previous evening if she could attempt to heal whatever was bothering him. He shrugged her off stating that it was simply seasickness. She had her doubts though.

Kay was pointing frantically in the direction of Bibo's island, and lines of worry streaked Alamin's face. The wizard looked to the smoke that was beginning to roll over the bow and nodded.

Planting his feet firmly on the deck and holding his staff rigidly before him, Alamin called out to all those aboard the *Albatross*.

"Everybody, hold on tight!"

Alamin raised his staff, and a bright-blue beam shot straight up into the clouds.

At first nothing happened. Jerra assumed something might have gone wrong with Alamin's spell. But then the wind picked up, and the sails filled to capacity. The *Albatross* lurched forward as a gale-force wind came from directly behind the ship, propelling it through the water. Some sailors lost their footing on the slippery wood and crashed to the deck, but most hooted and hollered at the excitement of moving so fast through the water. The *Albatross* skipped across the tops of the waves, and in no time Bibo's island lay directly in front of them.

Jerra's heart sank. Broken and burnt canoes littered the beach, while smoldering husks of trees were all that remained of a once-verdant jungle. Everything was still on the island.

Bibo appeared by Jerra's side and poked his head over the edge of the rail. "Who do this? Where are teloks?" His eyes welled up with tears, and he started to shake.

Jerra wrapped her arms around her friend and hugged him fiercely. "I don't know, Bibo. But we're going to find out. And they're going to pay for this…dearly."

Captain Errohd called out, "All hands on deck! Ready the landing boats! Arm yourselves well!"

The sailors headed down to their berths and returned with a hodgepodge of weapons that ranged from daggers and swords to bows, crossbows, and slings.

Bibo was the first to jump into one of the skiffs, followed closely behind by Jerra, Kay, and Felix. Alamin boarded one on the opposite side of the ship along with Captain Errohd. The two small landing crafts were soon bobbing up and down in the waves as the sailors rowed them skillfully and swiftly toward shore. When they were a short way from the beach, Bibo hopped out of the skiff and sloshed through the rough surf.

"Bibo, wait!" Jerra called out, but the telok paid her no heed.

Bibo swam with much more agility than Jerra imagined he could, based on his teetering walk when on land. The telok ran onto the shore and commenced a frantic search through the debris. Something appeared to catch his attention; he stopped near the hull of a capsized canoe and sank to his knees.

"That can't be good," Felix said with a concern that Jerra was unaccustomed to hearing from the sprite. "I'll fly ahead and check on him."

Jerra and Kay waited impatiently in the bow of the boat and jumped out on the beach as soon as the skiff struck the sand. They raced to where Bibo huddled and stopped short when they saw what was behind the canoe.

A telok with matted black fur lay soaking wet and caked with blood. Its lifeless eyes stared up at them, and it wore an expression of disbelief and horror.

"Oh, Bibo…" Jerra said putting a hand to her mouth. "Did you know him?"

Bibo nodded slowly. "He was Bibo's friend. Mali and Bibo friends long, long time," he said sadly while holding Mali's limp and lifeless hand.

Bibo turned his tear-filled eyes to Jerra. "Who do this? Why? Teloks kind. No hurt anyone."

Kay picked something up from nearby. "I bet I know. Look at this." He held up a dagger with a curved blade. "This looks just like the one Deets attacked me with. The pirates have been here!"

Chapter 29

"How did the pirates know to come to this island?" Jerra asked, raising her voice above the sound of the driving rain and pounding surf. "It's far from where they were searching. They would have had to sail leagues out of their way to get here. Could it be a coincidence?"

Kay turned the blade over and over in his hand. He shook his head. "They must have found out the location of the ring."

"But how?"

"Maybe Carnac told them, too?" Felix suggested. "I've never trusted a gnome."

Kay shook his head. "They couldn't have sailed all the way to Carnac's island and then come here." He threw the dagger down into the sand in frustration. "They must have found out that we were coming here."

"But that doesn't make any sense," Felix protested. "There's no way they could have gotten word."

"Maybe Asok has a way of signaling them," Kay suggested.

"Him again? When are you going to give up on that theory?" Felix chided.

"Never," Kay said stubbornly.

"What did you find?" Alamin called out. He trudged through the sand accompanied by a large group of sailors. The wizard stopped short when he saw the dead form of the telok on the ground. "Oh no…"

Captain Errohd called to his men, "Stick close together, and be on your guard."

"Could the pirates still be here?" Kay wondered.

"Aye," Errohd replied. "They could be anchored on the blind side of the island. We need to be wary."

Kay helped Bibo to his feet. "Come on, Bibo. This isn't going to be easy, but we need to keep going. You're the only one who is familiar with this island. Where should we go?"

Bibo looked to the burnt husks of trees that lined the beach and then back down at his friend. He sighed heavily and beat his chest twice. Bending down, Bibo put a hand on Mali's chest and used two furry fingers to close the telok's eyes one final time.

"Bye-bye, Mali."

Bibo stood up with a look of resolute determination. "Follow Bibo," he ordered and then marched toward the smoldering trees and foliage.

Kay reached over his shoulder and drew his sword from the scabbard that lay strapped across his back. He hurried up to walk beside his friend. The sailors fell in behind while unsheathing their own blades and readying their bows and slings.

How could the pirates have gotten here first? Kay thought in frustration. *And does that mean that they've got the ring?*

Kay normally hated rainy days, but he was thankful for the downpour that drenched them that day. If not for the rain, the island would have been engulfed in flames. Kay looked at the burnt jungle before him and was at least a little relieved to see that the fire had been contained to a small portion of the island. Gigantic trees, covered in greenery, stretched off to the north and south.

Bibo's island was not flat like the one on which Carnac dwelled. A tall peak towered above the west end of the island, and there were sheer cliffs to the south.

As they entered the jungle, Kay stopped short in dismay. The burnt remains of Bibo's village spread out before him. It reminded Kay of the time he returned to Devonshire after the goblins had attacked his home. He couldn't believe that it was only a year since that happened. It seemed so long ago.

Shaking his head to clear his thoughts, he continued to follow Bibo.

At first, no one spoke. They simply walked behind the telok, allowing him to guide them through what remained of his home.

"Most huts in trees," Bibo explained, gesturing overhead. "Some on ground though." He pointed to the burnt shell of a long hut. "That one for council meetings of teloks. Meet there to make important decisions."

Kay followed the telok's gaze to a dilapidated hut. Palm fronds might have once covered the roof and walls, but all that remained of the structure were the charred poles that framed it.

Something caught Kay's eye in the center of the building. *Oh no. Not another one…*

Bibo must have noticed it too, for he let out a tiny gasp and rushed forward into the remains of the council hut.

Kay was about to follow when he heard a single word uttered from Bibo. He stopped in his tracks and signaled to the others to do the same.

"Why did you stop?" Jerra whispered in his ear.

Kay looked at her and did his best to speak past the lump in his throat, "It's his father."

Jerra bit her lip, apparently trying to hold back her own tears. She suddenly perked up and pushed past Kay. "Why are you just staring? He could still be alive!" She entered the hut and knelt down next to Bibo. The two spoke in hushed tones.

"He's alive!" Jerra called to the others. "Does anybody have fresh water on them?"

"I do," Seamus chimed in and brushed past Kay.

Kay wanted to shove the young sailor to the ground, but he knew it was neither the time nor the place. He had to content himself with following at Seamus's heels.

Seamus knelt down next to Jerra and handed her a leather waterskin.

Jerra pulled out the stopper and held it to the wounded telok's lips.

Bibo's father took a few sips and then opened his eyes. They just about bulged out of his head when he saw his son.

"Bibo? You back…you alive!" he stammered weakly.

"Yes, Bibo back," Bibo answered.

Bibo's father looked directly at him and took his hand. "Father not have much longer…Bad people come…do this…" He looked at the destruction around them, and then he focused back on his son.

Bibo shook his head. "No. Father live long time. Friend Jerra will heal." He looked expectantly at Jerra.

She looked at the telok's bent and burnt body. "Bibo, I can try, but there are some injuries I can't heal."

Jerra closed her eyes and placed her hands on Bibo's father.

Breathing deep, Kay braced himself for the onslaught of senses that accompanied Jerra's healings. It wasn't only the one being healed who felt her power—all who were close by were taken along for the ride. He waited, but nothing happened.

Jerra opened her eyes. "He's too far gone. If I try to heal him, it may actually kill him." She removed her hands from Bibo's father and put a hand on her furry friend's shoulder. "He may pull through, but his body is not strong enough right now. Healing requires energy from the healthy parts of the body to heal the injured areas. His body has to slowly mend on its own."

Jerra beckoned the others to gather around. "We're taking him with us, but he needs to be carried in some sort of stretcher."

"Here, use this," Seamus offered, laying his cloak on the ground.

"Looks like Mr. Chivalry beat you to the punch again," Felix chided in Kay's ear.

Kay grunted at Felix and then bent down to help Jerra and Seamus gently lift Bibo's father onto the cloak. Four of the sailors took the job of each grabbing a corner of the makeshift stretcher.

Not wanting to strain Bibo's father any more than necessary but needing to know, Kay signaled everybody to wait a moment. Turning to the injured telok, he began hesitantly, "Um...Bibo's dad..."

"Balo," the telok said, giving his name.

"Balo, where did the bad people who did this go?"

Balo opened his mouth to answer but winced in pain.

"Kay, he's too weak. Let him rest," Jerra urged.

"And what? Walk around the island hoping not to get ambushed?" Kay snapped back. He was afraid that he already knew the answer. If he was right, then they really were too late—not only to save Bibo's people but also to save the Kingdom of Gaspar.

Jerra opened her mouth to reply but then pursed her lips and folded her arms.

Knowing that he was aggravating Jerra, Kay made the interrogation as quick as possible. Looking at the telok lying in the cloak, he asked, "Where, Balo?"

Balo spoke with great effort. "Heal...healing...spring..."

Though gently spoken, the telok's words were like a punch in the gut.

Kay hung his head in despair. "We're too late."

Chapter 30

T HE landing party pressed on through Bibo's village. As they continued farther into the interior of the island, a sea of deep, dense green growth obliterated all evidence of the fire.

Bibo led the way, followed closely by Kay, Jerra, Alamin, and the sailors. Felix flew overhead to watch for signs of the pirates, but everything was quiet in the tropical jungle except for the steady sound of the falling rain.

"How much farther, Bibo?" Kay asked. He was impatient to get to the healing spring but dreaded what they would find when they arrived.

"Up mountain," Bibo said, pointing to the steady rise that lay before them. "Up and up to healing spring."

The rain abated, but the relief was short-lived. The humidity became so oppressive that it made breathing difficult. Kay could hear Alamin's breath coming in short gasps, and the wizard leaned heavily on his staff.

"Are you okay?" Kay asked quietly so that the others nearby couldn't hear.

Alamin looked to his apprentice with tired eyes. "Yes, Kay. I'm fine. This is just a tough trek for these old bones." The wizard focused his gaze on the trail ahead and dropped the subject.

Kay felt a wave of uneasiness pass through him. Something was not right with Alamin. Kay had seen Alamin travel tirelessly across rougher terrain. The last time he saw the wizard this worn out was after Krellia drained him of his magic abilities. The ordeal almost killed him, but Alamin was back on his feet in no time and led an expedition into the Land of Nyn.

Did something happen while Jerra and I were on the pirate ship? Kay wondered. Although Alamin was secretive about his personal business, Kay was determined to get to the root of the problem and find out what was going on.

Through breaks in the foliage, Kay caught occasional glimpses of the mountain on Bibo's island. Its sides were green and steep, rising up to the clouds. The path they were on led to a narrow trail that zigzagged its way up to the summit.

"Let me guess," Felix began as he fluttered around Bibo. "The healing spring is not halfway up."

"Healing spring at top of mountain," Bibo said, pointing toward the clouds.

"Great," Kay huffed. He was about to ask Bibo how long it would take to get to the top when something hard hit his shoulder.

"Ow!" Kay cried. Looking down, he saw a stone at his feet.

"What's the matter?" Jerra asked.

Kay picked up the stone. "Someone threw a rock at me." He looked around, but the vegetation was too thick to see very far.

Seconds later, a shower of small stones riddled the trail. A sailor grunted in pain as another projectile hit its mark.

"Get under cover, everyone!" Kay shouted.

They all dove off the trail and into the safety of the underbrush.

"Would pirates be throwing little rocks at us?" Felix asked from inside a hollow log.

"I doubt it," Kay responded.

"Right," Felix answered. "So if it's not the pirates, who could it be?"

Kay was about to respond, but Felix cut him off.

"Bibo!" the sprite yelled. "Tell your furball cousins to stop throwing stuff at us!"

"Can't be teloks. Teloks no hurt anybody!" Bibo said defensively from across the path.

"Well, maybe they changed their minds after somebody set their island on fire!" Felix retorted.

Bibo stepped out onto the path. "No throw rocks! We friends!"

The barrage of rocks came to a sudden halt, and chattering echoed from all around. Suddenly the jungle exploded with a flurry of furry humanoids coming out from every tree and bush. Many of them rushed toward Bibo and embraced him. It soon looked like a giant ball of fur was bouncing in the middle of the jungle path.

"Bibo back!"

"We thought you gone!"

"So happy! So, so happy!"

Felix shook his head. "Did they miss the part about their whole village going up in flames?"

Bibo emerged from the cluster of teloks and led them to where his father lay on the stretcher. "Father hurt. Need healing waters."

"No safe there. Bad men come. They go up mountain," one of the teloks said while pointing toward the peak that overshadowed the tiny island.

"They burn village!" another called out.

"So sad," a third said with an anguished sigh.

Felix landed on Kay's shoulder and whispered in his ear. "Okay, two seconds ago they were jubilant, and now they're on the verge of tears. Did we land on Bipolar Island?"

"Real nice, Felix," Kay said, shaking his head.

"Come to caves," a telok urged as he took Kay by the arm. "Safe there. Bad men no find. Jili take you. Jili lead way."

"No," Bibo said with a raised hand. "Bibo bring Father to healing spring. Bibo and friends battle pirates. Save Father. Get special ring," he said in conclusion.

Though Jili seemed quite confused by Bibo's insistence on going headlong into danger, the telok nodded and wished the group good luck on their journey. "Come to caves when you done. Teloks there. Many happy to see you."

***

The higher the group climbed, the rockier the terrain became. Moss-covered boulders replaced trees as the main features of the landscape.

At least there are not many places that the pirates can hide, Kay reasoned.

"I wish we knew when the pirates arrived," Jerra stated. "We could be right behind them, or they could be long gone and—" She stopped suddenly as they rounded a bend in the trail.

"Look!" Jerra cried, pointing to the sea far below them.

A ship was anchored just off the western side of the island. Though it was far off, Kay didn't need to be any closer to recognize the *Black Dagger!*

"They're still anchored, and we haven't seen any signs of them on the way up. We might have them cornered!" Kay said excitedly.

"Don't get too ahead of yourself," Alamin warned. "These are agents of Krellia. I'm sure they will have some surprises in store for us. Keep under cover as much as possible. We don't need a lookout on the ship seeing us and signaling a warning to anybody above."

"How could they get word to anybody on the summit?" Kay asked.

A series of bright flashes issued from the *Black Dagger.* Someone was signaling with a mirror.

"That's how," Alamin said. Then to the others, he commanded, "We've been seen! Quick! To the summit! We've got no time to lose!"

Chapter 31

K AY and his companions scrambled up the winding slope as fast as they could. A sheer, unclimbable wall of rock loomed on their left, while a steep cliff that dropped hundreds of feet to the jungle below greeted them on their right. The sailors who carried Balo strained under the extra load, but they managed to steadfastly keep up with the others. Alamin led the way with his staff clutched tightly in both hands. Kay couldn't help but imagine that it was as if the wizard was rowing an imaginary boat up the mountain.

A rumbling echoed from farther up the pathway, and Alamin called a halt. He held out his staff and shouted, *"Mithandril!"*

A glowing blue wall came into being not a moment too soon.

A giant boulder careened down the mountain. The shield easily deflected the rock, which tumbled over the side of the trail and crushed a grove of palm trees many feet below.

Alamin maintained the shield as they climbed closer and closer to the summit. Beads of sweat dripped down the wizard's forehead. Kay knew that, even with his staff, Alamin was pushing himself too hard.

"I got this," Kay said as he stepped alongside Alamin. *"Mithandril."* A second glowing wall appeared just behind the first.

Alamin looked like he was about to protest, but then his face softened. Without a word, he ended his spell and fell into step behind Kay. More boulders bounded down the pathway, but each was sent over the edge by Kay's shield.

"They're just toying with us," Alamin commented. "Probably trying to slow us down. We've got to hurry!"

"Soon be at top," Bibo announced. "Healing spring not far."

Up ahead, the trail led straight to a crude stone archway. A granite crossbeam, supported by two rectangular columns, marked the gateway to the summit. The top of the mountain appeared to be almost perfectly flat, as if some gigantic sword sheared off its peak.

The companions slowed their pace, wary of an attack. All was quiet as they crept closer and closer to the stone archway. Suddenly, a voice broke the silence, and a figure stepped out from behind one of the columns.

"Ahoy, mateys!"

Kay whispered to Alamin. "That's Deets, the first mate of the *Black Dagger.*"

"Now didn't your mum teach you that it was impolite to whisper?" Deets called down mockingly. "But you *are* a stubborn one."

Alamin stood straight and spoke directly to the pirate. "There's nowhere for you and your brethren to run. If you stand down, we'll let you leave this island in peace."

The pirate folded his arms across his chest and laughed heartily. "We'll leave on our own terms. And with what we came to get." Deets briskly turned around and walked behind the column and out of sight.

"Top of mountain like big bowl. Healing spring at bottom," Bibo explained.

Ignoring the weariness they felt from the long climb, the companions rushed up to the archway and paused.

"It's beautiful!" Jerra gasped.

The top of the mountain *was* like a bowl as Bibo had said, but a bowl filled with elegant trees, shrubs, and flowers of every color imaginable. A stone stairway led down to a cobblestone pathway that meandered around a small pond fed by a spring that flowed out of the rock. The most prominent feature, though, was a ring of stone monoliths that ran along the perimeter of the mountaintop garden.

"A ringinaring…" Kay mused, reflecting on Carnac's strange words in his song. "A ring in a ring! Jerra, you were right. The crazy old wizard told the truth."

The sound of metal striking stone and a series of raucous shouts that seemed blatantly out of place in the tranquil paradise drew Kay's attention. A clutch of raggedly dressed pirates swarmed around the spring with picks and shovels in hand. They were gesticulating wildly at something they had unearthed. One of them raised a small metal chest over his head, and the others let out a hearty cheer.

Deets rejoined his brethren. The first mate examined the chest admiringly and opened the lid. He gazed upon the contents with greedy eyes then quickly slammed it shut.

Tucking the metal chest under one arm, Deets waved to Kay and his companions. "Thank you for leading us to the ring. We wish we could stay and chat awhile, but we really must be going." With that, he pulled a small brass ball out of his jacket.

"You're not going anywhere!" Kay shouted. He ran down the stone staircase, taking two steps at a time.

The first mate smiled wickedly and hurled the brass sphere at Kay.

The projectile bounced off Kay's magical shield and landed harmlessly on the stairs before him.

"Ha! You missed!" Kay taunted. He reached down to grab the sphere; it was making a curious ticking sound.

Alamin's voice caused him to hesitate. "Kay, get away from that! It's a—"

The brass sphere ticked louder and faster until it exploded in a blinding flash.

Chapter 32

KAY shielded his eyes from the explosion. His body went strangely rigid for a split second and then relaxed. When he opened his eyes again, Deets and the other pirates were nowhere to be seen!

"What just happened? Where did they go?" Kay cried, looking wildly about.

"They're gone," Alamin called down to him. "That pirate threw a time bomb. We were all too close to it when it went off. It froze us in time long enough for the pirates to escape. Very powerful magic. I can only imagine that Krellia must have given it to them."

Utter despair flooded through Kay. *We failed. The pirates have the ring.* He let out an anguished cry and kicked at the nearest flowers that were at his feet, sending a spray of petals into the air. *The goblins will unleash the fire elemental. Gaspar will be destroyed.* He swung his blade in frustration, cutting through the ferns and shrubs that dared to get in his path.

"Hey, easy there!" Felix said, flying in front of Kay's nose. "This is no time to take up topiary."

"We lost, Felix." Kay jammed his sword into the soft earth in frustration. "Can't you see that?"

"All I can see is a young squapprentice having a temper tantrum."

Kay looked past Felix to where Jerra, Alamin, and the others stood halfway down the stone stairway. They stared back at him with concerned expressions.

Kay suddenly felt very foolish. Getting angry was not helping the situation. Krellia's pirates hadn't won yet. There had to be a way to get the ring back.

Kay bolted past his friends to the top of the stairs and looked out on the open sea. What Alamin had said was true; the pirates had gained precious time. The *Black Dagger* was no longer anchored near the island; it was under full sail and almost half a league away. The sun, too, was much lower in the sky than it had been just a moment before.

He sheathed his sword and looked down at the rope bracelet around his wrist. An idea began forming in his head. *That's it. They won't be expecting us so soon.* Looking down at the others, Kay smiled and whispered, "I'll be right back."

***

Jerra watched as Kay displayed his frustration by attacking the nearby shrubbery. She turned to Felix. "Can you talk any sense into him?"

"Sure, send me to calm down the berserker. Thanks a lot," the sprite huffed and then fluttered away in Kay's direction.

Jerra understood how Kay felt, but she didn't approve of how he flew off the handle when things didn't go right. "He's being a big baby," she said to Alamin.

"Yes," Alamin agreed. "But a big baby with a big heart. Let him blow off some steam."

Kay finally calmed down and jogged back up the stairs. He ran silently past them and stopped beneath the archway. He appeared thoughtful rather than mad.

Jerra breathed a sigh of relief. *What we need now are calm heads.* She looked up at Alamin just as the wizard's face suddenly contorted in fear and surprise.

Following his gaze, she watched in horror as Kay reached for his bracelet. Time seemed to slow down for Jerra. *He couldn't be that stupid. Could he?* Teleporting was only safe when you were intimately familiar with your destination. The only reason that Alamin's charms worked to get them to Carnac's island was that they were teleporting to Alamin.

Before she could say or do anything, Kay said something incoherent and was gone.

"That foolish, foolish boy!" Alamin exclaimed, slamming the end of his staff on the ground.

Jerra was taken aback. She had never seen the wizard angry.

"Felix," Alamin beckoned. "Fly as fast as you can to that pirate ship." His voice and expression softened greatly. "And see if he's all right."

The sprite darted away without a single sarcastic comment. He made a beeline between a pair of monoliths and over the rim of the basin. Within seconds, he was out of sight.

This isn't good. Even Felix is scared. "What do we do now?" Jerra asked. "They're not too far away. Maybe we can catch up with them."

Alamin's face wrinkled with concern. Speaking to Bibo, Alamin instructed, "Lead the sailors down to the healing spring. See if it will help your father." He gestured to Jerra. "Follow me," he commanded then turned on his heels and climbed up the stone staircase. He leaned heavily on his staff and slowed with each step.

Bibo's voice trailed away while he explained how to dip his father into the healing spring. "Not all at once. Feet. Then legs. Then..."

Jerra caught up to Alamin and took him by the elbow to assist him up the stairs. Something was wrong. She had noticed it at various points during their journey, but she felt that it would be better to wait until their mission was done to say anything. Now that they were alone, she decided to broach the subject.

"Alamin," she began hesitantly, "you're not feeling good. Are you?"

The wizard shrugged her off dismissively. "I feel fine."

Jerra wanted to stop and force him to look her in the eye, but they needed to get within sight of the pirate ship. She continued climbing the staircase with Alamin, but also continued her interrogation.

"No, you're not fine. Your skin is pale, you're panting like a dog, and you're using that staff to help you cast spells."

Alamin gazed up at the top of the basin. "You're a stubborn one. Reminds me of someone I knew long ago." He looked at her with a resigned expression and exhaled deeply. "My longevity is not natural. Long ago, I began taking a potion that would allow me to live much longer than normal. The problem is that I need to take it at particular intervals—once every ten years to be precise. I missed my latest dose, so I'm aging at an increased pace. Please, don't say anything to anyone else."

Jerra nodded solemnly in agreement. They stepped under the stone archway and back onto the mountain trail. In the distance, the *Black Dagger* sailed steadily north toward Gaspar. Felix was nowhere in sight, but a small falcon, definitely out of place so far at sea, was racing toward the pirate ship with all haste.

Alamin stared out at the ocean and closed his eyes. Jerra almost thought he was resting but quickly realized that he was scrying. Alamin was reaching out with his senses to see what was happening aboard the pirate ship. Kay was able to scry to some degree, but to Jerra's frustration, that particular ability eluded her.

After a moment, Alamin opened his eyes.

"What did you see?" Jerra asked anxiously.

"Well, he teleported safely, but he didn't quite make it to the pirate ship."

Chapter 33

Kay realized his mistake a second too late. He pictured the pirate ship all right—a nice bird's-eye view of it—thankfully not as high as the one he had atop the mountain. He popped into existence a short way off the stern of the pirate ship and immediately began freefalling toward the water about fifty feet below. Still disoriented from teleporting, Kay couldn't focus his mind to recall the one simple word he needed to stop his descent. He flailed his arms and legs as he tumbled head over heels.

"*Melin—*"

Splash!

The water surged over Kay's head. Struggling against the weight of his clothes and boots, he stroked and kicked with all his might. After what seemed like an eternity, he finally reached the surface and took a thankful gulp of air.

Kay bobbed in the open ocean. The *Black Dagger* was close by, but it was sailing swiftly away from him. Thankfully, there were no signs that the pirates had noticed his sudden appearance.

Kay swam frantically after the ship, but he knew that it was futile. His sopping wet clothes made every stroke laborious, and the *Black Dagger* was moving much faster than he could ever swim. Kay stopped and treaded water. He was going to need to use his head and magic to get him out of this situation.

"Now what?" he asked himself aloud. "I could—"

A high-pitched screech cut off his train of thought. Looking up, Kay saw a small falcon bearing down on him. Falcons didn't usually attack people, but he wasn't going to chance the bird's razor-sharp claws ripping his eyes out. He ducked under water and held his breath. When he thought the danger had passed, he resurfaced to find Felix hovering close by.

"Nice idea: Throw yourself into the water to strike fear in the hearts of the pirates," Felix jested. "Look, it worked! They're running away."

Kay seethed with aggravation and was about to tell the sprite where he could shove his comments, but a wave caught him just at that moment, sending a gush of salt water into his mouth and down his throat. Rather than answering the sarcastic fairy, Kay had to cough and sputter until his lungs cleared.

"Another great idea," Felix continued. "Make scary sounds. Yep, it's working. They're still sailing away as fast as they can."

"This isn't helping," Kay said through clenched teeth, afraid to open his mouth any wider than he had to. "What do we do now?"

"I would normally say that we shouldn't do anything. We should wait for Alamin. But since you're too pigheaded and stubborn to listen, we'll go with the next best thing. Luckily for you, I have a plan." Felix smiled. "And...*this*." He took off his shape-changing ring and handed it to Kay. "I'm sure that a dolphin would catch up to the ship in no time."

As the tiny ring fell into Kay's palm, it magically grew to be the perfect size for him. Kay carefully placed the ring on his left hand and looked up at Felix. "Then what?"

"Oh, you mean that you didn't have that all figured out back there on the top of the mountain when you teleported away from us so impulsively?" Felix had his arms folded as he hovered above the waves, his wings a faint blue blur behind him.

Kay pursed his lips and thought for a moment. His face brightened as an idea came to him all at once. "I'll levitate. As long as I'm not touching the ship, I can still cast spells. Captain Gallard has probably got the ring. Right? If I can catch him by surprise, I'll bring up a shield around the two of us and then cast a sleep spell on him. We'll take the ring and teleport back to Alamin." Kay smiled. "It will be like taking candy from a baby." Kay cringed inwardly as he remembered the last time he used that phrase.

Felix looked uncertain. "Yeah, a baby who's got fifty friends hanging around with swords and daggers."

"Got a better idea?"

"Right now? No."

"Then what are we waiting for?" Kay closed his eyes and imagined a dolphin. He immediately felt his arms folding up into flippers and his legs fusing together. This was the first time he had ever used Felix's ring, and the transformation wasn't at all uncomfortable as he had imagined it would be. Kay's body felt as if it were made of the softest and most pliable clay. His face elongated, and he took a large gulp of air through the new blowhole on the back of his head.

With a squeak that meant "Race you there," Kay dove beneath the waves and was soon quickly catching up with the *Black Dagger*.

Being in the form of a dolphin, Kay felt a rush of freedom like he had never known. He dove down and swam in loops and twists. The feeling of the water rushing past his body was exhilarating! Kay didn't lose sight of his mission, but he swam in a way so that he enjoyed every second of the chase.

The ocean was filled with sounds. At first Kay found it difficult to filter what he was hearing. There were low growling noises, high-pitched squeaks, the pounding of the waves as they rolled and crashed on the surface of the sea, and the creak of timbers from nearby and distant ships. He followed the loudest of the creaks and was soon within sight of the *Black Dagger*'s hull.

Kay ascended to the surface and cautiously lifted his head above the water. A pirate was stationed in the crow's nest, but he was staring off in the distance toward Bibo's island. The lookout didn't seem concerned with what was happening directly to the rear of the ship.

This is good, Kay thought. *They're expecting our ship to pursue them. I'll be able to catch them by surprise.* He heard a faint buzzing noise coming from behind him and turned to see Felix approaching. *Oh no! Why is he following me? If they see him coming, they'll be on their guard.*

The *Black Dagger* was moving at full sail, and Kay had to dive below the waves again to catch up with her. As soon as he reached the hull, he dove out of the water.

He squeaked and fell back in.

Dummy! He remonstrated himself. *Turn back into a human, and then cast the spell.*

Trying again, and with better timing, Kay leapt out of the water, returned to his regular form, and chanted, "*Jymphilay, jymphilay, jymphilay...*"

Kay hovered at the stern of the *Black Dagger*, being very careful not to come in contact with the vessel. He changed the chant from his voice to his mind. Kay levitated higher until he could just peek through the banisters of the railing at the stern of the ship.

The helmsman stood alone and was looking straight ahead, intent on keeping the course steady. Kay used this opportunity to scan the rest of the ship while making sure he kept most of his frame hidden behind the rail.

From his raised vantage point, Kay had a clear view of most of the ship. Captain Gallard and Deets stood toe-to-toe on the main deck. They appeared to be arguing, with most of the crew standing behind one or the other of the two pirates. Gallard and Deets spoke so boisterously that Kay could hear every word.

"This is beyond gold and silver. There is magic involved," Gallard said.

"Bah! You live in fear of magic and witches," Deets replied scornfully. "You say that this is beyond gold and silver. I agree with you, my dear captain. This is about gold, silver, gems, and jewels."

"You fool!" Gallard seethed. "In the dream—"

"In the dream?" Deets raised his voice with mocking incredulity. "You call me a fool and then begin to talk of dreams."

Gallard's face turned a deep red. He sipped in his breath through gritted teeth and stepped back from Deets to regain his composure. "Mr. Deets, you are welcome to leave my crew at any time if you feel that your fortunes would be better made elsewhere."

Ignoring Gallard's discomfort, Deets looked past his captain and addressed the other pirates. "The Ring of Carnac is the key to the Kingdom of Gaspar's survival or demise. If we play our cards right, Carival will open its coffers to us."

Greed glowed in the eyes of the pirates; it was easy to see that Deets's speech was swaying some of his brethren. They began talking eagerly among themselves; some were nodding vigorously.

"This is going to get *uuugly*!" Felix whispered. He had perched on Kay's shoulder to watch the confrontation. "I'm glad I've got a front-row seat."

"What do we do now?" Kay asked.

"Hmm…an all-out mutiny would put a damper on your plan," Felix commented. "You're welcome to step in the middle of the fray if you want. I wouldn't recommend it, but it would make a great painting in the king's gallery. I'd call it *Kay's Folly*."

"You're not helping," Kay huffed with a frown. He was finding it difficult to levitate and keep up with the speed of the pirate ship. It was one step away from flying—a spell that he had yet to cast correctly. His last attempt had landed him in the moat of Marco's Keep.

Kay made his way along the port side of the ship. He continued until he was roughly where he thought Captain Gallard had been standing, all the while being very careful not to come in contact with the hull. He had temporarily lost sight of the pirates, and the pounding of the waves blotted out their speech. When he hovered up to view the deck again, his jaw dropped.

Blades were drawn, and the pirates had divided into two distinct groups; one stood behind Gallard and the other behind Deets. Felix's prediction of a mutiny had come true! Unfortunately for the captain, the group loyal to him looked much smaller than the one that backed his challenger.

Chapter 34

"DEETS, you have no idea what powers you're toying with!" Gallard shouted.

"I think it's *you* that has no idea," Deets sneered back. "Look behind you. You've lost the faith of most of your crew. It's time for a new captain. One that will bring riches and glory to the *Black Dagger*."

Deets raised his sword and, with a shout that was echoed by the pirates behind him, rushed toward Gallard and his supporters.

Kay watched helplessly as the mutiny unfolded. Jumping into the fray would be pointless—and probably suicidal. He kept his eye on Captain Gallard, waiting for the opportunity to put his plan into action.

At first, Gallard and his smaller group of followers held back Deets and his gang, but the tide soon turned. Deets's greater numbers gradually overwhelmed Gallard's crew. Thankfully, they pressed them closer and closer to the spot where Kay and Felix were hiding.

As Deets's men decimated Gallard's group, the captain and his followers were forced to take on two and sometimes three foes at once. Though many of them fought valiantly, they couldn't sustain the onslaught. It wasn't long before most of Gallard's men were bleeding and dying on the *Black Dagger*'s deck.

A group of Deets's pirates had Gallard surrounded. They toyed with the captain like cats with a mouse. Gallard held them at bay, but then Deets jumped into the fray. One of the pirates distracted Gallard with a quick jab. The captain reached out to parry the thrust, but the leader of the mutiny raised his sword high and brought it down in a single, vicious stroke.

Gallard screamed in agony as his sword clattered to the deck with his hand still attached!

The captain reeled back, clutching his bloody stump of an arm. His four remaining followers forced their way between their captain and his attackers.

Gallard thrust his injured arm into his coat and fell to one knee. He was so close that Kay could have reached over the edge of the rail and touched his jacket.

"This is our chance," Kay whispered to Felix.

"Kay, there's something I just thought of," the sprite began. "It's about your plan—"

"No time, Felix," Kay said, levitating over the rail. "*Mithandril,*" he whispered, and a glowing dome encased him, Felix, and Gallard.

The pirate captain's head swung all about, and he staggered to his feet. Gallard had a wild look in his eyes, like that of a trapped animal, but an expression of something else—relief, perhaps— crossed his face when his eyes fell on Kay.

"Ah, young Master Thomas, we meet yet again," Gallard said with a grim smile. "To what do I owe the pleasure of this unexpected visit? Oh wait, you probably want this." He dug into his coat pocket and pulled out a ring with a brilliant aquamarine stone. "Problem is, they want it too." Gallard motioned over his shoulder to those beyond the force field. The pirates had stopped fighting and were watching the confrontation underneath the glowing dome with curiosity.

Kay tried to answer, but he couldn't. It took all his concentration and energy to maintain the force field and continue to levitate.

A tiny voice whispered in his ear. "This is what I was trying to tell you. If you wanted to put the captain to sleep, you had to do it before you cast the shield spell."

Felix flew into view from behind Kay and addressed the pirate captain. "Greetings. It seems my young friend had a great plan for capturing that ring from you. However, in his impetuousness, he apparently cast his spells out of order."

Felix, what are you doing? As the thought flew through his mind, he wavered in the air and the shield flickered. He renewed his concentration and listened, hoping Felix knew what he was doing.

Gallard grunted. "So here we are. Now what, sprite?"

"Funny you should ask. I have a proposition for you." Felix opened his arms wide and smiled like he was about to sell a chariot with a broken wheel. "Come with us back to the *Albatross*. You'll be safe from these people who obviously want to kill you, and we can drop you off on an island of your choice. After you give us the ring, of course."

Upon hearing the sprite's words, the pirates from both sides of the fray cried out in protest and pounded against the magical shield.

Gallard shook his head. "No go, little man." Sweat dripped down his forehead, and he looked extremely pale. "I'm sure that I'll be thrown in irons the second I set foot aboard your vessel."

"Would you rather remain here and get skewered by your buddies? You don't have any other—"

An explosion cut off the rest of Felix's words. A large cloud of black-and-orange smoke billowed from the *Black Dagger*'s main deck.

Kay lost his concentration and crashed to the ground. He felt the magic drain away from him the moment he hit the *Black Dagger*'s wooden deck. He lay prone and braced himself for the rush of pirates that he expected to swarm around him.

But all was quiet aboard the *Black Dagger*. That is, until the stillness was broken by a cackle that Kay heard only once before—deep in the Land of Nyn.

Chapter 35

K AY raised his head and saw a scene frozen in time. All of the pirates who had been clamoring to get through the shield stood as still as statues—their faces locked in expressions hungering for blood. The one exception was Gallard. He sat slumped on the deck and breathed heavily, cradling the stump of his arm. Blood dripped through the pirate's fingers and pooled around him. Kay couldn't help but glance at the pirate's severed hand that still clutched his sword a couple of paces away.

As gruesome of a sight as it was, Kay knew the worst was yet to come. He shakily rose to his feet and looked past the pirates to where the smoke rose from the main deck. A silhouette of a bent, old hag emerged from the dark clouds, and her cackle echoed once again throughout the *Black Dagger.*

Krellia, the witch of the Silent Swamps, had arrived.

Kay ducked behind a frozen pirate who faced away from Krellia. The man had his dagger drawn, and his face was contorted with rage. Kay gulped, hoping that Krellia wouldn't suddenly end her spell.

"The witch is back," Felix muttered.

Krellia hobbled forward through the throng of pirates. Occasionally, she tapped one on the shoulder and turned him to stone. As she crossed the deck, Krellia called out in a mockingly sweet tone, "Gaaaallard! Oh, Gaaaallard! Where are you?" Her shuffling footsteps and the tap of her cane grew ever closer.

As Krellia stepped past the ring of buccaneers that surrounded Kay, she turned the two pirates on either side of her to stone. The witch scanned the scene with her one good eye; the other was hidden by an eye patch. How she lost the eye in ages gone by, nobody knew, but it was said that whoever gazed into that unseeing socket went terribly and irreversibly insane.

Krellia glanced at the pirate captain on the ground before her and then looked over to his severed hand. Shaking her head, she scolded, "Tsk, tsk, tsk. Gallard, haven't I told you to keep your hands to yourself?" The witch laughed evilly at her dark humor.

Kay shifted his position behind the pirate so that he would be out of Krellia's line of sight.

"Oh, stop all that hiding and come out where I can see you," Krellia called out. "I know you're there."

Kay looked at Felix, and the sprite returned his gaze with a worried expression.

"You're not going to listen to her," Felix hissed.

"She can sense that we're here," Kay whispered back.

"So, let's stay *here* where she *isn't* instead of going *there* where she *is*."

"Oh, this is taking too long," Krellia said impatiently. The pirate that Kay and Felix were hiding behind toppled over and smacked the ground with a bone-cracking crunch.

"Kay Thatcher of Devonshire, we meet again. Except this time you don't have Alamin and those nifty little toys to protect you. By the way, where are the Sword of the Dragon's Flame and the Gauntlets of Might? You don't have them on you, or else I would feel their power. Does Alamin not trust you with them? Did he send you on this mission to die alone? Oh…and with your little, insignificant friend." She said the last part with a dismissive wave at Felix.

"Insignificant? I'll show you, you ugly, bearded hag!" Felix fumed.

"Flattery will get you nowhere, sprite," Krellia retorted. Her wrinkled, green-tinted skin crinkled up into a wicked grin, and her eye shone brightly and greedily. Looking back down at Gallard, she said, "I see that you've found Carnac's ring. Good boy."

"Why do you want the ring?" Kay asked. "It does you no good."

"No good? Of course, it does me no *good*. But with it, I can do a lot of *evil*," Krellia sneered. "Your master, Alamin, may be happy with a pet dog, but I set my sights higher. I think it's about time I had a familiar of my own. Oh, say a fire elemental!"

The witch held out her hand, and a flame appeared in her palm. The flame was twice the size of her hand, and it danced in a strange way. It didn't move in the random flickers of normal fire but rather in a slow and purposeful dance, as if it controlled the way it wanted to move. As Kay stared at the image, a sinister face emerged from the flames.

"With this power, I will be able to bring not only Gaspar but any kingdom and its little people to their knees," Krellia boasted.

While watching the miniature fire elemental float in Krellia's hand, a realization came to Kay. *She's casting magic! She must have removed the antimagic spell when she arrived.* Without waiting another second, he prepared the incantation in his mind and attempted to cast the simple spell that would reach into Gallard's pocket and bring the ring to him.

Kay waved his hand and reached for the flows of magic…but nothing happened.

Krellia's eye opened wide, and the witch cackled with renewed vigor. "Trying to cast a spell, boy?" Her words dripped with venom. "Yes, *I've* been using magic, but does a spider get caught in its own web?"

She swung her hand in an arc, and a force pushed Kay and Felix backward. Just as they were about to fly over the rail of the ship, some kind of netting stopped them. Kay struggled to pull himself free, but sticky strands stuck to his clothing and skin.

They were caught in a gigantic spider web!

Krellia turned her attention to the pirate captain. "Now, Gallard, first things first," she said while tapping her crooked cane on the ground. "This boy has been a nuisance to me for longer than necessary, and I have foreseen that he will continue to be a thorn in my side unless he is disposed of." Reaching into her black robes, she handed a short curved blade to Gallard. "Take this dagger and kill him. Now!"

"With pleasure," Gallard said with a grim nod of his head. The pirate captain took the weapon and put it between his teeth as he used his one remaining hand to push himself off the ground. Gallard winced and reached into his coat to clutch the stump of his arm. Shaking off the pain, the pirate removed the dagger from his mouth and took slow, purposeful steps toward Kay.

Gallard addressed the young apprentice. "It's time we parted ways. You're not welcome here anymore." Before Kay knew it, Gallard was directly in front of him.

"Time to say good-bye," Gallard grunted. He gripped Kay's collar, pulling him forward so they were face to face. Unexpectedly, the pirate captain shoved a wad of crumpled paper down Kay's shirt and whispered, "Don't you dare lose this." He raised the dagger high above his head and cut Kay and Felix free of the webbing in a few deft strokes.

"Now flee!" Gallard shouted.

"Traitor!" Krellia screamed. "None of you will ever leave this ship alive!" She raised her gnarled wooden cane and pointed it at Kay.

A ray of light issued forth from the ancient wood. It would have struck Kay square in the chest, but Gallard dove in front of him. Where the pirate captain had stood a moment before, only a stone statue remained.

Krellia seethed with anger. "That only bought you an extra moment, boy."

Kay dove for the closest open hatchway and slid down the ladder with Felix buzzing by his ear. As Kay's boots struck the lower deck, he felt the wooden ladder rails turn to stone in his hands.

Looking around frantically, Kay found himself in the wide-open expanse of the *Black Dagger*'s gun deck. Rows of cannons lined each side of the ship; light streamed in from the hatchways above and through each open portal where the cannons peeked out.

Kay fumbled around with his shirt and shoved the wad of paper that Gallard had given him into his pocket. Whatever it was would have to wait until later.

"There's nowhere to hide here, and we can't squeeze through those windows without moving a cannon," Kay said, running to a wooden ladder that led deeper into the hull of the ship.

"Wait! You don't have to go any farther," Felix said as he flew hurriedly to keep up with Kay.

"Are you nuts?" Kay called back without looking over his shoulder. He bounded down the ladder that led to the crew's quarters.

Hammocks hung from hooks on the ceiling. Several sailors, who must have been on the night watch, were snoring away, oblivious to the mutiny and all that had recently occurred aboard the *Black Dagger*.

The ladder that Kay had just descended creaked and suddenly turned to stone.

"Will you stop and listen to me?" Felix pleaded.

"Shhh," Kay hissed as he tiptoed across the room toward another ladder that led down to the darkness of the cargo hold. "Do you want to wake these guys? I need to buy us some time so I can figure out how to get us out of here."

"But…" Felix began, but Kay ignored him and climbed ever deeper into the bowels of the *Black Dagger*.

Barrels and crates were piled haphazardly, littering the area and creating a virtual maze through the belly of the ship. Kay scrambled his way through the pirates' booty, but his progress was greatly slowed by the lack of light.

Kay whacked his shin against a wooden crate and let out a grunt of pain.

Krellia's voice floated from the deck above in an artificial singsong. "Come out, come out, wherever you are." There was something so evil and so malicious in her tone that it sent a chill down Kay's spine.

Kay ducked behind a barrel and peered over it. The top of the ladder leading down to the cargo hold was illuminated by the lanterns that hung in the berthing deck above. A worn leather shoe stepped on the first rung. Its material was crackled with age, and the stitching was frayed in many places. The shoe's partner soon joined it, a wrinkled green ankle topping each one.

Kay's mind raced. Should he try to battle Krellia? He had his sword. He could try to catch her by surprise in the darkness. The image of Gallard and the other pirates flashed in his mind. No. One misstep and it would all be over. And the ring. Did it turn to stone along with Gallard? How would they ever get it now?

Krellia reached the bottom of the ladder and peered through the darkness. She had her back to Kay and waved her cane from side to side.

"End of the line, boy," the witch called out.

Felix landed lightly on Kay's shoulder. "Will you please listen to me now?"

Krellia's ears must have been sharper than her age let on, because she spun around and aimed her cane in Kay's direction.

Kay ducked just in time to avoid the beam that slammed into the crates behind him, turning them to stone.

"As long as you're not touching any part of the ship, you can activate that bracelet," Felix explained hurriedly.

"I thought we had to be off the ship," Kay replied while crawling on his hands and knees between two rows of crates.

"That's it, keep talking," Krellia beckoned. "I can find you much easier that way."

Felix lowered his voice to an almost inaudible whisper. "You don't need to be off the ship. All you need to do is not touch it. Jump and then activate the bracelet."

"I can't exactly jump now. She could turn me to stone before I can teleport." Kay didn't dare look up again, but the sound of footsteps told him that Krellia was getting ever closer to their hiding place. "Plus, we've got to get back up to the main deck and figure out how to get the ring from Gallard."

"No, we need to get off this ship and alert Alamin of everything that happened. I saw a door leading to another compartment toward the stern of the ship. Head for it while I distract the old bat."

Kay didn't have time to protest.

Felix flew out into open view and taunted Krellia. "Over here, you toothless hag!"

Krellia bellowed with rage and unleashed a steady barrage of blasts from her cane. Felix swooped and dove through the cargo hold, easily avoiding the deadly rays. Crates, barrels, and even the beams and hull of the ship turned to stone. The *Black Dagger* began to creak and groan precariously with the extra weight.

Crawling on his hands and knees, Kay snuck through the maze of odds and ends. The pirates stored everything down there, from worthless rags and extra tools to gold and jewels that would make even a king open his eyes wide with desire, but there was no time to gather souvenirs. Besides, it wasn't in Kay's nature to take what wasn't his. His only object was to make it out of that compartment without becoming one of Krellia's statues.

Water started pouring into the cargo hold from cracks that riddled the hull. *The ship can't take much more of this*, Kay thought. He was soon sloshing through brackish bilge water.

Finally reaching the door, Kay groped around for something to distract Krellia. His hand struck a solid object, and he pulled it out of the water. Even in the dim light, the bejeweled golden chalice gleamed luxuriously. *Well, this is probably the most expensive weapon I'll ever use*, Kay thought wryly as he dared to get to his feet.

"Hey, Krellia! Catch!" Kay yelled, and he heaved the cup at the witch with all his might.

Krellia attempted to block the blow with her cane. The chalice struck the brittle wood, snapping it in half with an explosion that sent her flying backward into a pile of canvas sails.

Felix flew to Kay's side. "Nice shot!" he commended. "Now let's get out of here!"

Kay and Felix slipped through the door, closing and latching it behind them.

They turned around and froze.

Deets stood with his hands on his hips. Light from an open hatchway illuminated him from behind like a dark angel. "Now, what do we have here?" the pirate sneered.

Chapter 36

"DON'T you like playing with Krellia?" Deets taunted. "Maybe you'd rather play with me instead." With that, the pirate drew his sword.

They were in a small, empty storage compartment. The only ways out were through the door they had just entered or up through the hatchway that Deets blocked. With the low ceiling, it was a terrible place to have a swordfight, and Kay was sure that Deets wouldn't be alone for long. Not to mention, Deets had already bested him in a fight.

Captain Errohd's voice echoed in Kay's head.

You've just got one flaw in your technique... You don't cheat enough.

Kay's hand strayed to his pocket. Digging past the paper that Gallard had given him, he fingered the glass marble. He had kept it since the day he lost the fight with Captain Errohd.

The tingling of magic emanated from behind him. *Uh-oh, this can't be good.* Pulling out the marble, he tossed it at Deets. "Here. Catch."

Deets caught the marble and halted his advance. He examined it with a curious eye and then glared suspiciously at Kay. "What trickery is this?"

Kay jumped away just as the door behind him blasted off its hinges and flew across the room, crashing into Deets and flattening him against the opposite wall. The door teetered for a moment and fell with a crash.

Deets, knocked out cold, collapsed to the ground.

"Felix, now!" Kay shouted. As soon as he felt the sprite land on his shoulder, Kay leapt into the air just long enough to picture Alamin in his mind and touch the bracelet.

Krellia's scream of rage faded into nothingness.

***

All was dark. Kay's first thought was that the bracelet didn't work, but he quickly sensed that he was definitely somewhere else—not aboard a ship. The air was cool and damp, and murmured conversations came from all around.

"Felix, can you see anything?" Kay whispered.

Felix groaned. "Unfortunately, yes. We're in furball central."

Kay's eyes gradually adjusted to the dark. Everywhere he looked, the short and furry forms of teloks mulled about a low-ceilinged cave. Alamin sat on the ground nearby with his back against the rock wall. His eyes were closed, and his breathing appeared shallow.

Jerra knelt over the wizard and held a hand to his forehead. Looking up at Kay, her face brightened with relief, but she wore a grim smile. She rushed over to Kay and hugged him.

"I'm glad you're back," Jerra said.

Kay tentatively hugged her back. "Did you think I wouldn't make it?"

Jerra let go and gave him a shove. "Yes, as a matter of fact, I did." Her expression changed from relief to frustration. "You teleported into a den of pirates without even a single thought of what could happen. How can you be so reckless?"

Felix interrupted, "Actually, I believe he did have a thought. It went like this: I'm going to do something *really* dumb."

Kay's temper began to rise, but he stifled it and knelt down next to Alamin. "He looks…"

"Older," Jerra said, completing his thought.

Kay nodded. The light was dim, but Kay saw that deeper wrinkles stretched across the wizard's face. Alamin's eyes were sunken, and even his hair seemed a little thinner. "What's happening?"

Jerra opened her mouth to respond, but a young telok came running over to her.

"Miss Jerra! Miss Jerra! Please come!" He looked imploringly at her and tugged her arm with two small, furry hands. "King Balo get worse. You come. Please help."

The telok led Jerra to where the last light of day illuminated the entrance of the cave. Jerra looked back at Kay and then motioned to Alamin. "He'll be okay...for now. You should come with us."

The other teloks filed out of the cave to be with their dying leader. Kay hesitated but then left his master and followed the flow of teloks. The low ceiling of the cave abruptly opened to a wide, high mouth. The jungle lay just beyond the opening; its heat and humidity battled at that location with the cool dampness of the cave. With every step Kay took, the heat gradually conquered until sweat was dripping down his face.

With Felix buzzing along by his side, Kay pushed through the curtain of vines that camouflaged the cave's entrance. Nearby, a large group of teloks stood in a silent circle with their heads bowed. In the center, bathed half in light and half in shadow, were Bibo and his father. The leader of the teloks lay on a bed of straw, and his son was sitting cross-legged by his side.

Seeing Jerra and Kay arrive, the teloks parted to let them through.

"How is he?" Jerra asked Bibo.

"Not good," Bibo replied with a sad, slow shake of his furry head. "Breathing slower."

Hearing his son's voice, Balo's eyes fluttered open. He gazed up at the darkening sky for a moment and then slowly turned his head toward Bibo. With short, shallow breaths, the leader of the teloks spoke in a hoarse whisper. "Getting dark. Balo's time almost done."

Jerra knelt down next to Balo and put her hands on his head and chest. She closed her eyes, and her hands glowed with a soft golden light.

Jerra opened her eyes, and Bibo looked expectantly at her. "Jerra help?"

The young healer pursed her lips and shook her head sorrowfully. "I wish I could, Bibo. He's too far gone. He's bleeding inside. It won't be much longer."

Jerra stood up and whispered to Kay, "After you left, we brought Balo to the healing spring, but the magic of the water was gone. The ring must have been the source of the spring's healing properties."

Bibo looked down at his father. "Father?"

Balo turned his head slightly in Bibo's direction. A trace of a smile crossed the elder telok's face. "Bibo must stay strong. Bibo brave warrior. Balo love." He swallowed and looked deeply into his son's eyes. "Now have friends and adventures beyond waves. Bibo must help new friends."

Bibo nodded and beat his chest three times. "Yes, father. Bibo do."

Balo coughed hoarsely, shook slightly, and breathed his last breath.

The teloks silently bent down on one knee and bowed their heads. Kay did the same, guessing that this was the way that they showed respect when someone passed on to the next world. He stared at the sand below his feet. *Poor Bibo. I can't imagine losing my dad. How long has it been since I've seen him? And Mom and my sister, Carolyn, for that matter?*

Kay's thoughts drifted back to the last time his family came to visit him at Marco's Keep. Jerra's Aunt Elle and Uncle Gabriel had come at the same time. Jerra appeared happy to see them—she laughed and smiled—but there was a sadness about her.

Jerra's parents had died while prisoners of the goblins. She didn't talk about them much, but Kay knew that she hadn't gotten over it, nor would she ever. It was like a scar that wouldn't heal, and one that sat in a very irritating place so that you couldn't forget about it.

A prickling at the back of Kay's mind broke into his thoughts. It left as soon as it came, but he was positive what it meant. Somebody nearby had used magic, and the flows were ones that he didn't recognize!

Not wanting to cause a scene, Kay casually slipped away from the silent circle of mourners and headed to where his instincts told him the magic had originated—inside the cave. He crept through the hanging ivy and was greeted by a sweet coolness. Holding his breath, he moved as quietly and stealthily as possible. Reaching a bend in the cave, Kay leaned and peered with one eye around an outcropping of rock. He stiffened, not believing what he saw.

The mysterious man they had seen at the Happy Wanderer—Zelok—was leaning over Alamin! Zelok's light blond hair almost glowed in the dim light of the cave. He reached into his cloak and pulled out something slender and silver.

"Stop right there!" Kay commanded. Taking a bold step toward the intruder, he drew his sword and cast a shield around Alamin's sleeping form.

Zelok stepped back and looked at Kay. He smiled in recognition, and a look of relief flashed across his face. Zelok spread his arms wide in a defenseless gesture but still held the silver object in his right hand.

"Drop the knife," Kay said.

Zelok appeared confused but then looked to what he held and chuckled. "It's not a knife. My people don't use weapons...at least not well. Believe it or not, I'm here to help."

Chapter 37

KAY faced Zelok in the silence of the cave. He realized that the intruder did not hold a knife, as he first thought, but rather a slender, silver flask. Zelok wore an honest and benign expression that Kay couldn't help but feel was genuine. Still, he wasn't going to take any chances.

"I don't trust you. You had a secret meeting with Asok. You knew about our mission and sent Krellia directly to us," Kay accused.

Zelok shook his head. "I can assure you that I did no such thing. Well, at least in regard to the second part of your statement." He shrugged good-naturedly. "Yes, I was keeping my eye on your mission. Its success is imperative not only for Gaspar but for those beyond its borders. I was hoping that you didn't discover Asok's identity. Was it the gold tooth? I told him that it was hideous, but he insisted upon it as part of his sailor's *look*." Zelok rolled his eyes and sighed. "I guess this means I'll have to call him away from the *Albatross*."

"So, you're a spy from the Island Federation? I thought your people didn't associate with wizards."

Zelok smiled and shook his head again. "The Island Federation? No. You've probably never heard of where Asok and I are from. Our people live on the far side of the Desert Waste, in the Charmed Lands."

Kay smirked. Did this guy think he was born yesterday? The Charmed Lands was a fairy-tale place where everyone could perform feats of magic.

"Yeah, right. And I'm from the moon," Kay said dismissively.

"You're young, and there is much that you don't know. Do you really think that the entire world is made up of Gaspar and the Island Federation?"

He got him on that one. Kay hadn't really put much thought into what lay beyond the borders of Gaspar. To the north lay the Land of Nyn and then nothing but mountains and snow. The eastern forests were the homes of fairy creatures, nomadic people, and then beyond that…who knew? The Desert Waste blocked all travel by land to the west. As far as Kay knew, nobody ventured that way—even by sea.

Not wanting a geography lesson at the moment, Kay focused on the flask in Zelok's hand. "What were you going to do with that?"

Zelok motioned to Alamin. "I was going to give it to him."

"Is that poison?" Kay asked, taking a step forward and readjusting his grip on his sword.

Smiling, Zelok sighed and shook his head once more. "No, of course not."

He offered the flask to Kay. "Here, take it. Give it to Alamin when he wakes. He'll know what it's for. I shouldn't be doing this, but Alamin is an old acquaintance of mine."

Old acquaintance? From his close proximity, Kay could see that Zelok wasn't as young as he first thought. Crow's feet stretched from the corners of his eyes, and deep laugh lines marked his cheeks.

"Why shouldn't you be doing this?" Kay asked curiously, taking the flask.

"Because of the rules," Zelok replied. "Rule one: observe and report. Rule two: do not interfere. Rule three: if you're not sure what to do, refer to rule two."

"Observe who? Interfere with what?" Kay asked. He was as curious as a cat, but Zelok would say no more and slowly backed away into the shadows of the cave.

"Wait!" Kay shouted. He ran forward into the darkness and crashed into a solid wall. His vision blurred with the impact. Kay stumbled backward and struggled to regain his balance. He spun his head in all directions expecting an attack. But none came.

Zelok was gone without a trace!

Rubbing the bruise that was forming on his forehead, Kay looked down at the sleeping form of Alamin and then to the silver flask in his hand.

"What is this?" he wondered aloud.

"What's what?"

Kay jumped back in surprise. Felix was hovering by his ear.

"Don't sneak up on me like that!" Kay scolded. His could feel his heart pounding in his chest.

"Oh, but it's so much fun," Felix chided.

"Did you see him?" Kay asked.

"Him who? I rounded the corner only to see you run into a stone wall," Felix answered. "Entertaining, but also a little disturbing."

"Zelok was here!" Kay whispered excitedly. "He gave me this and said that I should give it to Alamin when he wakes." Kay held out the silver flask for Felix to see.

"What's in it? And why would Zelok give us anything? Isn't he working for Krellia?"

"I have no idea," Kay said ruefully in answer to all three questions. "For all I know, it could be a trick, but Zelok said that he was an old friend of Alamin."

"I don't trust anybody who would turn me into a sign," Felix declared with a grimace.

"Kay?"

They both turned.

Jerra stood at the mouth of the cave. Her expression was sad and resolute.

"I don't know why you two are back here, but you should come out and pay your respects to Balo," she said. "They do things quickly here. After a short mourning period, they're going to cremate him and the other teloks who were killed by the pirates as soon as the moon rises over the horizon."

Without a word, Kay and Felix followed Jerra out of the cave. As Kay slipped the flask into his pocket, his hand brushed against something else in there. It was the crumbled piece of paper that Gallard had given him on board the *Black Dagger*. Curious, but having other pressing matters, Kay put it out of his mind. It was a brutal reminder of his failed attempt to reclaim the ring. Whatever Gallard had written, if anything, would have to wait for later.

***

The echo of Kay's footsteps faded, and Alamin slowly opened his eyes. He shifted stiffly and uncomfortably. Looking to the wall at the back of the cave, he murmured, "So…we meet again, my old friend. I sometimes wonder if I should have taken your advice and followed you."

Chapter 38

SPARKS danced into the night sky and toward the heavens. A circle of teloks, surrounded by the passengers and crew of the *Albatross*, watched silently as the flames consumed the bodies of the teloks who had fallen that day. Bibo's older brother, Gali—next in line to be chieftain—stood as a sentinel a couple of steps in front of the others and held his father's spear resolutely.

Although he had seen battles and death, Kay had never been to a funeral before. It gave him feelings that he couldn't quite put his finger on. He felt sad but peaceful, content but afraid, comforted but alone. One emotion would take over for a minute and then be pushed into the background as another rose to the surface.

Little by little, the teloks began to sing and sway from side to side. Kay expected it to be a mournful dirge, but the melody was lively and joyous. There were no words that he could distinguish, but simply a series of "oohs" and "ahs" that uplifted his spirits in a way he had never experienced. Jerra must have felt it too, for a peaceful smile stretched across her face as she closed her eyes and swayed along with the teloks. Even Felix couldn't remain unaffected; the sprite hummed softly from his perch on Kay's shoulder.

I'm sorry that Alamin is missing this, Kay thought, feeling that things were somehow incomplete without the wizard's presence. *I wonder how he's doing.*

Kay's mind wandered to his encounter aboard the pirate ship, and a knot formed in the pit of his stomach. He had failed. Shortly after his departure, the *Black Dagger* had sunk beneath the waves.

The ring was either in Krellia's possession, or it lay at the bottom of the ocean.

A group of hardy teloks and some of the sailors from the *Albatross* had easily captured the few pirates who had been able to use their last remaining strength to swim to shore. The pirates were now in shackles aboard the *Albatross* and would be taken to the authorities when they reached Dunport. Neither Krellia nor Captain Gallard was among the survivors. Kay had no doubts that the witch escaped, but he wondered if she had time to retrieve the ring from Gallard's frozen form before the *Black Dagger* went down.

Kay tried to shake off those unsettling thoughts and return to the peacefulness of the ceremony before him, but it was no use. The more he tried to escape his worries, the more they doubled up and came back on him again.

The fires gradually died down, and the ceremony ended. The mourners quietly dispersed and settled in for the night. The sailors crawled into hammocks that they had strung between the trees, and the teloks settled down to their beds of leaves. Kay, along with Jerra and Felix, walked back to the cave to check in on Alamin.

"*Lume*," Kay said quietly, cupping his hands together.

Streams of light issued forth from between his fingers. Kay opened his hands, and a small glowing orb appeared. Setting it adrift just above their heads, he led the way through the mouth of the cave.

Alamin was still sitting with his back against the cavern wall, but this time his eyes were open. He greeted the visitors with a smile and a nod as they approached. Strapper lay by his side while the wizard petted his dog fondly.

"How did he get here?" Felix asked in surprise. "I thought he was still aboard the ship."

"I called him," Alamin said simply.

Felix opened his mouth as if to answer but then closed it again with a roll of his eyes.

"How are you feeling?" Jerra asked.

"Old," Alamin replied with a melancholy smile.

Strapper barked and began jumping around.

"What's up with him?" Felix asked.

"I think he's just glad to be off the ship. Remember how much he hates water?" Kay suggested.

Strapper barked in agreement.

"Plus he was seasick for a good part of the trip," Kay added.

Strapper barked questioningly at Alamin.

"Well, that's what I told them," the wizard said through furrowed brows. "If I let them know that you were sleeping most of the time, they would have gotten suspicious."

Strapper barked reproachfully at his master.

Kay looked from Strapper to Alamin. "What does he mean about something that you should tell us?"

"He's going to feel bad," Alamin said to Strapper, ignoring Kay's question.

Strapper barked insistently.

"Okay, but you can deal with his moping when it comes about," Alamin said with a sidelong glance at Kay. "And by the expression on his face, it will be right around the corner."

"You should tell him," Jerra urged.

Kay felt a sudden wave of hurt and jealousy. *She knows what Strapper and Alamin are talking about. What kind of secret did Alamin entrust to Jerra and not to me?*

Alamin looked at his three companions as they stood—or in Felix's case, hovered—over him. The wizard took a deep breath and exhaled it through puffed out cheeks.

"You know that I'm very old—"

Felix burst out laughing. "If that's the big secret you're keeping, I can let you know that the cat's been out of the bag for quite some time now."

"Hmmph!" Alamin snorted. "You're no spring chicken either. How old are you now, Felix? Three hundred and twenty-five?"

"I'm not a day over three hundred and twenty-four," the sprite replied defensively with his arms folded. "And I'm not sharing any of my beauty secrets with you, Methuselah, so don't ask."

Kay and Jerra looked at each other in surprise. Kay had always thought of Felix as being not much older than he was. The sarcasm that the sprite dished out reminded him of the treatment he had received from the older boys back home in Devonshire.

Alamin addressed Kay and continued his explanation. "Every ten years, I need to take an elixir. It's a special longevity potion. I give it to Strapper, too. We've been together for almost as long as I've been a wizard." He patted Strapper on the head.

"I only had one dose left when we departed on our journey. Strap needed it more readily than I, and there wasn't time to make another one." Alamin looked hesitant to finish. "Plus, I was missing the most important ingredient."

"Which was?" Kay asked with a sickening feeling in his stomach.

"Wildfire root," Alamin replied.

"Which I couldn't find in time," Kay said. "So it's my fault that you're dying."

"See, Strap, I told you," Alamin declared, throwing his arms in the air.

Turning back to Kay, Alamin said, "First, I'm not dying. That will take much longer than just a couple of weeks without the potion. And second, it's *my* fault. I waited too long to prepare the elixir."

"But if I had found the root…" Kay protested.

Alamin waved his hand in a silencing gesture. "You would have found it if I gave you more time to look for it. What's done is done."

"What does this have to do with Strapper sleeping aboard the ship?" Kay asked.

"The potion's effects," Jerra said and looked to Alamin for confirmation of her theory.

Shifting his weight to a more comfortable position, Alamin nodded. "The elixir is very powerful and causes lethargy for a period of time after it is taken. It usually knocks Strapper out for a couple of days. The good thing is that I now have a fresh supply."

"But how?" Kay asked.

Alamin smiled. "I believe I received a visitor earlier this evening. He gave you something for me."

"Y-y-yes," Kay stammered. His mind was a jumble of thoughts: Krellia and the pirates, Balo's funeral, and the mysterious encounter with Zelok. He wanted to tell Alamin about all of them.

One thing at a time, he told himself.

"Yes," Kay repeated with more conviction. "Zelok was here. I caught him trying to give you a flask of something, but it could be poison."

Alamin shook his head. "We go way back. I thought I recognized his handiwork back in Carival, but I wasn't completely sure. Zelok must be a new alias that he's using. I've always known him as Laserrure."

"Who is he?" Jerra asked.

"A wizard...and a spy," Alamin answered.

"Who is he working for?" Kay pondered. "He said that he wasn't working for Krellia, but if he's a spy, he could be lying."

"No. You can bet he's not working for her," Alamin assured. "Otherwise, he wouldn't have brought along a dose of elixir for me."

"What!" Kay exclaimed in surprise. He rummaged through his pocket and pulled out the flask. As he did so, a wad of paper fell to the cavern floor.

"Hmm, what's that?" Alamin asked.

Kay handed the flask to Alamin and picked up the paper. "I don't know. Captain Gallard shoved it down my shirt right before he cut Felix and me free of Krellia's web."

Alamin's eyes widened in surprise. "Krellia was there? I thought I felt the flows of her magic, but it was a little too far away for me to be sure. You'll have to fill me in, but first I think you should open up that piece of paper and see what it contains."

"It's just a crumbled up piece of parchment," Kay said with a shrug. "Probably with some kind of death threat written on it." As he carelessly unraveled the paper, something fell out of it and landed on the stone floor with a barely audible *clink*.

Everyone froze and stared at what lay at Kay's feet.

Finally breaking the silence, Jerra asked tentatively, "Is that what I think it is?"

Alamin reached down and picked up the tiny object. The reflection of the silver ring with the glowing blue aquamarine danced in the wizard's eyes as he exclaimed, "Behold, the Ring of Carnac!"

Chapter 39

"BUT why would Gallard give Kay the ring?" Felix wondered aloud.

"Maybe that parchment holds the key," Alamin suggested.

"Read it," Jerra prodded.

Kay squinted at the tiny writing on the paper and read hesitantly.

If you're reading this, then either you're Krellia standing over my bones or a very lucky lubber indeed. Take this ring and bring it to the wizard, Alamin. How you will find him, I do not know. That's your problem now. Keep it, and you will be hunted by Krellia and all the minions that she has at her disposal for the rest of your very short life.

I have had a vision that I cannot ignore. Each night for as long as I can remember, my dreams have been plagued with images of fire and destruction. Last night, when we came within sight of the island where the ring resided, I had a new dream. This vision was not of fire and doom, but of light and hope. The wizard, Alamin, held the ring in his hand. How I recognized him, I cannot say, but a sense of peace—like none I have ever known—enveloped me. I now know that I must alter the path of the ring away from Krellia.

You may think these the ramblings of a crazed mind, but my thoughts are clear—as should be your path.

Captain Gallard

Felix whistled. "A pirate with a conscience, who'd have thought?"

Strapper barked.

Felix smirked. "Oh, very funny. Sprites do too have consciences. We just choose not to use the troublesome things." Turning to Alamin, he added, "Was that dream your handiwork?"

Alamin shook his head. The wizard looked as amazed as the rest. "No, Felix. I cannot explain it. All I can tell you is that there are things in this life bigger than us, and there are mysteries that we will never fathom."

Kay could hardly contain his excitement. Everything seemed so easy now. They had the Ring of Carnac. Krellia's pirates were no longer a problem. All they had to do was travel with Alamin—and hopefully an army of Gaspar's most elite soldiers—to confront the goblins.

What Alamin planned to do with the ring and how it would seal the fire elemental's prison was still a mystery, but Kay was sure that the wizard would reveal that when the time came.

Chapter 40

JERRA sat on the beach and stared out at the rippling waters and small waves that crashed onto the shore. The *Albatross* lay anchored nearby. The ship's silhouette glowed in the sunrise; a brilliant halo surrounded it, and beams of red and gold shot off in infinite distances across the horizon. Jerra tried to collect her thoughts, but they were just a jumble of emotions. She dug her toes into the sand and traced meaningless patterns with her fingers through the white granules.

What is the purpose of all this? Why do so many people have to die? My parents…and now Bibo's father…and for what? The goblins are still out there, more powerful than ever. Who knows, they may have released the fire elemental by now. We've got the ring, but we could be too late. Maybe we're doing all this for nothing. She shuddered as she imagined returning to a seaport cluttered with the burnt husks of ships, blackened buildings, and a shore covered in ash.

Shuffling footsteps approached from the jungle behind her. She didn't have to look to know it was a telok, and she had a pretty good guess which one it was. The footsteps sounded closer and closer until a furry shape plopped down beside her on the beach.

"Why is friend Jerra all alone?" Bibo asked.

Jerra turned toward him with a grim smile. "Just thinking."

Bibo looked at Jerra's feet and mimicked her position by burying his own fury toes in the sand. "Ooooh, this nice!" he remarked.

Jerra glanced at Bibo and was surprised by the expression on his face. She had expected her friend to be terribly depressed this morning. Rather, the telok had a peaceful look about him while he stared off toward the ocean.

"I'm sorry about your father," Jerra said.

"Thank you," Bibo replied. "But why you sorry?"

Feeling suddenly very awkward, Jerra struggled to find an appropriate reply. "Um…well…because he's gone."

Bibo looked quizzically at her. "Not all gone. Father still here." Bibo patted his chest. "And here," the telok added, spreading his arms wide and gesturing to the island and sea around them.

"Bibo lucky," the telok went on to explain. "Bibo no see Father for many season. We come here just in time to see Father again. Talk to Father. Tell Father how much Bibo love him. Father love Bibo, too." Bibo finished with a broad smile.

Jerra fought back tears that welled up inside while a flood of emotions threatened to take her over. *A chance that I didn't get.*

"That's beautiful Bibo," Jerra said sincerely. She really was happy for her friend, but the memory of her own loss rushed back.

Her parents had been healers. One night, goblins had raided Jerra's home village of Eaglewood, capturing her and her parents along with most of the other inhabitants. Her mother and father suffered the worst kind of death a healer could imagine in the clutches of those foul creatures. They were both burned out—their life essence stripped away—by being forced to use their powers beyond their capacity.

She didn't get to say her last good-byes. Jerra and her parents were separated soon after they were brought to the underground Goblin Realm. She only heard of their fate through her aunt and uncle.

As if reading her thoughts, Bibo asked. "Jerra miss mother and father?"

She nodded, afraid that she would burst into tears of both sorrow and frustration if she tried to speak.

"Think of parents," Bibo said simply. "When Bibo close eyes, Bibo can feel his father. Mother too."

Jerra looked at him. "Your mother…?"

"Bibo never know mother. She die when Bibo a baby. But Bibo think of her. Bibo feel her too."

Putting a furry hand on Jerra's shoulder, Bibo repeated, "Think of Jerra's mother. Think of father."

Jerra stared into his large, liquid eyes. Bibo's head tilted slowly from side to side, and he smiled encouragingly. She closed her eyes and thought about her mother and father, how they must have suffered, and how much she wished she could see them again. She thought about their separation and the cruelty of the goblins. She dug her hands into the soft sand of the beach. Tiny grains spewed out from between the fingers of her clenched fists.

Opening her eyes, she stared out again at the ocean.

"Jerra feel parents?" Bibo asked curiously.

"Yes," Jerra lied. She swallowed hard and decided it was time for a change of subject. "I heard you promise your father that you would come with us."

Bibo nodded. "Bibo need to help friends."

"You don't want to stay here on the island with the other teloks?" Jerra asked. "You're here with your people, and they need you right now. You've already done so much for us. You guided us out of Nyn when no one else could. You risked your life to find out what the goblins were planning. Those two things alone are worth being able to stay here with your people."

"Your people now Bibo's people. Bibo want to help," the telok insisted. "Brother Gili brave and smart. He lead teloks. Rebuild village."

Jerra smiled. Her anger and frustration were melting away. "And you're our people...um, person...I mean telok," she finished with a giggle.

Bibo hugged her and then took her by the hand. "Come. Teloks make breakfast of fruit, coconut milk, and nuts. You like."

Jerra stood up and followed Bibo along the beach. She forced herself not to look at the charred remains of his village as they continued on to where the foliage remained green and vibrant.

Jerra suddenly stopped and hugged her friend.

"Thank you, Bibo," she said as she buried her face in the matted fur on his shoulder. Then, like the sudden opening of a floodgate, Jerra began to sob uncontrollably.

Bibo patted her on the back. "No cry, friend Jerra. Better to live with happy hope than sad sorrow."

Jerra straightened up and smiled at her friend. "I'm going to try my best to remember that." She rubbed a sleeve across her tear-streaked face and clutched Bibo's hand tightly as they walked to the teloks' camp at the foot of the mountain.

Chapter 41

KAY leaned on the railing at the stern of the ship. The farther they sailed out to sea, the smaller the little specks on the island became. The teloks didn't see big ships often, so they had stayed on the shore to bid a fond farewell as the *Albatross* sailed into the horizon.

It reminded Kay of the day he had left his home to begin his studies at Marco's Keep. It was a bittersweet memory. He had to leave his family and friends behind while the villagers rebuilt Devonshire after the goblin attack. He wished he could have stayed with his family, but he was forced to move away after his apprenticeship to Alamin had become common knowledge.

"Bye! Bye!" Bibo waved while hopping up and down next to Kay. Then quietly he added, "Bye, Mali. Bye, Father."

Felix sat on the rail alongside Kay and also waved at the island. "Bye, Furball Number One! Bye, Furball Number Two!"

"Really, Felix? How about a little sensitivity?" Kay scolded.

The sprite shrugged. "I can try, but being nice isn't exactly my strong point."

Light, running footsteps approached from behind them. "Kay! Felix! Bibo! Alamin wants to see us all right away," Jerra announced.

"What's it about?" Kay asked.

"I think it's about the potion," Jerra said with a worried look on her face.

Kay followed silently. He was still upset that Alamin had confided in Jerra about the longevity potion. *Why didn't he tell me first? Why keep it a secret? After all, I was the one Alamin had sent to trek through the Jirambe Swamp to find that stupid root. And what about Zelok and Asok. Are they wizards too? Zelok said they were from the Charmed Lands, but he's obviously lying.*

Kay had never felt that Alamin didn't trust him. But now…

They descended the ladder to the lower deck and slipped into Alamin's cabin. The wizard sat propped up in his bunk and motioned for them to close the door. Strapper lay curled on the blanket at Alamin's feet.

Kay, Jerra, and Bibo sat side by side in the berth opposite Alamin and waited for the wizard to speak. Felix fluttered down and perched comfortably on a shelf over the wizard's bunk.

Alamin held Zelok's flask in his wrinkled hands; he looked from the flask to his young companions and then back to the flask. Lines of worry scarred his face.

Sighing deeply, he began, "The time is growing short. Shorter than I expected. I had hoped to hold off taking this elixir until the whole affair with the fire elemental was complete, but I see now that I cannot. I have already tarried much longer than I should have."

"What's the harm in taking it now?" Kay asked. "If you need it, take it."

"Back in the cave, I said the good news was that I had a fresh supply."

"Yes?" Kay implored.

"We discovered the ring, so I didn't get to tell you the bad news. Once I take the elixir, I will fall into a deep sleep," Alamin answered.

Felix piped up. "Let me guess. It's not just a cat nap."

Alamin shook his head gravely. "No," he admitted.

A deep worry settled on Kay. "You said that Strapper slept for a couple of days. We've still got a few days before we reach Dunport. If you take the elixir now, you'll be awake by then, right?"

"I wish that were so," Alamin said.

"Then how long do you usually sleep when you take it?" Kay asked, dreading to hear the answer.

"Usually…a fortnight," the wizard answered. "But sometimes less," he added hastily.

"Two weeks!" Kay exclaimed. "The goblins will probably free the fire elemental by then!"

"You're right. That's why you have to go on without me."

"What?" Kay exclaimed, rising from the bunk. "We can't do that! How will we use the ring? How will we get past the goblins? How in the world will we even know where to find them?"

Alamin signaled for Kay to simmer down. "Yes, you can. I'll tell you. You'll have help. You should already know the answer."

Kay shook his head to clear it. "Huh?" He looked to the others, but they seemed just as mystified by the wizard's response. They stared back at Kay with blank expressions and shrugged their shoulders.

"I just answered all of your questions and concerns," Alamin stated. "First. Yes, you can do it. Secondly, I will tell you how to use the ring. Third, you're not going alone. You're to make all haste to the outlying village of Rathbourne. There you'll meet up with Deriah. I was afraid this situation might happen, so I sent word to her before we left for Carival."

"Oh, great. My favorite elf," Felix mumbled under his breath.

"She also happens to be the best ranger and tracker this side of the Desert Waste," Jerra said defensively. "Alamin, that's good news. I feel better already."

"Better?" Kay asked in astonishment. He was still trying to wrap his head around the situation. Yes, Alamin was quirky, but he was a safety net. No matter what dangers Kay had faced, Alamin was always there somehow to back him up. Except, of course, when he faced the Lord of Nyn. But then he also had the power of the Helm of Truth—not to mention a magical sword and a pair of gauntlets. This time, that would not happen. The Helm was destroyed, and the other artifacts of power were locked away in King Roland's armory. This time there would be no safety net.

"Lastly," Alamin said in conclusion, "are you forgetting that one among you has already made the trip to the goblin camp?"

Bibo hopped off the bunk and beat his chest. "Yes! Bibo know the way. Show brave friends where nasty goblins are." The telok said the last part with a scrunched up face and mimicked claws.

Despite his trepidation and weariness, Kay couldn't help but crack a smile. Sighing, he asked, "Assuming that we can get past the goblins, what do we do then? Jerra and I can't cast a spell powerful enough to imprison a fire elemental."

Alamin nodded in understanding. "That is one thing you do not have to worry about. There's a carved stone that marks the site of the elemental's prison, and on that stone is a small and inconspicuous notch. Simply put the ring in the notch. It will activate the spell and renew the bonds of the elemental's prison. The goblins won't be able to try again for another thousand years."

"Simply?" Felix squealed. "*Simply* waltz through an army of goblins, past an array of bloodthirsty shamans, and place a ring in a little hole that has a fire elemental on the other side."

"It's a notch, not a hole," Alamin said defensively. "All the other stuff is correct though."

"We're dead meat," Felix sighed.

Alamin shifted his position on his bunk and looked at them with a serious expression. Kay hated that look; it always meant danger.

"Something else has been troubling me," the wizard continued. "When we caught up with the pirates at the healing spring…that pirate…what was his name again?"

"Deets." Kay grunted in disgust.

"Ah, yes. Deets. He thanked us for leading them to the ring."

"So?" Felix asked.

"Did we lead them to the ring?"

"Well…no," the sprite admitted hesitantly.

Alamin stroked his long white beard. "Kay and Jerra said that Gallard's logbook stated that the pirates came close to 'the wizard's ship'—obviously this one—but that they never made visual contact. How would he know that we were nearby without seeing us? Krellia's pirates somehow knew where we were. They probably also knew that we were sailing toward Bibo's island. Bibo's island is remote; if the pirates knew our general heading, they could easily have guessed where we were bound."

Alamin grabbed his staff and tapped the floor, which immediately transformed into a map of the Southern Islands. "We encountered the pirate ship here—about three days' sail due east of the teloks' island. We continued south to Carnac's island, which is here." Each time Alamin pointed to an area, little ships appeared to mark the spots.

"It seems that the pirates sailed west by southwest to this tiny island. Felix's description of your time aboard the *Black Dagger* confirms this. If the pirates were somehow alerted to our heading, they could have set a course directly for the teloks' island and beat us there."

Jerra frowned with concern. "You think Krellia has a spy among this crew," she stated slowly and deliberately.

Alamin nodded gravely. "There is a snake in the grass."

Kay pounded his fist into his hand. He was more confused than ever. He had been so sure that Zelok and Asok were Krellia's agents, but that theory had been blown out of the water. *So if not them, then who?* There were about fifteen members of the crew, and it could be any one of them.

The companions shared anecdotes of their time on the *Albatross*, trying to discover any suspicious actions of the crew, but they came up blank.

"The only suspicious act I saw was when Asok snuck off to meet Zelok the night we departed Carival," Kay insisted.

"But, as I've told you, there is nothing to fear from him," Alamin reminded his apprentice.

Kay grunted in disagreement. Asok had mysteriously disappeared the night after they departed from Bibo's island. The crew assumed that he had fallen overboard during his night watch, but Kay knew that was most likely not the case.

"Alamin," Jerra began, "how could they have notified Krellia? If anybody cast a spell, we would have felt the flows of magic."

"True," Alamin confirmed. "That's why I think they are using some sort of magic item or talisman to communicate our whereabouts."

"So it could be anybody." Kay sighed.

"Unfortunately," Alamin agreed.

"Can you do anything to find it before we reach Dunport?" Jerra asked expectantly.

Alamin's face gained a sheepish expression. "Well, that's another thing that I need to discuss. As soon as we're done with this conversation, Strapper and I need to teleport back to my cabin. It's the only place I can be completely safe during my wizard's sleep."

"So after tonight, we're on our own," Jerra said resolutely.

"Until you meet with Deriah, yes," Alamin stated with finality.

Chapter 42

WHEN the city of Dunport appeared over the horizon, Kay wasn't sure whether his heart was filled with more joy or dread. The first portion of their journey was finally over. No more pirates. No more storms at sea. But also no more Alamin. Kay hoped the wizard was wrong for once and that he would come out of his wizard's sleep early.

Peering over his shoulder, Kay's face twisted into a grimace. Seamus was busy working the riggings. *No more sailors. That, at least, is a good thing,* Kay thought.

Jerra and Seamus had apparently been spending too much time together, especially when Seamus was supposed to be working, so Captain Errohd put the sailor on double duty for the remainder of the voyage. Kay couldn't help but feel pleased with the captain's decision. Why he was so happy, he couldn't quite put his finger on it. Jerra was his friend, and what made her happy should make him happy. Shouldn't it? *What does she see in him anyway?*

The wind picked up, and an extremely large wave loomed ahead. Kay gripped the bulwark tighter in preparation for the lurching of both the ship and his stomach. He felt the full motion of the boat from his position on the bow; the *Albatross* sank in the wave's trough and then rose steeply through its crest.

"Woo-hoo!" cried Seamus from nearby. "That was a big one! Looks like a storm's brewing to our south. It's a good thing we'll be in port tonight."

For once, Kay had to agree with his rival, albeit begrudgingly. "Yep. It's a shame we'll be parting ways soon," he added.

"Oh, you never know, Kay," the sailor said with a benign smile. "You never know when friends will bump into each other."

"Seamus, are you bantering again?" Captain Errohd bellowed. "Do I have to put you on triple duty?"

"No, sir!" Seamus answered.

"Then help hoist up the staysails. We've got to beat this storm to port," Errohd commanded.

"Aye, aye, captain," Seamus answered and hastily went back to work.

Thankful for Seamus's departure, Kay turned his sights to Dunport and his thoughts to the journey ahead. Alamin was true to his word and had departed five nights past. Try as they might, neither Kay, Jerra, Bibo, nor Felix could find the least sign of a magic talisman aboard the ship or any evidence of a sailor trying to use one. Jerra suggested that Krellia could have put a cloaking spell on it similar to how she cast an antimagic spell on the *Black Dagger*. If that were true, it would be almost impossible to find.

Well, at least it won't follow us off the Albatross, Kay thought hopefully. *Once we're ashore, we can travel in secrecy.*

***

It was late in the afternoon when the *Albatross* pulled into Dunport harbor. Kay and his three friends tried their best to stay out of the sailors' way as they readied the ship for port. Every sailor was on deck and helping to prepare for the extremely late arrival of the cargo from Carival.

Errohd shook his head ruefully as he watched his men move crates and barrels onto the main deck. "There'll be no tips from the merchants for a quick delivery," he mourned.

The city of Dunport was nothing like Carival or any of the ports they passed in the Southern Islands. The first word that came to Kay's mind was *dirty*. Even from the vantage of the open sea, the city held an aura of filth and deprivation. The buildings along the waterfront were in disrepair and seemed to have not been given a fresh coat of paint in many years. Even Dunport's castle was constructed of a dark brownstone that gave the illusion that the structure had suffered a fire. The towers were streaked and stained with deeper browns and blacks. The only splashes of color were the maroon-roofed turrets that stood like bloodstained bookends on the castle's ramparts.

The *Albatross* pulled into a weather-beaten dock with workers whose garments were as drab as their surroundings.

Felix screwed up his face in disgust. "Ugh, this looks like a pleasant place. When do we leave?"

"At the first light of day," Kay answered. "There's no reason to tarry here. We'll stock up on provisions and then hit the road."

"Oh no! No road," Bibo chimed in. "Alamin say to stay off road. Travel through woods and tall grass."

"It's just an expression," Jerra said, putting a hand on Bibo's shoulder. She heaved a sigh and looked around the ship with a melancholy expression. Even in the cloudy, overcast light, the Ring of Carnac gleamed brightly on her finger.

Kay gritted his teeth. That was another slap in the face that Alamin dealt him before teleporting to his cabin in the Western Woods. Alamin had ordered that Jerra was to be the one to carry the ring. Yes, it looked more natural on her finger, but Kay could have hidden it in his pocket or worn it on a chain around his neck.

Kay followed Jerra's gaze; she was staring off to where Seamus was working the sails.

"Yep, just an expression," Kay said briskly. "And the sooner we get off this ship the better, if you ask me."

"I didn't ask you," Jerra snapped.

"Oh, do I need to ask permission to talk?" Kay asked.

"Ouch, not so hard!" Bibo exclaimed, grabbing Jerra's hand, which was now clutching his shoulder tightly.

"Oh, sorry Bibo," Jerra said in earnest and let go of the telok.

Bibo rubbed his shoulder.

Turning to Kay, Jerra pointed her finger at him and said, "You...ugh! I've had enough!" She stormed off and went down the hatch to the cabins below.

Kay huffed and dropped his elbows forcefully on the ship's railing. He rested his chin in his palms and stared gloomily at the city before him.

"Well, Bibo," he heard Felix whisper, "it looks like we're going to have some entertainment on this trip." The sprite rubbed his tiny hands together and sighed happily. "I do love a good drama."

***

As night fell on the city of Dunport, a dreary mist filled the air and turned the wooden docks slick with moisture. A skeleton crew manned the *Albatross* while most of the sailors went ashore to enjoy the games and nightlife that the city offered.

Captain Errohd had advised Kay and his companions not to follow them. "It's a dangerous city in the daytime," he had explained. "At night, it only gets worse. The streets are ripe with thieves and pickpockets. For those as young as you, nighttime is best spent safely aboard the ship."

Seamus had been among those who went ashore. Jerra had pleaded with him to stay, but the young sailor insisted that he had to go with his shipmates or he would never hear the end of it. Kay had caught the scene on the deck and thoroughly enjoyed the pouting and foot stomping that had continued until Seamus promised that he would be there to say "good-bye" in the morning. Jerra then disappeared below deck and hadn't been seen since.

Felix sat on Kay's shoulder. "The rain is on its way. We should go below for cover soon," the sprite suggested.

"Yeah, or we could find out where the sailors went," Kay said with a furtive sidelong glance. "One of them has been working for Krellia."

"Hmm. If you want to get off the SS *Boring* for a while, I won't raise an alarm," the sprite cajoled.

"We'll have to be careful," Kay said. "Krellia's agents may know we're here, and we don't have Jerra to turn us invisible."

"We could ask—" the sprite began, but Kay cut him off.

"No," Kay said curtly.

"You're probably right not to ask her. Even if she turned us invisible, the entire city would hear the two of you arguing from a mile away."

"Let's go," Kay said, doing his best not to let the sprite's comment get him rattled.

The *Albatross* was the last ship into port, so it had the mooring that was farthest out. The dock, like the city it belonged to, was in disrepair and cluttered with discarded or forgotten crates—their contents never to reach their destinations.

"Oh, this is a little slippery," Kay noted, stepping on the rickety boards of the gangplank.

Out of the corner of his eye, Kay caught a sudden movement on the dock.

A dark figure slid out from behind a nearby pile of crates.

Kay spun to face this unknown adversary and lost his footing on the slick, wobbly surface. He crashed to the gangplank, heard a pair of almost simultaneous *thuds* just above his head, and fell headlong into the brackish water of Dunport Harbor.

Kay surfaced, choking and gasping for breath. He spit out a mouthful of filthy water.

Felix's voice resounded through the night. "Help! Help! Jerra! Bibo! Come quick!"

Retreating footsteps pounded down the wooden dock toward the city.

Kay clambered onto the dock just in time to see the mysterious figure disappear through a swirling patch of fog with a cloak billowing behind.

"What happened?" asked Jerra, appearing at the top of the gangplank.

"I'm not sure, I…" Kay stopped short.

Two wicked-looking knives were buried in the hull of the *Albatross* just above the gangplank!

"Um…it looks like someone just tried to kill me," Kay said with more than a little thanks for his lucky slip.

"That could be Krellia's spy," Jerra said. "Let's go get him."

Before Kay could protest the dangers of pursuing an unknown adversary through the streets of an unknown city, Jerra was on the dock and three steps ahead of him.

"Felix, come with us," Kay called over his shoulder, trying to catch up with Jerra. "Bibo, stay here and let Captain Errohd know what happened if he returns before we do."

"Bibo stay," the telok replied, thumping his chest. "Friends, be careful. What Bibo do if you no come back?"

Kay left Bibo's question unanswered as he concentrated on running as quickly and quietly as possible. He and Felix caught up with Jerra at the end of the dock. They stopped and looked around for any sign of Kay's attacker.

Dunport was even more dismal by night than by day. The waterfront was almost completely deserted. The few torches that lit the docks were scattered sparsely, leaving most areas in darkness.

Faint running footsteps echoed along the cobblestones.

"There!" Felix exclaimed. "He went down that street."

Kay and his companions plunged into the darkness and shadows. As they ran, Captain Errohd's warning about Dunport echoed in Kay's head.

It's a dangerous city in the daytime. At night, it only gets worse.

Chapter 43

KAY and Jerra chased the cloaked figure through the streets of Dunport. Fog swirled around their feet, and their footsteps echoed off the stone facades of the dilapidated buildings. Although the city was in disrepair, it wasn't dead. Raucous laughter and the sound of breaking glass were the telltale signs of a brawl as they passed a tavern. Greedy cheers and cries of frustration bellowed from the many gambling halls that dotted Dunport. Bedraggled wanderers standing in the light of torches peered curiously at the companions as they sped by.

Felix flew just overhead. The cloaked figure couldn't escape his sharp fairy eyesight. "He ducked down that alley," the sprite cried.

"Felix, keep an eye on him and make sure he doesn't get away," Kay panted. His legs were still wobbly from the weeks they spent at sea, and he was afraid that they would lose their quarry.

"Sure." Felix shrugged. "What's the worst thing that can happen to me all alone in a dark alley with the person who just tried to kill you?" Nonetheless, the sprite dutifully sped up his flight and swooped around the corner.

Kay and Jerra screeched to a halt at the entrance to the alley. Kay reached for the flows of magic, and a glowing orb appeared above the palm of his hand.

Gazing down the alley, Jerra's face lit up into a smile. "We've got him."

The alleyway led to a dead end. The object of their pursuit stood with his back against a blank brick wall.

"End of the road, buddy," Felix said, hovering above Kay and Jerra with his arms folded authoritatively.

The figure drew a pair of throwing knives from under his cloak.

Felix sighed. "And then again, maybe not."

Kay drew his sword. "Don't be foolish. It's three against one, and you've got nowhere to run."

"I'm not going down without a fight," said a familiar voice.

The cloaked figure removed his hood.

Jerra gasped. "No...not you."

Seamus sneered. "Aw, did I disappoint you?" He spun the deadly blades in his hands. "You're foolish to waste your time with that ragged, old has-been Alamin. The goblins are coming, and there's nothing you can do to stop them."

"Are you mad?" Kay exclaimed. *Who filled his head with this nonsense?*

Continuing to approach in a slow, steady stride, Seamus waved the knives in slashing motions. "Krellia will be queen of all the land, and the goblins her servants."

Well, there's my answer, Kay thought. "But I don't understand," he said bewilderedly. "You helped Alamin on Carnac's island."

"Of course I did," Seamus scoffed. "Alamin was the only one that batty old wizard, Carnac, was likely to speak to. Once we had set course for the teloks' island, I made sure that the pirates beat us to the ring. Unfortunately, you and that turncoat, Gallard, messed things up. But I plan to fix it."

Seamus eyed Jerra's hand greedily. "Thank you for bringing the ring. When I place it in Krellia's hands, she will grant me riches and power."

Jerra covered the aquamarine ring that adorned her left hand. "Krellia? The goblins?" she asked with an astonished shake of her head. "You would choose them over your own people?"

"I choose the winners," Seamus sneered and charged forward.

"*Lume!*" Jerra unleashed a light spell directly in Seamus's eyes.

"Ah! I can't see!" Seamus screamed. He veered from side to side and crashed into a pile of rubbish, falling flat on his face. His throwing knives slid across the ground, skidding harmlessly out of his reach.

Kay picked up the weapons while keeping an eye on Seamus.

The sailor struggled to his feet and wildly flailed his hands to ward off any oncoming attacks. Seamus took a step forward, slipped in a puddle of muck, and crashed to the cobblestones.

"It's over, Seamus." Kay almost felt sorry for the pathetic young sailor, who was sloshing through trash and puddles of dirty water.

"No, it's not over," Jerra stated with a hard look in her eyes.

Kay shook his head. "Jerra, what are you talking about?"

Ignoring him, Jerra strode to where Seamus was struggling to keep his feet. "You want to be with Krellia and the goblins so badly? Then I'm going to grant your wish."

Seamus reached out with his hands to steady himself on the alley wall. He turned toward the sound of Jerra's approaching footsteps, took a step forward, and—

"*Pousarra!*" Jerra shouted and thrust out her hand.

The push spell sent Seamus flying backward down the alley. He crashed into the brick wall and slumped to the ground.

"What is she doing?" Kay whispered to Felix.

"I have no idea," Felix answered. "But something tells me she is *really* mad."

Taking another step toward Seamus, Jerra whispered and moved her arms in the motions of a spell.

Kay recognized the incantation. *What in the world…?*

Before Kay could protest, Jerra opened her hands and unleashed the spell at Seamus. Then she did something strange— she continued chanting and twisted her arms, folding them in front of her chest.

Seamus writhed and twisted, his body completely hidden beneath the cloak. His voice changed; it became harsher deeper. "Arrrgh! What's happening? What are you doing to me?"

Jerra stood silently and watched until Seamus stopped his convulsions.

Panting heavily, the sailor rose shakily to his feet and lifted his head.

Kay let out a horrified gasp. From under Seamus's hood, the green, warty face of a goblin stared back at him!

Chapter 44

"WHAT did you do?" Seamus asked in a guttural voice. He examined his long yellow fingernails and stubby green fingers. "What's wrong with my hands? I've got claws. Why are they like this?" He clutched at his throat. "And my voice…?"

"You like the goblins so much. You can join them." Jerra turned her back on Seamus and walked past Kay. "Let's go."

Seamus called out after her. "I'll be hunted through this city like an animal!"

Without looking back, Jerra replied, "Then you better leave before daybreak. Head north and join the goblins that you are so fond of."

Kay slowly backed away. *What's Jerra thinking? The effects of the spell will wear off in a day or two, and he'll be back on our trail. We should have brought him to Dunport's city watch.*

Kay and Felix found Jerra waiting for them on the wide deserted street. The oil lamps were starting to flicker out; soon the city would be in darkness. They needed to head straight back to the *Albatross*.

They walked in silence for a while. Kay kept looking over his shoulder in case Seamus decided to follow them. His mind strayed back to the scene in the alleyway and the strange arm folding Jerra had performed at the end of the spell.

Breaking the silence, Kay turned to Jerra and asked, "What was that final gesture you made? I've never seen that before."

Jerra pursed her lips and continued to stare straight ahead. At last she spoke, answering Kay's question with one of her own.

"Remember those old spell books that we found in Marco's Keep?" she asked.

"The ones in that dusty old back room? Those were from past apprentices that Alamin had. I looked through a couple of them, but they were filled with spells that we already knew."

"Did you look through all of them?"

She had him there. Kay had scanned through only four or five of the more than fifty small spell books. "No, not really," he admitted. The night was becoming chilly, and Kay pulled his cloak around him.

"Well, I did," Jerra continued. "And in one book, I found a little gem." She paused as if contemplating continuing or not. "It was a spell that an apprentice created on his own."

Kay stopped abruptly. "A rogue spell? You know that we're supposed to avoid those at all costs."

Rogue spells were created by magic-users who were not full wizards. The problem with rogue spells was that they sometimes had unfortunate side effects. One of Kay's biggest problems when he began studying magic was that he would accidentally change a word or motion to a spell and cast a rogue spell inadvertently. Luckily, Alamin had always been there to fix his mistakes.

When a wizard put a newly created spell down in his or her spell book, it was only after careful testing and approval by another wizard. Apprentices were only allowed to copy known spells into their books.

"I tested it," Jerra said with a shrug. "There were no side effects."

"Did you tell Alamin?"

"I didn't have a chance. It was right before we were called to go on this mission."

Felix chimed in. "Yeah, and there was no time to tell him on that short cruise we've been on. You were too busy playing with Gaspar's newest goblin."

Jerra glared at Felix but didn't reply.

"So what did that spell do?" Kay pressed.

"It was a permanency knot." Jerra looked down at the ground guiltily. She began walking again, this time more briskly.

Kay jogged to catch up with her. "Wait! You mean…"

Not looking at Kay, Jerra said matter-of-factly, "He's never changing back. He'll be a goblin forever."

A chill ran down Kay's spine. He didn't like Seamus. If anything, he probably hated the sailor. But this was going too far. "Jerra, that was cruel."

Stopping again, Jerra turned to Kay and poked him hard in the chest. "It's not all happily ever after, Kay. After escaping from Nyn, you got to have the storybook reunion with your family while I found out that the goblins killed my parents. When your mom, dad, and sister visit us at Marco's Keep, I'm dying inside. My Aunt Elle and Uncle Gabriel have a baby now, so I probably won't be seeing them anymore. It's just me. I'm alone!"

"But to take it out on—"

"He made me feel like I was special. He paid attention to me." Jerra flung her hands up in exasperation. "But it was all an act. He was just trying to find out more about our mission. And he's the one responsible for what happened to Bibo's people."

Jerra paused and glared at Kay. "You don't get it," she huffed and resumed walking.

The wind picked up, and a steady rain started to fall. Kay looked at Felix and sighed heavily. They followed Jerra at a close but safe distance.

***

What did I do?

Biting her lip and fighting back tears of frustration, Jerra stared straight ahead at the darkening street before her. A knot formed in the pit of her stomach. She knew that she had let her emotions get the best of her.

What did Kay call it? Oh, yes…cruel. That word stung.

Jerra halted and abruptly turned around.

Kay stopped in his tracks, and Felix hovered by his side. Both looked fearful and wary.

Her mind raced with everything that she wanted to say right then and there in the rain-soaked street, but the words were lost in a jumble of thoughts and emotions. Seamus betrayed her trust. He made a fool of her. He tried to kill her best friend.

Clenching her fists, Jerra let out an agitated "hmmph!" and continued on her way.

It took a few seconds, but the footsteps behind her began again, only this time they followed a little farther behind and seemed to step more gingerly in her path.

Chapter 45

THE sun's first rays were just peeking over the horizon when Kay and his companions bid farewell to Captain Errohd and his crew. They had explained Seamus's treachery but purposefully left out his new goblin look.

"He seemed like such a nice young lad," Errohd said with a rueful shake of his head. "You just never know, I guess."

Kay was more confused than ever and fervently wished that Alamin was there to help sort things out. He had been convinced that Asok was the one in league with Krellia. That turned out to be completely wrong. And although Seamus was his least favorite sailor, Kay never would have thought him to be Krellia's pawn. Wrong again. How many more times would his instincts fail?

Kay and his friends walked along the dock toward Dunport's waterfront. Bibo was back in his beekeeper disguise, and Felix had taken on the form of a small parrot. As they passed the other ships on the dock, Kay kept a wary eye out for signs of another attack. Seamus was certainly not Krellia's only agent. Alamin had once stated that she had eyes and ears throughout the kingdom. They needed to get out of the city and disappear in the countryside.

The vendors were already busy setting up their carts on the cobblestone waterfront in preparation for the day's commerce. Similar to the street vendors in Carival, men and women wheeled carts overloaded with fruits and vegetables, jewelry and trinkets, and clothing and linens in a variety of hues and materials. Though their wares brought splashes of color to the otherwise drab city, their carts—complete with chipped paint and splintered wood— fit in quite well with the rest of Dunport.

Kay motioned to a fruit vendor who had arrived early and was already prepared to make the first sale of the day. "We should get some fresh fruit while we can. Errohd stocked us up well, but mainly with hardtack and dried beef."

The others nodded in agreement and followed Kay to the fruit vendor's cart.

"Good morning," Kay greeted the woman cheerfully.

"Ah, good mornin'. And *interestin'* mornin'," the woman replied with a twinkle in her eyes. She was visibly eager to share the day's gossip.

"Now don't you go blabbin', Elsa," the cloth merchant next to her remonstrated. "It's my story to tell."

"How is it your story? Do you own it, Libby?"

"Well, it happened to me, so I should be the one to tell it first," the other declared with a curt nod of her head and a quick fold of cloth. Without waiting for a response, she stepped out from behind her cart and addressed the companions with wide, excited eyes. "There is a goblin in the city!"

Kay's heart caught in his throat; he didn't know how to react or what to say. None of the others ventured to utter a peep either.

"Oh, now don't be scared, children," Elsa chimed in, apparently mistaking their silence for fear. "Don't believe everythin' that comes out of that one's mouth. Why just last week, she claimed to have seen a ghost."

"Two ghosts," Libby corrected.

"Come back next week, and it will be a whole family of ghosts," Elsa whispered confidentially.

"I heard that," Libby said indignantly, but her face regained its eager expression as she continued her story. "I saw it with me own eyes. It was in the wee hours of the mornin'. I heard someone rattlin' at the lock on me cart. Well, no horse thief was goin' to get the best of me. I grabbed me stoutest broom, opened the door wide, and screamed at the top of me lungs.

"Well, you could just imagine the shock and fright I got when I saw it was none other than an ugly green and warty goblin staring me right in the face. I didn't know what to do but keep screamin' and wavin' me broom."

"What happened then?" Jerra asked with concern in her voice.

"The funniest thing," Libby said with a cock of her head. "I wouldn't have believed it if I didn't see it. The goblin screamed too, and then it ran off. It was as if he was as scared of me as I was of him."

Felix, still in parrot form, landed on Kay's shoulder and whispered in his ear. "With the amount of warts she's got, coupled with her broom waving, maybe he thought Krellia was coming to get him."

"Shhh," Kay hushed out of the corner of his mouth. Addressing Libby, he inquired, "Which way did he head?"

"Goin' goblin chasin', are ye?" Libby chided. "It went north, toward the city gates." The merchant waved her thumb over her shoulder.

A chapman was laying out a cloth on the ground nearby and preparing his display of needles, lace, and silk scarves. Without stopping his work or looking up, he jumped into the conversation. "She speaks the truth. I was at the city gates at dawn. Before the great doors were fully opened, a goblin bolted out past those of us waiting to enter the city. He took everyone by surprise, even the guards. They didn't have time to get off a shot with their crossbows before he disappeared into the orchards."

"Aye, ask the guards if you don't believe me," Libby suggested, poking Elsa in the arm.

"The guards will never admit to it," the chapman said. "Otherwise, they'd have to explain how they let him *in*."

"Goblin chasin' or not, I wouldn't be flashin' that pretty ring in these streets, missy," Libby said as she gently grabbed Jerra by the hand and looked admiringly at the ring on her finger.

Jerra pulled her hand away. "It...it's a family heirloom," she stammered nervously.

Kay and Jerra exchanged uncomfortable looks, and Bibo teetered nervously. They choose some fruit that had the least amount of brown spots and a few that were not quite ripe, so they would have stock for the days ahead. Paying Elsa and bidding farewell to the vendors, the companions struck out for the city gates.

∗∗∗

As soon as the children were out of sight, the chapman gathered his wares. He rolled up his cloth and tucked it under his arm.

"Givin' up so soon, me love?" Elsa asked, watching him perplexedly.

"Just because the children didn't buy anythin' from you is no reason to quit right away," Libby added.

The chapman smiled good-naturedly and walked up to the women, flashing his icy-blue eyes. He waved his hand as if to say good-bye, blinked twice, and said, "You will remember none of this."

Chapter 46

THE Great Doors of Dunport were open wide. Streams of carts and wagons passed in and out of the city in such a haphazard fashion that it was a small wonder that there were not constant collisions.

Kay stood close to the walls of the buildings that lined the main thoroughfare to avoid being trampled. Even then, he was constantly bumped and shoved this way and that as he made his way out of the city.

As in Carival, the companions decided that it would be best to separate so that they would not call attention to themselves. Jerra traveled with Bibo, while Felix had flown ahead to meet them outside the gates. Kay, preferring to spend some time alone, offered to go solo.

The Great Doors of Dunport were just as their name suggested—stout doors, as thick and as tall as a tree, reinforced with wide bands of iron and painted black as night. A series of handles adorned the bottom of the doors, so that teams of guards could open and close them—most likely with great struggle.

Making his way through the throngs of people and traffic that clogged the city's entrance, Kay wove, dodged, and shoved until he was free of the confines of Dunport. When he stepped outside the city walls for the first time, he had to catch his breath.

The countryside that surrounded Dunport was as beautiful as the city was ugly. Peach and apple orchards lined a pleasant, wide, dirt road, allowing the mass of comings and goings to have plenty of room to pass comfortably. Other roads led off to the east and west, and tidy cottages with whitewashed walls and newly thatched roofs dotted the landscape.

Kay chose the road heading north.

"Ah, this is more like it," a parrot said joyfully, swooping overhead.

"You're telling me," Kay assented. "I hope we never have to return there again." Looking up the road, Kay asked, "Do you see Jerra and Bibo?"

"Yep, they're up ahead," Felix replied. "Head off to the apple orchards on the left where the road bends east."

Kay did as the sprite suggested, and soon all the companions were reunited in a secluded grove off the main road.

Jerra looked all about as if expecting something to sneak up on them.

"Seamus?" Kay asked simply, afraid to get too deeply into the subject.

Jerra nodded. "Kay, what did I do? I…I shouldn't have…" She bit her lip.

Kay wanted to agree emphatically, but he held back. "What's done is done," he replied. "If we do encounter him again, do you think you could reverse the spell?"

"I think I can, but he would have to be willing," Jerra answered.

"I don't think you'll have a problem with that," Felix commented.

"Sailor no want to be nasty goblin," Bibo added. He stepped out of his beekeeper's garb and tucked it into his leather satchel.

Kay decided to change the subject. "From this point on, we have to stay off the main roads. If the goblins are nearby, they may be searching for us. We'll head northwest through the grasslands and hug the western shore of Greenfern Lake."

The others agreed and picked their way through the apple orchard. The apples were just past peak season, and many lay on the ground, creating a sweet, sugary smell as they decomposed. Kay wished he had a beekeeper's suit because the discarded apples attracted swarms of yellow jackets.

"Stay clear of the rotten apples," Kay warned. "We don't need to have wasps *and* goblins on our trail."

They carefully navigated through the orchard until they emerged upon a narrow road, not much wider than a footpath. Two small ruts marked the frequent passage of farmers' carts. On the opposite side of the road were rows and rows of corn. The stalks soared above their heads and were ready for the fall harvest.

Seeing no one about, the companions traveled this route north, occasionally ducking amid the cornstalks or orchards when they came close to a farmer's cottage or when a cart rolled past. The farms eventually became fewer and farther between, and the cultivated fields gave way to rolling hills.

The companions made camp for the night in a secluded tree-sheltered dell, thankful to rest their travel-weary feet.

***

The next day dawned with the air already hot, quite unusual for early autumn.

The hill country was devoid of any roads, so Kay and his friends picked their way across the terrain in a steady northern route. The hills gradually became smaller and smaller until Gaspar's grasslands stretched out before them.

The warm autumn breezes blew across the prairie, making ripples flow through the grass like waves on the ocean. Kay had expected the grasslands to be easier to traverse than the ups and downs of the hill country, but he was sorely mistaken. The tall blades pulled at the companions' arms and legs as they waded through the sea of grass.

"Bibo no see anything," the telok complained, straining to look above the grass that stood as tall as he. Bibo gave up trying to see where they were going and took out his compass. "North, north, north," he mumbled.

"I don't like this," Jerra said, looking around nervously. "It's too easy to hide in this stuff."

"I think you're right," Kay agreed. Turning to Felix, he asked, "Can you get a bird's-eye view of the area? We don't need any surprises."

The sprite shrugged. "Sure. But who's going to find us out here? We're in the middle of nowhere."

Felix changed into a tiny hummingbird and took to the air, flying in ever-widening circles high above the grasslands.

The minutes ticked by, and Kay grew impatient to be on the move. He was about to call the sprite back, when Felix stopped in midflight and made a beeline back to the companions.

"This can't be good," Jerra gulped.

"Goblins!" Felix shrieked as he approached, back in his original form. "Just to the west. And they're coming in fast!"

Chapter 47

"HEAD back the way we came!" Kay commanded. "It's got to be a coincidence. They can't possibly know we're here."

The companions turned and ran, following the clear path of trampled grass back toward the hills. Kay figured that they would retreat a short distance, let the goblins pass, and then continue on their way.

"Felix, how many of them did you see?" Kay asked, panting as he ran.

"Maybe about twenty, but I can't be sure," the sprite responded.

"This might be far enough away," Kay suggested and signaled for a halt. "We'll duck down in this high grass and let them pass."

"Good idea," Jerra said. "We could hold them off for a while, but we wouldn't stand a chance against that many."

Felix fluttered up and quickly came back down. "This isn't good," he said. "They've changed direction and are heading straight for us again."

"But that's impossible!" Kay said, dumbfounded. "They can't see us."

Felix tilted his head. "You can let them know it's impossible when they get here."

"Can you turn us all invisible?" Kay asked Jerra.

She shook her head. "I can only do two people at once. Bibo and Felix would be on their own. Besides, the goblins seem to know exactly how to find us. I doubt being invisible will help."

"Felix, how long before they get here?" Kay asked.

Before the sprite could respond, a whizzing came from overhead, and several arrows thumped to the ground in the nearby grasses.

"Everybody, huddle close!" Kay commanded.

The others immediately complied and formed a defensive circle.

"*Mithandril,*" Kay chanted, and created a glowing shield that encompassed the companions not a second too soon.

A new spray of arrows flew through the air, some of which bounced harmlessly off the force field.

"Now what?" Jerra asked. "We can't sit here forever."

"Too bad you don't have the Sword of the Dragon's Flame and the Gauntlets of Might," Felix mused. "You'd make short work of the goblins with those gadgets."

Kay's mind raced for a solution. He wished more than ever that King Roland had entrusted the sword and gauntlets to him. "You're right," he agreed. "They would come in handy now."

"Well, you don't have them, and that's all there is to it," Jerra snapped. "Sometimes you can't have something back from the past."

Kay fought the urge to retort. *That would only be helping the goblins,* he thought grimly.

"Did Alamin ever teach you how to throw a fireball?" Felix asked hopefully.

Kay shook his head. "Jerra and I know mainly defensive spells."

"Great." Felix turned to Jerra. "How about you turn them all into chipmunks?"

"That would work for only a couple, and then I would need to rest. It takes a lot of energy just to do one transformation."

"How about…" Kay stopped short. "Uh-oh."

The shield began to flicker.

"What's wrong?" Jerra asked.

"Something from out there is causing it," Kay said in wonder. "Could they have a shaman with them?"

Kay's shield winked out, and Jerra immediately cast a shield to replace it.

Heavy steps and the trampling of grass filled the air as a new spray of arrows crashed into Jerra's shield. A moment later, the glowing dome winked out.

"It's the arrows!" Jerra exclaimed. "They're enchanted."

"Sitting ducks," Bibo said with wide, fear-filled eyes.

Not wanting to go down without a fight, Kay drew his sword. He heard Jerra unsheathe her dagger from her belt, and she slipped into position beside him. Bibo crouched in a defensive stance, and even Felix brandished his tiny rapier.

Yip.

Yip.

Yip.

The high-pitched barks came from all around. More and more, faster and faster, the *yips* filled the air. Soon, it was all Kay could hear. He looked questioningly at the others, but they stared back with confused expressions of their own.

A yellow dog's face suddenly appeared out of the grass as if from behind a curtain. It reminded Kay of a traveling puppet show he had once seen. The dog wore streaks of red and blue paint around its eyes. Stepping silently out of the grass on its hind paws, it stood eye to eye with Kay. The doglike creature was dressed in a plain leather loincloth; in one paw, it held a spear wrapped in colorful, decorative grasses.

Kay raised his sword, but the dog-man did not attack. Rather, it signaled for him to be quiet and to follow. Turning, it disappeared among the grasses.

"Should we go with him?" Kay asked.

"What other choice do we have?" Jerra whispered. "Let's go!" She emphasized her point by giving him a shove.

Kay raced after the dog-man. He caught random glances of it through the tall grass as he pursued.

"They're prairie dogs," Felix explained. "Normally, they're a fidgety bunch. They shy away from strangers and retreat to their underground tunnels. But when forced to fight, you don't want to mess with them. They're fast and fierce warriors."

The yipping continued and grew louder. Kay looked over his shoulder and saw prairie dog heads popping up and down in the tall grass. The clash of spear on shield and the cries of battle rang through the air.

"Why are they helping us?" Kay asked.

"Who knows?" Felix said. "They live underground just like the goblins. And goblins are probably not the best neighbors."

They ran on and on. Kay's heart pounded in his chest as tall blades of grass slapped mercilessly at his face and exposed skin. He could feel the sting of multiple tiny gashes that the stiff grasses were inflicting.

"Where do you think he's taking us?" Jerra asked, huffing from behind. "My legs can't take too much more of this."

"East, east, east," Bibo said, still holding his compass. The telok had amazing stamina for a creature with legs that needed to take two steps for every one of Kay's.

The grasses came to an abrupt end.

The companions spilled out onto the rocky shore of a vast lake. The coastline stretched to the north and south as far as the eye could see, and the opposite side of the lake was just a small shadowy line on the horizon.

The prairie dog raised its spear and tapped it on the ground two times. With a curt "*Yip*" it did a quick about-face and disappeared into the grasses to join its brethren in battle with the goblins.

***

Jerra looked away from the prairie dog and out at the expanse of water before her. The strong smell of salt flittered on the breeze, and a lump began to form in her throat.

She knew this body of water—Greenfern Lake—the great saltwater lake that took up much of western Gaspar. In a way, it was part of her home; her village of Eaglewood was situated on its banks, far to the northeast.

Memories of pleasant summers spent fishing with her father and picnics by the water filled her mind. Then there was that brutally cold winter when the lake froze. Some had feared it was a bad omen, but not Jerra and her friends. They had been filled with glee upon discovering the pleasure of sliding on the slippery ice.

Something tugged at the edge of her consciousness. Soft, pleasant whispers. How long had it been since she'd been home? Over a year now. She remembered the last time she laid eyes on Eaglewood and shuddered. Flames. Screaming. Goblins. The happy memories faded, and whatever was tugging at her dissipated like a passing breeze.

"Let's keep moving," Kay said, breaking up her thoughts.

"Oh, uh...y-yes," Jerra stammered. "We should."

"Are you okay?" Kay asked.

"I'm fine," Jerra said, wiping a sleeve across her face. "I just got a little sand in my eye."

The companions traveled along the shoreline and continued their journey north. They wanted to put as much distance between themselves and the goblins as possible. Not long after they began their trek along the shore, a faint yipping sounded in the distance.

Jerra looked to the tall grasses and saw a solitary prairie dog approaching. Its head bobbed in and out of the grass, appearing closer and closer with each *yip*.

"Something tells me that this isn't good," Jerra commented. "He's pointing to the north."

"Let me check," Felix said and immediately soared overhead.

The prairie dog bounded out of the grasses and onto the sandy beach. It yipped, gestured to the north once again, and shook its head.

Felix returned from his reconnaissance and gave his report. "More goblins!" he shrieked. "And this time it looks like they've brought the whole clan for a reunion."

The prairie dog yipped, confirming Felix's words, and shook its head. Its people couldn't help them against a foe this powerful. Tapping its spear on the ground twice, the prairie dog disappeared into the grasses.

"We're dead meat," Felix sighed.

For once, Jerra had to agree with the sprite.

Suddenly, Kay looked to the lake with a curious expression and bolted into the water. When he was about knee-deep, he cupped his hands and frantically called for help. He sloshed deeper and deeper into the lake, and then he dunked his head in the water.

"I think he's finally lost it," Felix said, shaking his head.

"Kay, what are you doing?" Jerra called out in concern. "This isn't helping."

Kay lifted his head out of the water and continued to cry out, this time invoking a name for aid. "In the name of Queen Nalla of the merfolk, please help us!"

"Oh!" Jerra exclaimed with a start. "I get it now!" She ran into the water to join Kay. Behind her, she could hear Felix and Bibo bantering as they followed.

"Oh no," the sprite moaned. "They don't like me down there."

"Bibo think they like you better than goblins do."

"That's to be seen," Felix replied.

Soon they were all waist-deep in Greenfern Lake and calling out to the merfolk. They continued on and on until their voices were hoarse.

But nobody came, and their cries were replaced by heavy marching footsteps that reverberated across the grasslands.

Chapter 48

JERRA took a deep breath.

Stay calm.

There was nowhere to hide. Nothing but open shoreline. *The goblins seem to know every step we take*, Jerra thought anxiously. She felt the weight of responsibility that was on all of them. *Why did Alamin let us go on our own? This was too much for us.*

She glanced down at the ring on her finger. Deep in the depths of the gem, a tiny spark of liquid light flared to life and flowed out toward the precious stone's surface.

Kay must have noticed it too. "Jerra, the ring," he said, pointing.

Jerra felt a tug on her hand like the ring wanted to go down into the water. It was calling to her. A longing. A longing for the water and all its vastness. She made a fist and plunged her hand into Greenfern Lake.

In her thoughts, Jerra called out, *Help us!*

Immediately, a male voice called back. She heard it in her mind rather than her ears.

Who summons us?

Before Jerra could answer, a voice came from the ring.

I do not have a name, yet you know me, rely on me, and honor me. Help these wanderers in their quest, for they are good, and their need desperate.

With only a second's pause, the voice answered. *We come.*

***

Kay looked back toward the grasslands, and fear knotted up in his stomach. The goblins' spears rose above the tall fronds, heralding the evil creatures' arrival, while the distant prairie grass fluttered haphazardly as the goblins trampled it underfoot.

Then came a sound that he remembered all too well...

Boom!

Boom!

Boom!

The goblins' war drums reverberated across Greenfern Lake.

"They're coming!" Jerra exclaimed.

"No kidding," Felix snapped. "Were the drums your first clue?"

"Not the goblins," Jerra corrected. "The merfolk!" She looked over Kay's shoulder to the approaching spear tips and added, "I just hope they come in time."

A familiar but stern voice interrupted their conversation, "What trickery is this?"

Five mermen waded in the shallow water.

Kay recognized the one in the forefront as Keet, a member of Queen Nalla's royal guards. Once, Kay and Felix stumbled upon one of the entrances to the merkingdom. Keet and two of the other royal guards captured them and held them prisoner for a short time.

"Hi, Keet," Felix called out good-naturedly. "We seem to be in a little jam."

"You again? I should leave you here," the merman replied, folding his arms.

"Please, we need your help," Kay pleaded. "There's a whole host of goblins on our tail."

Felix fluttered in front of the merman. "What do you say? For old time's sake?" he urged.

Keet grimaced. He looked off into the distance and then back at Kay. "Where is it?" he demanded.

"Where's what?" Kay asked.

"We were summoned by a water elemental," Keet answered. "You could not have imitated its call."

"I summoned you," Jerra said, jumping into the conversation. "Well...it's more like the ring did." She held up her hand and displayed the Ring of Carnac.

Keet's eyes opened wide with surprise, but then a look of quiet understanding crossed his face. "Come with us," he said, and then he raised his trident and waved it in an arc.

A curtain of water rose out of the lake, shimmering with all the colors of the rainbow. Millions of water droplets coalesced into a protective sphere around the companions. Then, without warning, the sphere lurched forward. Kay and Bibo bumped into each other, while Jerra reached out to the sphere's watery wall to balance herself.

"I can't see through," Jerra said, pressing her face against the globe of water as if trying to peer out a foggy window. "Where do you think they're taking us?"

Kay shrugged. "Somewhere safer than where we were."

"Ooooh...squishy!" Bibo exclaimed, repeatedly pressing his finger against the soft surface of the watery sphere.

"Careful!" reprimanded Felix. "You don't want to poke a hole in it."

Bibo hastily withdrew his finger and examined the sphere for leaks.

"Don't let him fool you," Kay said, rolling his eyes. "I'm sure that we couldn't break out of this if we wanted to. The merfolk are very protective of their kingdom. That's why we can't see where we're going."

"I remember you telling me," Jerra said. "Their kingdom is actually below the bottom of the lake in an enormous underwater cavern."

Kay nodded. "It's beautiful. I hope you get to see it." He and Jerra locked eyes, and a funny feeling overtook him. He suddenly didn't know what to say. Jerra must have felt something too, because she cleared her throat awkwardly and turned away. The two young apprentices traveled the rest of the way in silence.

It wasn't long before the companions felt the watery sphere stop moving. It melted around them like rain, leaving them all damp but safe.

They stood in a small, cozy room with coral walls, a couple of chairs with colorful and decorative upholstery, and a round window that looked out on the merfolk's underwater realm.

"Is this where you were brought last time you were here?" Jerra asked, breaking the silence.

"I don't think so," Kay said, looking around hesitantly. "Unless they refurnished it. There was a tapestry there…and a bed of pillows here."

Kay walked over to the window. A school of silvery fish swam by in zigzag patterns, and clumps of tall, green seaweed gently swayed like graceful dancers. Brilliant fluorescent rocks of pinks and blues lay scattered about the lakebed, but no other structures similar to the one they were in could be seen.

"No, this is definitely a different place," Kay announced with confidence. "I had been in the heart of their kingdom. This may be an outpost of some sort."

The room contained no doors. Instead, its only entrance was a hole in the floor, about as wide as Kay was tall. Keet and one of the other mermen popped up through the watery portal.

"The goblins are camped by the water's edge," Keet reported. "Do you seek out quarrels with these creatures?"

"Not on purpose," Kay answered. "They're tracking us, and the strange thing is that they seem to know our every move. We escaped one band of goblins only to be found immediately by another. I don't get it."

Bibo looked out the window and examined the brass compass in his hand. "Window faces west," the telok announced. "Back toward nasty goblins."

Kay looked at the simple-looking compass in Bibo's hands. "Bibo, which sailor did you say gave you that compass?"

"Seamus give," Bibo replied. The telok's eyes opened wide, and he put a furry hand to his mouth. Bibo dropped the compass as if it had suddenly become red hot and backed away from it.

Kay and Jerra looked at each other with identical grim expressions.

"I think we've found the answer," Kay said to Keet, picking the compass from the floor. "This device is enchanted. It somehow leads the goblins straight to us."

"That must be taken out of our realm immediately," Keet declared urgently. He waved his trident, and the compass flew to his hand. Turning to the other merman, he said, "Come, Nalo, and gather the others. I know what to do with this."

The two mermen disappeared below the surface of the water and were gone from sight as if they were never there.

Jerra wrung out the end of her shirt. "They made that sphere around us without getting us wet. You'd think they could have kept us dry when they made it disappear."

"Merfolk aren't exactly concerned with keeping their visitors dry," Felix commented. "But at least they make sure we can breathe," he added, motioning to the room around them.

"Now what we do?" Bibo asked.

"I think we have to just sit and wait," Kay said.

The companions hunkered down and discussed their path that would lead to the village of Rathbourne and then ultimately to the Desert Waste. None of them spoke with eagerness, but rather with a fear and uneasiness of the journey ahead.

Bibo described his visit to the Desert Waste and what they could expect there. "Sunny and sandy all around," the telok said with squinted eyes as if the sun glared directly above him. "Sometimes strong winds come. Blow storms of sand and dust. No move then. Bury self in sand to protect."

Felix snorted. "Sounds like a jolly place. I can't wait to get there."

Bibo continued and marched about the small room. "Not far into dry place is where we go. Old stone tower. Many goblins."

"It's not going to be easy to get past them," Kay remarked. "What if—"

A splashing in the pool made him stop short. *They're back so soon?* Kay wondered. His breath caught in his throat when he turned around and saw the mermaid, Laurel, bobbing in the water.

"Hi, Kay!" she said excitedly. "I heard the call. Well, actually we all did. So I had to come and investigate." Looking around conspiratorially, she whispered, "Don't tell Seral. She'd be *very* upset."

"Who's your friend?" Jerra asked with a raised eyebrow.

Kay and Jerra had shared many tales of their prior adventures during the past year together at Marco's Keep. On their days free from studying, Kay had told Jerra how he had met Felix the day his village was destroyed by goblins, of his capture by mermen because of Felix's mischief, and how he had come to be a captive—as Jerra had also been—in the underground Goblin Realm. However, for some reason, he had always glanced over meeting Laurel—a mermaid to whom he had made a solemn promise to return someday.

"Um…th-th-this is Laurel," Kay stammered. "Laurel, this is Jerra. Oh, and Bibo too. I think you may remember Felix."

Laurel, either not noticing any awkwardness or choosing to ignore it, nodded a polite hello and then continued to speak directly to Kay as if they were the only two in the room.

"So have you seen it? Have you been to the ocean? You did promise that you would come back and tell me all about it," Laurel said with a bright eagerness in her eyes.

"Uh…yes. That's not why we're here though," Kay admitted.

Laurel pouted and splashed her tailfin in the water while the gills on the sides of her neck flared in and out discontentedly.

"But since we're here for who knows how long, I can tell you all about it," Kay added hastily.

Laurel's pout flowed into a sweet smile. She hopped out of the water and took a seat at the edge of the pool. The mermaid's long bluish-black tresses cascaded all around her. Patting the spot next to her, she indicated for Kay to take a seat.

Kay's nerves relaxed a little, and he settled down next to Laurel. He didn't even bother to take off his boots before dangling his legs in the water.

Kay talked in earnest about their adventures aboard the *Albatross* and the dangers they faced from pirates, goblins, and mysterious wizards.

The time flew by. Laurel was such an enthusiastic listener that Kay felt he could talk with her forever and ever. The mermaid interspersed Kay's tale with giggles and exclamations of delight.

"Tell me more!" she urged with a raptured expression.

"How about being seasick," Felix interrupted. "Don't forget that part." Turning to Laurel, Felix continued, "He was so green, I thought he might turn into a goblin. And the smell…it was so much worse than usual."

Laurel giggled, and Kay began to feel uncomfortable again. Looking down into the water, he noticed the shadow of an approaching mermaid. "I think we've got company," Kay said, pointing.

"Oh no!" Laurel cried in dismay. "It's Seral, my guardian. She'll be so angry if she finds me here."

"I think she just did," Felix noted. "She's coming straight for us."

Seconds later, a middle-aged merwoman surfaced in the pool. She had a handsome face, but she wore an expression that told everybody in the room she wasn't pleased.

"Laurel, I've been looking all over for you," Seral said with crossed arms and a disapproving stare. "I should have known that you would come here."

"I was just swimming by and—" Laurel explained.

Seral held up her hand to silence the young mermaid. "Just swimming by the outer reaches of our kingdom? I think not. Come with me, young lady."

The elder mermaid dropped below the surface of the water, not waiting for an answer or debate.

Laurel's face drooped, and she slid into the water. With a small wave and a sad smile, she bade Kay and his companions good-bye. A moment later, she was gone.

"Bye, nice mermaid." Bibo waved and teetered to the pool's edge.

Kay looked with a melancholy air at the rippling waters. He was glad that he kept his promise, but he wished for more time with the mermaid. She was always so full of excitement. *Yes, a little moody*, he had to admit, *but those bursts were quick and short-lived. Not like Jerra. When she's mad, you know it…and it doesn't go away in a flash.*

"So—" Jerra began, but she was interrupted as Laurel suddenly reappeared in the pool.

"I didn't thank you for telling me about the ocean," Laurel said hurriedly. She wrapped her arms around Kay and kissed him full on the lips. She lingered for only a second and then was gone again as quickly as she'd appeared.

Kay was speechless. He gingerly touched his fingers to his lips, which slowly spread out in a huge grin.

Jerra let out a loud "hmmph!" and plopped into the chair with her arms crossed.

"Impressive," Felix said. "Getting your first kiss from a mermaid. Now that's one for the storybooks."

Chapter 49

THE others were soon napping, but Kay couldn't have slept if he tried. *Wow!* he kept saying over and over in his head.

His gaze strayed to the pool in the center of the room, hoping that Laurel would suddenly reappear. He thought back on the time they swam together through the merkingdom. Granted, she was escorting him to his trial before Queen Nalla, but he wished he could relive that moment...and the kiss.

Kay closed his eyes and let out a self-satisfied sigh when a splash in the pool interrupted his daydreaming.

"Laurel?" Kay asked, opening his eyes wide with anticipation.

"Ahem...not quite," a deep voice replied stoically.

Keet floated waist-deep in the water with Nalo by his side. Both bore tridents in their hands.

"Really, Kay?" Jerra asked, rubbing the sleep from her eyes. "That's the first thing you think of when you wake up?"

"We led the goblins far to the south," Keet announced. "That particular war party will bother you no more," he added with a grim finality.

Kay noticed that both mermen bore fresh cuts and bruises.

"Does that mean we can go now?" Jerra asked with a hint of impatience in her voice.

"Yes," Keet replied. "Now that we've saved you. You may leave our realm and go about your way."

Jerra flushed. "I didn't mean that the way it sounded. It's just that we have an important quest to complete. One that may in turn save you."

Keet nodded. "You hold a talisman of great power," he said, pointing his trident at the ring on her finger. "Normally, we wouldn't let that leave our realm for fear of the damage it could do if it fell into the wrong hands. But we have seen your dreams and know that your mission is of utmost importance."

The merfolk had the enviable ability of telepathy; they could read people's minds and find their way to the truth. If Keet had decided that the Ring of Carnac needed to stay in the merkingdom, it could have been a costly, and possibly deadly, delay for Kay and his friends.

"Gather together," Keet commanded, and, without any further words, he raised his trident.

The water from the pool cascaded over the companions and surrounded them in a shimmering sphere.

***

The underwater voyage lasted longer than the previous one, and the companions became restless and were anxious to continue their journey.

"Long ride," Bibo commented. "Where they take us?"

Kay paced back and forth in the limited space that the bubble offered. "I wish I knew. Last time they brought Felix and me back to where they found us. This time I hope they're bringing us closer to our destination."

"If Bibo have compass, Bibo could tell direction," the telok said sadly.

"If Bibo have compass, we have goblins," Felix said mockingly.

Bibo folded his arms and sat down sullenly.

Great. Now we've got two pouters, Kay thought, glancing from Bibo to Jerra. She hadn't said a word to him since they had left the merkingdom.

The sphere suddenly shuddered like a boat when it beaches on the shore, causing Kay and Jerra to stumble to their knees. The watery globe disintegrated into a rain of mist, and warm sunlight streamed down on the companions. Shallow waves of water rushed in from all sides, submerging all of them but Felix up to their elbows.

Kay pushed off the soft sand, and he clumsily gained his footing in the shallows.

They were on a sandy beach, nestled in a cove and surrounded by a grove of pine trees. The smells of salt and pine mingled to create a tangy aroma so strong that Kay could even taste it on the back of his tongue. He had never been to this part of Greenfern Lake, but he guessed that they were much farther north than they had been.

"The human village of Rathbourne is due west of this spot," Keet said, confirming Kay's suspicions. "Just follow the setting sun."

"Sure, right after we dry off," Felix said, wringing out his tiny tunic.

Keet bid a curt farewell and then turned and dove beneath the waves, his tail giving a powerful splash as he departed.

The companions sloshed out of the water and onto the warm sand. Kay and Jerra removed their boots, each of which seemed to hold half the contents of Greenfern Lake. Bibo stretched out and shook himself dry like a dog, sending a spray all over the others.

"Hey, watch it!" Felix cried while shielding himself against the onslaught. "It's bad enough that I have to smell you. I don't want to smell *like* you."

"Oh, Bibo sorry," the telok said sincerely and tottered off a short distance to continue his drying process.

It didn't take long before the warm autumn sun dried them and their belongings. Kay and Jerra hefted their backpacks while Bibo slung his satchel over his shoulder. With Felix fluttering overhead, they trudged up a steep embankment that marked the boundary between the forest and the beach.

As they were about to enter the shade of the forest, Jerra stopped abruptly and turned toward the lake. She seemed to be staring at something on the distant shore.

The others halted and looked back at her. Kay was going to ask what she was doing when Jerra faced them again. With an audible sigh and a sag of her shoulders, she resumed her trek through the grove of pines.

The companions hiked through the pine forest and soon came to a well-rutted trail that led west toward the village of Rathbourne. Deciding that it would be safer to stay off the beaten path, they traveled just south of it. The going was easy, and the soft bed of pine needles cushioned their travel-weary feet.

***

Felix hovered above the others. He was glad to be free of the merkingdom and longed for the forests—all of which he called "home."

Bibo looked about nervously. "You think goblins in woods?"

Kay shrugged his shoulders. "At least we'll be able to see them approaching."

The kid is right, Felix thought. Only spotty patches of scrub brush grew in the shade of the tall pines, so they could see for great distances all around.

"Goblins also see us," Bibo noted.

Ugh, the furball is right too.

Before anybody could make the suggestion, Felix decided to beat them to the punch. "I'll fly ahead and make sure we don't get surprised by any goblins or bandits. They may not know we're coming, but if there are any about, we don't need to walk into an ambush."

Felix headed straight up and alighted on a stout branch where the boughs of the great pines created a canopy over the forest. The upper pines were alive with birds and squirrels flittering and scampering about. Soon they would be readying for the coming winter, but the sun's warmth made that time seem very far away.

In years past, the fairy folk would have also been easy to find in these parts; however, with the return of the goblins, many had departed Gaspar. Some had withdrawn to the dense forests far to the east, where few humans dwelt or visited. Others disappeared to lands farther away beyond the Southern Islands or the Desert Waste. Others though, like Felix, had decided to stay.

And this is the type of out-of-the-way place to find one, Felix thought.

Fairies could always find one of their kind when they needed to. Felix reached out with his mind and looked all about. His vision changed. The trees and their inhabitants faded into foggy shadows. Mist covered the land in all directions.

Felix strained to see as far as he could, and suddenly there it was! A faint, pink glow fluttered in the trees just to the south.

Ah, a pixie, Felix thought. He searched his memories, wondering if he had offended one of the female fairy creatures in the past. "Hmm…probably," he said nonchalantly.

Felix flew cautiously toward the pixie—partly not to spook her, and partly because the foggy boughs were hard to navigate when he was using his fairy sight. She had apparently seen his approach, for she alighted on a branch and turned to face him.

He hovered near the branch and cleared his vision of his fairy sight. When she came into focus, Felix's mind suddenly flooded with recognition. *Uh-oh...*

"Hello, Felix," the pixie greeted with terse lips. She was clutching one of the pine's branches and had it bent almost to the breaking point. With a whimsical sigh and a sweet smile, she said, "Good-bye, Felix," and let go of the branch.

The bough snapped back into place like a whip. It hit Felix directly in the chest and sent him plummeting toward the forest floor!

Chapter 50

FELIX spiraled out of control.

The sky, trees, and ground all blurred together in a whirl of light and color. Luckily, the bed of soft pine needles that coated the ground broke the sprite's fall. He landed facedown with a muffled "ooff!"

Flipping over to a sitting position, Felix called up to the denizen of the tree, "Hey, Breena! Is that any way to greet an old friend?"

He raised his head just in time to see a barrage of pinecones heading his way.

"Bombs away!" the pixie yelled from above.

Felix folded in his wings and flung his arms over his head as pinecones rained down all around him. He was soon covered up to his neck in a sticky, sappy pyramid of conifer seedpods. As a final touch, an acorn bounced off the top of his head.

"Ow! That hurt!" Felix cried. "Where'd you find an acorn in the middle of a pine grove?"

"I was saving it for a special occasion," Breena retorted with a sharp tongue as she flew down from the tree. The pixie brandished a pine bough in her hands and raised it above her head with a menacing expression carved into her face.

Felix did his best to scramble out from the pile of pinecones; however, those that didn't trip him stuck to his wings and body, encumbering his movements. Before he could free himself, Breena landed in front of him and began beating him with the tiny branch.

"Take that...and that!" she said each time she struck. "How *dare* you come back here?"

"I didn't come back on purpose," Felix replied while doing his best to shield himself from the onslaught.

"What?" Breena screeched. "That's even worse!" She raised the branch and whipped Felix with renewed vigor.

Kay's voice rang out from nearby. "What in the world is going on here?"

The beating stopped abruptly, and Felix looked up to see his friends jogging toward him. *Thank goodness*, he thought.

"Are you trying to alert every goblin for miles around?" Jerra hissed while kneeling down beside Felix. "What are you doing?"

"Defending myself from..." Felix whipped his head around from side to side. Breena was nowhere to be found. "Where'd she go?"

"Where'd who go?" Jerra asked. She cleared away the pinecones from around the sprite and brushed him off. She opened her palm, giving him a platform to stand upon.

Felix sighed. "A pixie named Breena. We kinda go way back," Felix replied with a guilty slouch of his shoulders.

"Hmm. Somebody that you've upset in the past," Kay said with a wry grin. "What a surprise."

"Who's that hussy holding you?" Breena shrieked as she flew down from the pine's upper boughs. She circled down around the tree with her arms folded and the pine branch still clutched in one hand. "Not that I care," she added with a snort.

"Ooooh, female fairy." Bibo smiled. "Friend of Felix?"

"We *were* friends," Breena replied tersely. "That is until he convinced my betrothed not to marry me." She finished her tirade by striking Felix with the branch.

Felix flew from Jerra's hand and hovered face to face with the pixie. "I didn't tell Narl not to marry you," the sprite said with his hands on his hips.

"Oh, then what *did* you say?" Breena asked scornfully, swinging the branch but missing this time.

"All I did was point out the obvious," Felix retorted. "Sure, humans get married all the time, but they only have to deal with the other person for fifty or sixty years, tops. Then, well...they die. Sorry guys," Felix added, looking at Kay and Jerra. "I just pointed out to Narl that fairies live a *looooong* time, and…"

"And?" Breena asked.

"And he'd have to deal with you for a *looooong* time."

"Why, you!" Breena exclaimed. She threw the branch on the ground and pummeled Felix on the head with her tiny fists.

"Hey, that's enough!" Kay said and thrust his hand between the battling fairies.

"She started it!" Felix exclaimed.

"He started it!" Breena cried.

"I don't care who started it. Just stop it!" Kay said in exasperation.

Felix took a deep breath and drew back. Breena was just as beautiful as he remembered. Her translucent wings fluttered behind her while her silver hair fell on shoulders that were covered by a petite emerald-green dress of shimmery, finely woven silk. Unfortunately, Breena also wore the same scowl that she had the last time Felix saw her.

Felix opened his mouth to speak, but something in the distance caught his ears.

Breena must have heard it too, for her head snapped in the direction of the faint sounds.

"What is it?" Kay asked.

"Bandits or goblins," Felix replied. "Take your pick."

Chapter 51

A<small>LL</small> of Kay's senses were on high alert as he and his companions hurried through the dense pine grove toward the sounds of battle.

Up ahead, a covered wagon sat in the middle of the forest trail. A woman stood on the wagon tongue, wildly swinging a bo staff in an attempt to keep a goblin away from a team of two gaunt horses. Her long dress didn't seem an encumbrance at all as her boots danced on the slim wooden beam, although the horses whinnied wildly and tossed their heads in fright.

At the rear of the wagon, a stocky bald-headed man wielded a short sword. He was doing his best to fend off a pair of goblins, while he bled heavily from a gash on his head.

I guess it's better that we found the goblins rather than them finding us, Kay thought ruefully as he released his sword from its scabbard. He scanned the area and tried to formulate a plan of attack. There were only three goblins, but more could be nearby. This had to be neat and quick.

"What are we waiting for?" Breena asked as she sped by him. "Attaaaaaack!"

The pixie drew back the string of a small golden bow and released a glowing arrow. The tiny missile expanded into dozens of other smaller glowing tendrils that coalesced into a mesh of vines. The net landed on the goblin who was tormenting the woman and the horses. The fibers wrapped around the creature and constricted him like a cocoon.

"One down!" she exclaimed. The bow disappeared in her hands.

"Can you do that again?" Kay asked hopefully.

Breena shook her head. "Not until the moon rises and falls."

Kay couldn't think of a spell exactly like the pixie's trick, but her magical net gave him an idea. He stopped by the nearest tree and dug through the pine needles at its base until he came to a pair of shallow roots.

"*Leganta*," Kay chanted. *Grow.*

The ground rippled in a pair of parallel lines that shot directly toward the goblins who were attacking the man at the rear of the wagon. The dirt exploded at their feet. Roots reached up and wrapped around the goblins, dragging them to the ground and pinning them in place.

The man and woman stared wordlessly at the scene around them. The goblins, on the other hand, cried out and struggled to free themselves.

"I'd better quiet them down," Jerra said. She waved her hand and whispered. "*Galana.*"

The goblins became suddenly silent, although they continued to bare their teeth and wrestle with their bonds.

"Thank you," the woman said in a gruff drawl, hopping down from the wagon tongue. She looked at the goblins and then at Kay and his companions. "I'm not even goin' to ask how you did that, but thank you again."

The man mopped his brow with a worn and dirty handkerchief. The blood smeared on the cloth, but his head showed just a small scratch. "Darn head wounds bleed like crazy," he grumbled.

"You're lucky they only hit you with a glancing blow," Kay noted. "It was two against one."

The man looked at Kay indignantly. "You think one of those clumsy varmints did this? Not a chance! I whacked my head on the bottom of the wagon bed," he declared, slapping the side of the wagon. "We snapped an axel in that darn rut over there. I was underneath the wagon just finishin' the repairs when these goblins attacked us. Guess I sat up too quickly."

"Aren't all traders supposed to have an armed escort to protect against attacks like this?" Kay asked.

"Yes, aren't they?" the woman said, giving the man a whack in the arm. She rolled her eyes and continued in a mocking tone. "There hasn't been an attack in weeks. We don't need an escort.

Why spend the extra money?" She finished by whacking the man again.

Rubbing his arm, the man said, "It's a good thing you came by when you did. What are you kids and...um...others...doin' out here?"

"We're on our way to Rathbourne," Jerra answered simply.

"Hmm. I'm sure there's more to it than that, but I'm not one to ask nosy questions," the woman said, looking at the group as if she wanted to ask a slew of nosy questions. "That just happens to be where we're headin'. You're welcome to come along for the ride. Rathbourne is a long walk from here."

Kay wanted to stay off the road, but hiding in the back of the wagon would also provide the cover that they needed. In turn, they could make sure that the traders arrived at their destination safely. Kay looked to the others, and they silently nodded in agreement.

"Then it's settled," the man said. "Hop aboard. The name's Jonah. This razor-tongued woman is my wife, Ezra."

"Wait," Bibo said. "What we do with goblins?"

The three creatures were still desperately trying to wriggle out of their bonds. It wouldn't be long before the magic wore off and they were free to follow the companions or return with reinforcements.

"We can't leave them here in my forest," Breena noted.

"Well, we can't exactly take them with us," Felix said in reply.

"I know what to do," Jerra said, sheathing her knife and stepping toward the goblin that was near the horses. She chanted and gracefully waved her arms.

The creature stopped struggling and looked up at her with frightened eyes.

Jerra finished the spell by pointing her index finger at the goblin. The creature convulsed and writhed in its bonds, gradually shrinking until it disappeared in the pile of vines. A chipmunk scurried out of the pile of netting that once held a menacing goblin. As a final touch, Jerra added a permanency knot to the spell.

"Hey, you took my advice and turned him into a chipmunk," Felix exclaimed proudly. "I think you're finally warming up to me."

Jerra gave the sprite a sidelong glance and repeated the process with the goblins at the back of the wagon. As the forest's newest denizens retreated into the woods, Jerra sat down heavily among the pine needles that blanketed the ground.

"Bye chipmunks!" Bibo waved as the creatures disappeared into the undergrowth.

Jonah whistled. "We've heard rumors that magic was afloat again. Didn't believe the tales at first. Guess we do now."

"And glad that we lived to see it," Ezra added, slapping her husband yet again.

"So, where are we going?" Breena asked with a clap of her hands and a colorful flutter of her wings.

The companions hesitated and looked to one another.

"Um, we're going very far..." Kay said awkwardly. He looked nervously at Jonah and Ezra, not wanting to say too much about their mission in front of the traders.

Breena chortled with a harshness that seemed out of place with her delicate features. "Hey, I was only kidding. Anyway, you think I'd want to spend more time with *him* than necessary?" she said with an accusatory glare in Felix's direction. "Enjoy your secret little club, Felix. And try to stay away from any more goblins."

Without a backward glance, the pixie shot up into the pine trees and wove her way through the forest. Soon she was lost from sight.

Kay sheathed his sword and thanked the traders for their offer to bring him and his friends to Rathbourne. Ezra tended to the horses to make sure they were still securely in their harnesses while Jonah pulled down a short ladder and hooked it to the back of the wagon. Bibo headed in first, nimbly scrambling up the wooden rungs. Jerra stood up groggily and shuffled toward the wagon. Kay put out his hand to assist her, but she shrugged him off. She climbed into the wagon, huddled in a corner, and instantly fell asleep.

As he crested the ladder, Kay looked back to see Felix staring off into the forest.

"Are you coming?" Kay asked good-naturedly.

"Huh?" Felix responded distractedly. "Of course!" The sprite took one last look at the pines and blew a halfhearted raspberry in Breena's direction.

They were soon rumbling down the bumpy trail toward Rathbourne. Jonah and Ezra sat up front, while Kay and his friends crammed in close quarters under the bonnet. The bed of the wagon was filled with an assortment of haphazardly stacked odds and ends that included fruits and vegetables, dried fish, books, clothing, hats, an ornate chair, a couple of saddles, and carefully packed glassware.

The wagon bumped and bounced so much that Kay felt like his teeth were going to rattle out of his head. Several times, items fell into his lap. He tried to place them in more secure spots, but the jostling always won out in the end, and the objects usually tumbled down again.

Kay sat in the rear of the wagon bed and occasionally pulled back the canvas flap to peer at the passing countryside. The pine forest eventually gave way to shorter scrub brush, and they were soon in the midst of the grasslands again. The narrow trail cut a straight and true path across the prairie while the tall blades of grass swished against the wheels and sides of the wagon.

It was a few hours past nightfall when the sturdy wooden stockade that surrounded Rathbourne came into view in the light of the waxing half moon.

"Make sure you stay outta sight when we get to the gates," Jonah instructed. "The people of Rathbourne are mighty skittish around strangers, especially those arrivin' at night."

Kay ducked his head back inside the cover of the wagon but continued to peek through a small hole in the canvas.

The horses clomped to a halt, and the wagon stopped shaking for the first time in many a mile. All was still until trudging footsteps resounded on a creaky wooden battlement.

"Who goes there?" a guard challenged in a gruff tone, his head and shoulders poking above the wooden spikes. The conical helmet that adorned his head appeared at least two sizes too big.

"Who do you think it is, Eli?" Ezra called out. "If you don't recognize our wagon by now, I'll slap your behind like I did when you were a troublesome little toddler."

"Sorry, ma'am," Eli replied with a slight crack in his voice. The young guard had evidently feigned the grit in his initial challenge. His head disappeared, and footsteps rang out on the wooden boards.

The grinding of a heavy beam sliding from its resting spot echoed through the night, followed by the hard clinking of a metal latch. A moment later, the massive wooden door slowly shuddered open with the young guard laboring against its weight. Once the entrance to Rathbourne was completely open, Eli gave an awkward salute to the traders. Jonah clicked his tongue while snapping the horses' reins, and the wagon rambled through the gate.

As they wound their way through the sleeping village, Kay felt a sudden unease. They were one step closer to the end of their mission, but that also meant one step closer to the unknown. He wondered where and when Deriah would catch up with them. Kay was sure that she would show up in her own time and in her own unexpected way.

His eyes strayed to the ring on Jerra's finger, and questions flooded his mind. How would they get through all those goblins that were waiting for them at the end of their journey? Would the Ring of Carnac work? What if the goblins freed the fire elemental before they arrived? And if they failed, what would happen to the Kingdom of Gaspar?

***

The amulet's blue glow intensified.

They were getting closer. *Finally.*

Rathbourne's spiked wooden wall loomed over her, but Deriah did not fear the occupants of the village—only their overzealous laws. The people of Rathbourne were suspicious of strangers almost to the point of delirium. She needed to meet up with Kay and the others before they entered the village, or they could be stuck behind its walls for who knows how long.

The sound of an approaching wagon reached her ears, and the elf-maiden slid further into the shadows.

The wagon pulled up to the gate, and the guard hailed its occupants. Based on the banter between the guard and one of the riders, the wagoners were definitely locals. The gates opened and the wagon's wooden wheels rolled behind the walls.

Once the gate shut, Deriah risked another look at the amulet.

Maybe they were following the wagon, she thought. To her dismay, the glow was fading.

She looked to the village's barred entrance and then to the amulet.

Oh no. I was afraid of this.

Chapter 52

THE streets of Rathbourne were well lit by numerous torches on tall poles. Kay watched silently as Jonah and Ezra tethered the horses on a post outside their tiny cottage.

"If any goblins or bandits are sneakin' about, we want to see 'em," Ezra explained when she saw Kay looking curiously at the array of torches.

The traders invited the companions to stay the night, explaining that Rathbourne did not boast any inns for travelers. Jonah reached under the front seat of the wagon and opened the lid of a small wooden box. He drew out a candle, walked to a nearby torch to light the wick, and then led the procession into his home.

The inside of the cottage reminded Kay of the back of the wagon. There was hardly any room to walk among the hodgepodge of boxes and random items that littered the room.

Jonah handed the candle to Ezra, who used its flame to light the tinder in the fireplace. Soon a roaring fire burned in the hearth, taking the chill from the night air.

"You'll have to present yourself to our magistrate before you depart," Jonah announced, plopping down in a wicker chair that he had pulled off a pile of crates.

"We're not staying in Rathbourne," Jerra protested through a stifled yawn. "We're only passing through."

Jonah shook his head. "All strangers in Rathbourne have to present themselves to Judge Harrow or they wind up in the stockades," Jonah explained. "That's the rules."

"Well, I hope he's an early riser, because we're leaving at dawn," Kay said with determination.

"Oh, that won't be possible," Jonah declared with a shake of his head. "He's not due back in town for a couple of days. You'll just have to stay in Rathbourne and wait until he gets back."

"Don't worry," Ezra piped in, seeing the troubled looks on the companions' faces. "You'll be able to stay here with us. We wouldn't make you sleep on the street."

"Not worried about streets," Bibo said, correcting their host. "Worried about time. No time to stay!"

"Don't be in such a rush. Look what happened to us out on the road," Ezra said with a dark look at her husband. "Wherever you're goin' or whoever you're lookin' for will be waitin' for you when you get there."

"That's what we're afraid of," Felix mumbled.

"We'll just explain our situation to the guard at the gate," Kay said hopefully.

"Won't make no use," Jonah said with another shake of his head. "Rules is rules. You're going to have to wait until the magistrate gets here. Good night, all." He got up from his chair and headed into the back bedroom.

Ezra brought out a load of blankets and pillows. "We normally unload right away, but it's late," she explained. "We'll take care of the inventory in the mornin'. Maybe you could help. It'll earn you some money while you're here. Say, a copper a day each?"

Without waiting for an answer, Ezra followed the way her husband had gone. The door creaked shut behind her, followed by the soft click of the latch. Soon the couple's snoring reverberated throughout the small house.

"What do you think we should do?" Kay whispered. He finished with a heavy yawn.

Nobody answered. The others were already sleeping soundly.

Kay wanted to stay awake to formulate an escape plan, but the exhaustion took over, and he was soon sound asleep.

***

Hours later, the gray light of dawn peeked in through the one tiny window that was not blocked by piles of junk.

Kay yawned and stretched stiffly; his muscles still ached from all the jostling of the previous day's ride.

He attempted to sit up, but someone pulled him back down from behind and clamped a hand over his mouth!

Chapter 53

KAY fought to free himself, but it felt as if iron bands were holding him down. When his captor's face appeared above him, his panic immediately subsided. Although he had an upside-down view, he recognized the elf-maiden immediately.

"Shhh, little warrior," Deriah said in a barely audible tone. Her short brown locks fell around an ageless face that bore a broad grin.

Little warrior. Kay would have hated that nickname, but he knew she meant no disrespect. To her, he *was* little and young. Though Deriah appeared only a couple of years older than Kay and Jerra, she had seen almost as many winters as Alamin—and as much trouble. Deriah was a ranger—a warrior who was as at home in the woods as she was on a battlefield. Her ability with the blade was equal to any of the greatest knights in Gaspar, but Deriah's weapon of choice was the longbow that always hung over her shoulder.

"We need to be on our way before the villagers wake up," Deriah whispered.

Kay nodded and quickly roused the others.

Jerra and Bibo squeezed Deriah with silent hugs of greeting, while Felix gave a strained smile and merely waved at the elf.

They gathered their belongings and tiptoed out of the cottage. Kay felt bad that they weren't able to bid farewell to Jonah and Ezra, but he knew that Deriah spoke the truth. If the people of Rathbourne were as suspicious of strangers as Jonah had suggested, the sight of their entourage would definitely cause a stir.

In the breaking dawn, Rathbourne reminded Kay a little of Devonshire. The cottages were unassuming but neatly kept; although, rather than being of wood construction, the dwellings in Rathbourne were predominantly made of stone. They sat short and stout with thatched roofs that hung over on all sides like wide-brimmed hats. As with the other villages in Gaspar, the presence of the surrounding wall was evident in every direction.

Kay remembered the freedom that he had felt in his home village before the return of the goblins. Everywhere you had looked, the fields and forest had stretched off into the unknown. There had been mystery and adventure beyond every horizon. Now, there was a blockade—a wall. The people of Gaspar had caged themselves in as efficiently as the goblins did to their human slaves in the underground labyrinth of the Goblin Realm.

The main gates and the guardhouse were close by, but Deriah led the group in the opposite direction.

"Are we going out another gate?" Jerra asked.

"No," Deriah answered. "Rathbourne has only one entrance on its eastern side. There's no way to get by the guards without being seen. We're going over the wall on the opposite end of the village."

The streets of Rathbourne meandered to and fro as if wandering cows had chosen the paths. One minute the companions were heading west, but then the street turned to the north and then northeast. They kept to the shadows as much as possible and ducked in the narrow alleys between houses and shops whenever they heard the cart of an early riser rumble in their direction. Thankfully, Rathbourne was small, and they were soon just a stone's throw from the western outer wall.

A guard paced along a narrow wooden plank that served as a walkway along the top of the wall. He carried a short spear that he shifted from hand to hand each time he changed direction. Luckily for Kay and his friends, the guard had his attention focused on the expanse of countryside beyond the wall.

The companions ducked behind a small granary and formulated a plan of escape.

"Sounds easy," Felix said when they finished. "That means something is going to go very, very wrong."

"Do you have a better idea?" Kay asked.

"Nope. I just like to point out the obvious," Felix retorted.

Kay gritted his teeth; he had neither the time nor the energy to get into a debate with the sprite. The plan was simple. It had to work.

"We need to act now," Deriah said with urgency. "Go ahead, Jerra."

Jerra nodded and quietly stepped out from behind the granary. She walked over to a ladder that led up to the guard's platform.

The others carefully peered around the corner of the building and watched the scene unfold. All Jerra needed to do was convince the guard to let her have a look over the wall. She would put him to sleep, and they would quietly leave the village.

The guard swung around just as Jerra stepped on the first rung of the ladder. "Who goes there?" he asked in a booming voice.

"Too loud," Bibo said, nervously looking over his shoulder in the direction of Rathbourne's cottages.

"He's going to wake the whole village," Felix hissed.

Jerra seemed taken aback by the sudden, sharp question and faltered in her speech. "Uh...I...I wanted to get a view from up there. I always wanted to see what it was like." She took a step up the ladder, but the guard shifted his position on the parapet to block her way.

"Who are you?" the guard asked sternly. "You're not from around here."

"I am so. It's just been a while," Jerra retorted, climbing another rung. "I left when I was a little girl. My family and I came back last evening."

The guard didn't seem convinced. He brandished his spear in front of him and asked, "Who are your parents?"

"Their names are Percy and Lace," Jerra answered.

That at least was true. Kay was surprised that she used her parents' real names.

"There's never been anybody here by those names," The guard replied. "I don't know what game you're up to, but I suggest that—"

"They were my parents," Jerra cried, tears welling up in her eyes.

"Hey, I didn't mean any harm," the guard said awkwardly.

"They were my parents! They were my parents! They were my parents!" Jerra screamed.

"Uh, this wasn't part of the plan," Felix said.

Kay looked on with concern…then he felt the flows of magic. *Uh-oh.*

Jerra gripped the ladder in both hands; her whole body was shaking. Smoke seeped out from between her fingers and rose from the rails.

The young guard looked on with wide, frightened eyes. "W-w-witchcraft," he stammered. He cupped his hands and cried out in a loud voice, "To arms! To arms!"

Jerra regained her composure and immediately cast the sleep spell. The original plan was for her to be on the parapet with the guard so he wouldn't be injured falling from the walkway. Instead, the guard's eyes drooped, and he slumped off the platform. Jerra took the full weight of his body, and the two of them tumbled backward down the ladder.

Kay rushed to Jerra's side and rolled the guard off her. She lay unconscious with one leg tangled in the ladder's rungs. "Oh, great! Now what?"

Shouts echoed from the nearby cottages.

Deriah arrived by Kay's side. The elf-maiden heaved Jerra over her shoulder with an ease that shocked him. "What are you waiting for?" she asked and gave Kay a hearty shove up the ladder.

Kay crested the battlement and stepped to the side to allow the others to join him on the walkway. Deriah placed Jerra on the plank and wrapped a thin rope around one of the wooden spikes that adorned the top of the wall.

Just as Kay swung his leg over the barricade, he heard a *thunk* and turned to see an arrow buried in the wall behind him.

"Don't they know we're on their side?" Felix screeched.

"Apparently not," Kay shouted. He slid down the rope so fast that it stung his hands. Landing with a thud, he held the rope steady as Bibo clambered down with amazing agility.

Kay heard many more arrows strike the wall, but thankfully the people of Rathbourne were not very good archers.

Felix fluttered over the wall, and Deriah was able to rouse Jerra enough for the girl to cling to the elf's neck as she slid down the rope. When Deriah hit the ground, she gave the line a snap. The rope flipped off the wooden spike, and she wrapped it around her shoulder.

"Run!" Deriah commanded. "I kicked over the ladder, so we've got a short headway before they climb up. We should be out of bow range by the time they can replace it and get on the battlement."

"Do you think they'll follow us?" Kay asked.

"Not if we're heading toward the Desert Waste," Deriah replied. "The people of Rathbourne don't travel very far west of their village unless they absolutely have to."

"So they'll probably bid us good riddance," Felix noted.

Deriah grunted in agreement. She adjusted her hold on Jerra and led the group westward.

Scattered fields and small farms dotted the landscape around Rathbourne. A few farmhands mulled about in the distance, but they tended to their work and ignored the passing companions on their journey. Soon, even these small farms and fields were swallowed up by the endless grasslands.

Once they were safely out of sight of any dwellings, Deriah paused and placed Jerra on the ground. She roused the girl by splashing a small amount of water on her face.

"What happened?" Jerra asked.

"Let's just say that things didn't exactly go according to plan," Deriah said.

Jerra looked down and blushed with embarrassment. "Yeah. I remember that much. Sorry."

"What's done is done," Deriah said and helped Jerra to her feet. "Let's keep moving."

The day wore on monotonously—each step looked the same as the last—but Kay knew that the Desert Waste lay just beyond the horizon.

"Are we there yet?" Felix complained from his cross-legged perch on Kay's shoulder. "Grass, grass, grass. This place is as boring as the frontier."

"We'll be there soon enough," assured Deriah. "And when we arrive, you'll long for these boring grasslands."

Felix grimaced. "It's like eating liver and onions for dinner and then finding out that you're having spinach for dessert."

They camped out for the night and chose to do without a fire for fear that there may be goblin patrols guarding the area. Kay lay on his back and looked at the star-filled sky. On their journey through the forest, the trees had hidden what was on the edges of the horizon. But now, in the grasslands, the stars seemed so close he imagined that he could reach up and pluck them from the sky.

He closed his eyes and thought about Alamin. The wizard could read signs in the stars. Kay wondered if there were any messages that he could see. He opened his eyes and looked up at the constellations; however, try as he might, they just looked like stars—tiny globes of light, far, far away and impossible to touch.

***

Not far to the southwest, where the grasses met the sands, a lone goblin trudged along a solitary path. The bloody carcass of a half-eaten rabbit drooped in its hand. The goblin stared straight ahead, and its thoughts fixed on one thing—revenge.

Chapter 54

THE companions awoke with the sun's first rays. They enjoyed what might be one of their last leisurely meals, dining on a breakfast of fruit and bread that Deriah had brought along. After eating, they hefted their backpacks and continued on their journey.

Bibo stared off into the distance. "Not far to sea of sand. Little by little, less and less grass. More and more sand until nothing. Nothing but sand, dunes, and heat. Oh, so hot."

By midday, the telok's words came true. The carpet of grass had gradually ended, leaving only scattered tufts that clung to dry, cracked soil. Even the air became more arid, causing Kay's lungs to sear with every breath, and the sun's heat increased dramatically. A short distance more, and they stood at the edge of an ocean of sand.

"So, this is the Desert Waste." Kay reached for his waterskin and took a long, thankful draught.

"Don't drink it all now," Deriah warned. "There's no place to refill it in the Desert Waste. We've got enough water to get to the tower and back but no more."

Deriah passed out scarves from her backpack. Kay and the others wrapped the fabric around their faces to guard from the constant spray of sand. She even had a miniature scarf for Felix.

"Hmm, thanks," the sprite said begrudgingly as he took the gift.

"Are we close, Bibo?" Jerra asked.

"Not too far. We should reach by nightfall."

"Oh, great!" Felix exclaimed. "A night with the goblins. They're ugly enough during the daytime. But by the firelight…ugh…twice as ugly."

Their slow march continued; the desert was as monotonous as the grasslands. Up one dune, and down the other side. Up one, down another. It seemed to go on forever.

As they crested the top of one of the dunes, Deriah ushered everyone to huddle down.

"What is it?" Kay asked.

"We're here," the elf announced.

Kay lay flat on his belly and peered over the top of the dune.

A crumbled stone tower lay nestled in a dry valley encompassed by lofty mounds of sand. The tower was probably half its original height; broken stones littered the ground around it. But it was not the desolate, decrepit sentinel that sent a chill of fear through Kay—it was the army of goblins that surrounded it. Hundreds of crude tents made of animal skins encircled the tower like tiny worshippers bowing before an idol.

"Do you think they've freed the fire elemental yet?" Jerra wondered.

"No," said Deriah. "We would know. All of Gaspar would know. We're still not too late."

"So now what do we do?" asked Felix. "March in and say, 'Excuse us. Excuse us. Coming through. Just trying to close that portal that you're trying to open.'"

"They've got that tower completely surrounded," Kay noted. "It'll be impossible to sneak in."

"You're right," Deriah agreed. "That's why we're going to let them know we're here."

Chapter 55

THE sun's last rays streaked between a gap in the dunes, and shadowy forms danced laboriously before newly lit fires. The goblins' chanting grew steadily louder, and soon their drums began to beat.

Bibo covered his ears. "Ooooh. Bad music. That what Bibo hear when he come before. Soon tower make evil glow."

A low rumbling reverberated from the tower, and the ground shook violently. The companions looked to each other with fright and uncertainty.

"Did that happen the last time?" Kay asked.

Bibo gulped and shook his head.

"We need to act fast," Deriah said urgently. "Felix, hand me your ring."

Deriah had designed a plan to infiltrate the goblin camp and gain access to the tower. The first part seemed simple enough. Deriah would disguise herself as a goblin who was bringing a sacrifice—Bibo—to the shamans. Kay and Jerra would turn invisible and follow them to the tower. Once inside…that was a different story. Nobody knew what to expect.

The sprite obediently passed his ring to the elf. "Just make sure you survive so you can give it back," he said.

Deriah pursed her lips and slipped the shape-changing ring on her finger. "I plan to." She rummaged through her backpack and took out a short cord, which she used to bind Bibo's wrists.

"Ouch," Bibo yelped. "Too tight."

"Sorry," Deriah said and loosened the rope a little.

It was time for Kay and Jerra to become invisible. For some reason, as soon as Deriah had mentioned this part of her plan, Kay felt uneasy. It wasn't his fear of the goblins, but rather his fear of Jerra. He wasn't afraid that she would hurt him; it was a different kind of fear. They used to be the best of friends, but they had hardly spoken a word to each other lately.

"Here we go," Jerra said grimly and grabbed Kay's hand with a cold firmness. She cast the invisibility spell, and Kay watched as their bodies faded into the sandy landscape.

"Be sure to walk in my footsteps," Deriah directed. "Even dim-witted goblins will know that something is amiss when footprints appear in the sand as of their own accord."

"What about me?" Felix asked. "I'm not just going to wait here while you have all the fun."

"You can ride in the hood of my cloak," Kay offered. "If you duck inside, it should make you invisible too." Jerra gave his hand a little squeeze, and he took it as an acknowledgment that this would work.

Deriah peered over the top of the dune. She took a long moment to scan the area and then commanded, "Let's move."

Deriah closed her eyes and used the power of Felix's ring; her features contorted and her figure bulged until a goblin stood where the elf-maiden had been. Taking hold of the strand of rope that was connected to Bibo's wrists, she led him over the top of the rise. Kay and Jerra followed, carefully plodding in Deriah and Bibo's tracks.

As they approached the camp, Kay found the goblin horde to be even more numerous than it had appeared from a distance. His one consolation was that the goblins seemed to be worse for wear from their long exposure to the heat and sun; they moved about their camp with dull and weary steps. The drums were calling them to formation, but most ignored the signal and continued bantering, while others sat in the sand engaged in games of stones. As they passed, Kay picked up bits and pieces of the goblins' conversations.

"You hear drums? We must get in formation."

"Me sure false alarm. Always false alarm. Your turn. Roll stone."

"Shamans no like this."

"Who care? Shamans no come out of tower for days."

A sentry who was more alert than most of his brethren hailed Deriah and Bibo. "Who you? What you have?"

"Me bring sacrifice," Deriah said, giving Bibo's leash a sharp tug for effect.

The sentry eyed Deriah suspiciously. "Shamans busy. Gurg say go away."

Deriah shrugged and looked back at Bibo. "Then maybe we eat."

Gurg eyed Bibo up and down as if appraising his possible taste. Shaking his head, he replied, "No. We may still need. Shamans say elemental almost free. Drums beat, then they tell drums to stop. Elemental no free." The goblin counted on his pudgy fingers and held up his calloused digits. "This many times since last moon."

"Four," Deriah answered.

Gurg looked at his hand and then back at Deriah. His eyes narrowed, and he said slowly, "Yeeees."

It took the goblin a moment before he spoke again. The drums' pounding increased, and the troops were coalescing into battalions with their spears at the ready. Deriah held her ground steadily, but Bibo was quaking. Kay could tell that it was more than just an act; his telok friend was genuinely scared.

Finally, the sentry broke his silence. "Go. Bring him to tower."

Deriah nodded and yanked gruffly on Bibo's tether.

Kay and Jerra carefully stepped past the sentry. As they entered the mass of goblins, following Deriah and Bibo became more difficult; the foul creatures, having no concept of common courtesies, pushed and shoved their way among each other.

A goblin bumped into Kay, and he almost lost his grip on Jerra's hand. Thankfully, the creature thought it had collided with Bibo. It shouted an expletive and shoved the poor little telok to the sand.

***

Gurg watched as the goblin and the furry creature walked toward the tower. Something didn't seem right.

He glanced down at his hand and held up his fingers again. The stranger had a word for the number of fingers he held up. A word he didn't know. "Where that goblin from?" he wondered. "Gurg no like."

Shaking his head, Gurg decided that it didn't matter. Soon the goblins would have lots of new things more important than words. *Elemental help us conquer humans,* he thought with an evil smile. *Have their treasure and make people our slaves.*

Gurg turned his gaze once again to the dunes and resumed his sentry duty. A speck appeared at the top of one of the sandy hills to the south. He watched it approach until he was convinced that it was another wandering goblin. It was not unusual for bands of fresh troops or supply trains to arrive...but a lone goblin bearing a sacrifice and now this solitary wanderer?

"This strange," Gurg muttered. He hefted his spear and headed out to meet the newcomer. The sentry adjusted the battle horn that hung over his shoulder and prepared to raise it to his lips to call the alarm if necessary.

The approaching goblin stumbled several times and shakily rose to his feet in the soft and yielding sand. Soon they were only a few paces from each other. The wanderer looked at Gurg with vacant eyes.

This goblin looked horrible—even for a goblin. His parched skin spoke of many days without much food or water. He was not dressed in battle armor, but rather in torn and threadbare clothes, most likely stolen from a human.

Gurg eased his grip on his spear and battle horn. This one would not give him any trouble.

"Wi...wi..." the ragged goblin began, but then fell to his knees in a series of violent coughs. Some blood splattered on the ground.

Caught in sandstorm, Gurg thought as he watched the pathetic creature gradually gain his composure.

On hands and knees, the lone goblin looked up at Gurg. This time, his face wore an expression of malice that caused Gurg to step back involuntarily.

With great effort, the wanderer boldly spoke a single word, "Wizards!"

Gurg looked over his shoulder. He spotted the goblin and the furry captive making their way through the camp. Something didn't seem right. The rope was slack. The furry creature was following willingly.

Gurg raised the horn to his lips and sounded the alarm.

Chapter 56

THE long, shrill cry of a battle horn echoed through the desert.
The goblin camp exploded into a frenzy of activity—games of stones were abandoned, swords were released from their scabbards, pikes were raised, and shields were strapped into place. The goblins fell into formation causing Deriah and Bibo to stick out like a sore thumb amid the straight lines of battalions.

Kay saw Jerra's image flicker, and he knew that he must have flashed into sight too. "Concentrate, or you'll get us all killed," he hissed.

Jerra squeezed his hand so hard that he thought the bones would crack.

"Breaking my hand is not going to help us," Kay whispered, but then he felt the crushing pressure once again.

"Both of you, knock it off," Deriah scolded with a sidelong glance over her shoulder. "And hurry up," she added.

They quickened their pace, which made it difficult to stay in Deriah and Bibo's footsteps. A couple of the goblins pointed at the ground where Jerra and Kay's invisible feet were making very visible divots in the sand.

The horn sounded again, only much closer this time.

Kay risked a quick glance over his shoulder, and he realized their ruse was over. The goblin sentry was running straight for them!

"Intruders! Intruders!" the sentry shouted. He pointed to Deriah and Bibo. "Stop them! No let them get to tower!"

The goblins closed ranks around the companions.

Kay released Jerra's hand and drew his sword, ending the invisibility spell on himself. A second later, Jerra popped into view with her dagger ready.

The sudden appearance of two humans materializing in the middle of their camp startled the goblins. The creatures jumped back, buying the companions a little time and space. Kay and his friends formed a defensive circle and prepared to fight what could be their last battle.

The goblins grunted and pounded their swords and spears on their shields. They wanted blood.

"Why aren't they attacking?" Felix asked, lifting his head out of Kay's hood.

"I think they want to scare us first," Kay said, adjusting his grip on his sword.

"I think it's working," Felix whimpered.

The goblins rushed forward with a roar.

Kay and Jerra unleashed light spells into the eyes of their nearest foes. The blinded creatures swung their weapons wildly and struck down some of their own comrades, causing confusion among the goblin ranks.

Deriah changed back to her original form and unleashed a flurry of arrows in all directions that pushed the goblins back.

"I can cast a shield around us," Kay suggested. "That will hold them off."

"No, we need to get to the tower," Deriah said. "We've got to push our way through these goblins or die trying. Once the fire elemental is free, all is lost."

"But there are too many of them!" Kay argued.

He and Jerra sent fresh blasts of light spells into the nearest goblins' eyes, but the creatures continued advancing.

"Ahhh!" Bibo screamed.

Kay spun around. A pair of goblins had entangled Bibo in a crude net, and they dragged the telok along the ground by a rope that extended from the mesh.

"Oh, no you don't!" Kay shouted and raised his sword to cut through the line. He took only one step toward his friend when he felt a pair of strong arms grip him from behind.

"You no go nowhere, little human," a goblin grunted in his ear.

Kay fought back a sudden urge to vomit at the creature's rank breath, but he twisted faster than the goblin expected and freed himself from its grip.

"Pousarra!" Kay shouted and extended his hand toward the goblin.

If they were not fighting for their lives, Kay would have probably laughed at the creature's surprised expression as it flew backward, flung by an unseen force. The goblin crashed into a wall of its brethren, creating a jumble of yellow claws, green feet, and leather armor.

"Now would be a good time for a fireball," Felix called from Kay's hood.

"How many times do I have to tell you—" Kay began, but he was cut off by a powerful goblin voice that bellowed above the noise of the battle.

"ENOUGH!"

An exceptionally large goblin towered above its brethren. Its armor was covered in spikes—like a gigantic, evil porcupine. In one hand, it held a spear, and, in the other, a net that contained Bibo's wriggling form. The goblin barbed the telok with its weapon, producing screams of agony from the poor creature.

"You no stop. I stab harder," the goblin announced.

"This isn't good," Felix whispered. "That's Garr."

Kay's blood boiled in his veins. Garr. The goblin warlord who had burned Devonshire and took his family as slaves to the Land of Nyn.

The other goblins looked at Garr and trembled. They gave him a wide berth as their monstrous leader stepped forward.

"You stop," Garr continued. "Put down weapons. No magic, or me kill right now." He accentuated his point by prodding Bibo once again, forcing the telok to issue a fresh squeal of pain.

Despite his desperate situation, the brave telok called out, "No give up! Bibo brave. Bibo give life if have to."

Kay was fraught with indecision. If they dropped their weapons, they were all doomed. However, if they made the slightest hint that they would continue the fight, he had no doubt that Garr would fulfill his promise and end Bibo's life immediately.

"What you say, little human?" Garr snarled. "You want fight, so me can kill..."

Kay had encountered this many goblins before, but he had the benefit of magical artifacts from ancient times. *If only I had them now*, he thought desperately.

"I guess it's about time I gave you this," Deriah whispered and took a sapphire amulet from the folds of her cloak. He didn't need the elf to tell him what the charm contained. He knew. He felt their power calling to him—the Gauntlets of Might and the Sword of the Dragon's Flame.

"Why didn't you give it to me earlier?" Kay demanded.

"Because you would have insisted on doing this all on your own, probably run off in the middle of the night to play hero, and got yourself killed," Deriah replied in a matter-of-fact tone. She swung the amulet on its golden chain and tossed it lightly in Kay's direction.

Time slowed. Kay couldn't believe his eyes. He watched the amulet swirl through the air. Joy and rapture surged through his whole being! *How did Deriah get it?* It didn't matter. Now they were safe.

Kay confidently held up his hands to catch the amulet, but it was lost from view as a black shape suddenly appeared before him. He grasped at empty air.

A gnarled, wrinkled green hand clutched the amulet and rose above what seemed to be a pile of old dirty rags. The black shape began to shake, and then it issued forth a wicked cackle.

The intruder turned to face Kay. "Aw, were you hoping to get this?" Krellia asked mockingly while dangling the blue amulet in front of Kay's face. Her eye glowed greedily at the prize in her hand. Krellia stepped back to join the goblins and smiled maliciously. "It seems I've arrived just in time for the fun. And it was so nice of you to bring me such an unexpected present," the witch said, tapping the amulet.

"You can wear it to the next Witches' Ball, you old bat," Felix shouted, drawing his tiny blade as he flew out of Kay's hood.

"Oh, sprite, it would be such fun to pluck your wings," Krellia sneered. "One feather at a time, as you scream in agony." She clapped her hands together and sighed. "Yes, such fun.

Unfortunately, I have an elemental to release, so I'll have to leave that to my servants."

Krellia's gaze traveled to Jerra's finger, and her eyes opened wide with desire. Motioning to the goblins closest to her, she demanded, "Disarm them, and bring the girl to me."

"Not without a fight," Kay challenged, brandishing his sword.

"Oh, my little, young pup," Krellia said with a sigh and a *tsk, tsk, tsk*. "You are a feisty one. Aren't you?" She waved her hand. "With what weapons are you going to fight me?"

"With…" Kay began, but he stopped. His sword disappeared from his hand! Spinning about, he saw that all their weapons were gone—Deriah's bow, Jerra's dagger, and even Felix's tiny rapier.

"And no magic," Krellia said dismissively. "You really don't want to duel with me. It would be quick, but extremely painful—for you. Now stop all this nonsense and hand over the girl with the beautiful ring."

A pair of goblins grabbed Jerra by each arm and led her to the witch's side.

Kay watched in helpless frustration as Krellia stroked Jerra's chin with her long, sharp fingernails. "Give me the ring, my dear, or I'll have to take it from you—finger and all."

"What about others?" Garr asked expectantly, giving Bibo a fresh prod with his spear.

Krellia gestured nonchalantly at Kay and his companions. "Kill them," she ordered.

The witch turned and marched toward the tower, dragging Jerra with her.

Chapter 57

THE goblins pounded their weapons on their shields and chanted as one gigantic, hideous voice.

"Death! Death! Death!"

With each word, they edged closer and closer to Kay and his companions.

Krellia was moving away, pushing through the host of goblins, but she stopped short and slowly turned with an evil look in her eye. "No! Wait!" she shouted above the goblins' clamor.

The goblins immediately stopped chanting and looked to Krellia. They shuffled their feet and adjusted their grips on their weapons, awaiting her next command with impatience.

Krellia regarded her captives with an expression so evil, so full of hate and malice, that Kay wished that she ordered the goblins to attack again. He had a feeling that whatever was coming next was going to be worse. Much worse.

Krellia glanced over her shoulder at the crumbled stone tower, and then she addressed the goblins. "Your shamans' magic is not the only thing that feeds on the blood of others. The fire elemental's power will have waned from its long imprisonment."

Pointing a bony finger at Kay and his companions, Krellia commanded, "Capture them alive. And prepare them for sacrifice!"

Garr scowled, eyeing the squirming telok in his net. "Even this one?" he asked Krellia. "Me want kill something today."

"Hmm. Such a pathetic creature," Krellia said, squinting disdainfully at Bibo. "We don't want to insult the fire elemental with…" Krellia hesitated and snapped her head about. "What's that sound?"

Kay strained his ears. All had gone silent. At first, the only thing he could hear was the creaking of the goblins' armor and the occasional tap of sword upon shield. But then he heard it—a strong buzzing sound, like a ginormous swarm of angry bees—and it was growing louder and heading their way!

The goblins looked about in confusion. They turned away from the companions and faced a glowing wave of light that approached from all directions.

"Well, I'll be," Felix said in awe.

"What is it?" Kay asked.

"Reinforcements," Felix answered with a smile.

Before Kay could ask any more questions, a high-pitched squeal echoed through the sandy valley.

"Attaaaaaack!"

A legion of fairy creatures, with Breena at its forefront, overran the goblin horde. Pixies fired barrages of tiny arrows into the throngs of goblins, both stinging them and ensnaring the foul creatures in magical nets. Glowing will-o'-the-wisps flew among the goblins, bringing bad luck to the evil creatures; swords and spears missed their marks, and weapons shattered in the goblins' claws. Sprites slashed the goblins from every direction with their swords while the wingless brownies danced across the heads of the goblins, whacking them with their tiny staves.

The fairies' sneak attack had distracted Krellia. Jerra slammed her heel onto Krellia's foot and pushed the witch with all her might. Krellia toppled over, screaming in rage. As the witch lost her balance, Krellia's hands flew up in the air, and she released the amulet. Jerra deftly caught it and ran to her friends.

"I think it's time you used this," Jerra said, handing the amulet to Kay.

Without hesitation, Kay threw the chain over his head and chanted the magic words to release the artifacts from their confinement.

"*Ignol frobus wessar!*"

The amulet flared with a brilliant light that blocked out all other sights from his vision. When the glow subsided, he felt power rush through his arms as the Gauntlets of Might fitted themselves on his hands. The Sword of the Dragon's Flame burned fiercely, and Kay knew instinctively that the witch was powerless to take these weapons away from him now.

A multitude of fairies attacked Garr from every angle, forcing him to ward off their attack and drop the net that contained Bibo. The telok nimbly scrambled out of the tangle of ropes and ran to Kay's side.

"Quick, this way!" Kay shouted and charged through an opening in the goblin ranks. Deriah took up the rear while Jerra and Bibo followed Kay through the mass confusion of swinging weapons and flying fairies.

"Where's Krellia?" Deriah shouted as she picked up a discarded sword. The elf grabbed what weapons she could from fallen goblins. She tossed a short club to Bibo and a mace to Jerra.

"I see her!" Jerra said pointing to a crooked hat that was winding its way toward the tower.

The companions ducked and dashed through the melee, occasionally stopping to ward off an attack from a goblin. They pulled free from the horde, but when they arrived at the base of the tower, the witch was nowhere to be found.

"How do we get inside?" Kay asked. "The main passageway looks like it was over there, but it's blocked by rubble."

Bibo tottered over to where Kay had indicated and waved to the others. "Entrance still here. Behind big rocks." The others joined Bibo and saw that the goblins had dug a small tunnel through the debris.

Kay looked at the ring on Jerra's hand. None of this was going as planned. They were supposed to sneak in, place the Ring of Carnac on the seal that bound the fire elemental, and let the ring do its magic. Now Krellia was here, the fire elemental was about to be freed, and they were on the fringe of a raging battle.

"What are we waiting for?" Felix asked impatiently. Turning to Deriah, he gestured with feigned politeness, "Ladies first."

The elf-maiden led the way into the low-ceilinged tunnel followed closely by the others. Up ahead, the flickering lights of torches danced against the stone walls.

A faint chanting flowed down the tunnel. It was musical but harsh. Though the words were unintelligible, Kay knew what their purpose was—the goblin shamans were casting the final part of the spell to free the fire elemental!

Chapter 58

THE tunnel opened up into a wide corridor that circled the tower. The companions peered cautiously from the shadows. A chain of archways revealed a circular central chamber dimly lit by several torches. There, a dozen goblin shamans huddled around a central point, and flows of dark magic permeated the air.

The shamans were dressed in animal skins with the heads still attached. The faces of wolves, bears, and mountain lions topped the goblins like hideous crowns, their dead eyes looking forever and forlornly out at nothing. Each shaman held a feathered staff that they tapped on the ground to an uneven beat that accentuated the words of their foul chant.

Krellia stood at a distance from the shamans, crouched in an alcove at the far end of the chamber. She watched with what seemed to be a mingling of desire and caution as the shamans' chanting grew louder and faster.

With the witch's attention on the goblins, the companions crept out of the tunnel and slipped stealthily to flank both sides of the nearest archway. Kay stood next to Deriah with Felix fluttering close by, while Jerra and Bibo hid across from them.

The shamans' chanting filled the chamber like a whirlwind. They held their staves with two hands and forcefully pounded the stone floor until Kay thought the wood would splinter and shatter. The bizarre ceremony reached a climax and then abruptly stopped.

All was quiet except for the muffled sounds of the battle that still raged outside the tower.

Maybe their magic failed, Kay thought hopefully. But then the ground rumbled anew, and his hope turned to dread.

The goblin shamans slowly backed away, and their faces glowed with a reddish light that emitted from a source at the center of the chamber. The light grew more intense until all the room had changed from the tan of the desert to the red of a furnace. The air grew hotter and hotter, and breathing became difficult. A noxious, sulfurous smell forced the companions to cover their mouths and noses with their desert scarves.

Kay gripped the wall for fear of passing out. He had to squint and shield his eyes, but he refused to look away.

The goblin shamans choked on the foul air; their expressions bespoke surprise, and even fear, as they stared at one another with red, glowing eyes. Even Krellia backed away into the shadows.

A red orb rose from the floor. Power radiated from it. Power and greed. It wanted something. It wanted to consume. It wanted to destroy. It wanted revenge.

The orb pulsed, and with each pulse, it grew larger and brighter. Waves of an unseen force pressed out, each one bringing a different emotion or desire.

Fear.

Greed.

Power.

Destruction.

Tongues of flame burst forth from the orb, and bubbling globules formed on its surface. The orb expanded and elongated until it towered above the occupants of the chamber, blasting out waves of heat that made the air shimmer. The flames coalesced into an enormous torso, and two fiery bands extended into arms. A bulbous head topped with flames stretched forth; it bore two dark spots that blinked at their first sight of the surface world in more than a millennium. Lastly, it opened its newly formed mouth, and a malicious roar blasted the chamber.

"Free!" the fire elemental bellowed.

Kay's knees buckled, and Deriah reached out a hand to steady him. A despair like none that Kay had ever known—not even when he had stood before the Lord of Nyn—flooded over him. The Dark Lord had been flesh and blood, albeit most of his mortal being had been well past saving, but this entity was something different. The fire elemental was pure spirit and pure power. It did not possess the confining human emotions of fear

Brian G. Michaud

and doubt, but rather a palpable desire to consume and destroy for no other reason but to satisfy its hunger.

Kay looked across at his friends. Jerra was staring straight ahead with a look of terror and awe carved onto her face, while Bibo hid behind the stone wall of the archway and quivered with his face in his hands.

Kay's eyes strayed for a moment to the sword and gauntlets, and he realized that even their power would be useless against such a being. *If the elemental desires power as much as I think it does, these will only call attention to us.* With a twinge of regret, he sent the magical artifacts back into the amulet.

The most venerable and grizzled of the shamans boldly stepped forward and spoke directly to the fire elemental. "We summoned you. We freed you. You will serve us!" He emphasized each of his points by slamming his stout feathered staff on the floor of the chamber.

The fire elemental's eyes changed from black to deep-red. It let out a mighty bellow that evolved into a laugh and then a low rumble that resembled a snicker. The sound was terrible and mocking, and it caused the younger goblins to retreat a step.

The venerable shaman stood before the others and brandished his staff before the elemental. "Why you laugh?" The goblin appeared to be trying his best to be bold, but there was a definite quiver in his voice. "You our slave!"

The fire elemental laughed again and spread its arms out wide. "Slave? No, you insignificant bug. I am not your slave."

"You must obey!" the shaman shrieked.

The other shamans were looking to one another with fright and indecision. They shuffled away from the elemental, leaving their leader exposed and on his own.

With a move as fast as lightning, the fire elemental swung its arms around the lead shaman. The goblin didn't even have a chance to scream. The shaman's body burst into flames as the fire elemental pulled the goblin into its enormous frame.

Krellia stepped out from her hiding place. The witch beamed like a proud parent on a child's naming day. She took a deep breath then slowly and deliberately shifted her gaze to Kay. For a split second, Krellia's eye met his. It was aglow with triumph. The witch let out a wicked cackle and disappeared in a cloud of black smoke.

Kay gasped. *Krellia knew that the goblins wouldn't be able to control the fire elemental.* The realization hit Kay like a punch in the stomach. *She wanted this to happen! Destruction. Chaos. The end of Gaspar. The end of everything.*

The fire elemental swelled in size, and the chamber grew dramatically hotter. "Yes! The power! It has been so long!" Setting its sights on the other shamans, it smiled evilly. "And I want more!"

The goblins turned tail and stumbled over each other as they tried to escape, but it was no use. The elemental flew from one to the other, engulfing each one in flames until the chamber was empty.

The fire elemental closed its eyes and let out a satisfied sigh, like a king after completing a feast. It hovered in the center of the chamber while the soft crackling of fire issued from its body.

Without warning, the fire elemental's eyes snapped open. It looked directly at Kay and roared, "Ah! There's more!"

Kay realized his mistake too late. In looking for Krellia, he had leaned out from the archway and exposed himself to the fire elemental. Now the creature stared at him with the same hunger in its fiery eyes as when it consumed the goblins. Kay's mouth went dry. He thought about every spell he knew; however, none came to mind that could combat such a foe. *The Ring of Carnac was supposed to seal the prison*, Kay thought desperately. *Now what do we do?*

He glanced at Jerra and watched in shocked disbelief as she stepped out from behind the archway and stood in full view of the elemental.

Bibo tugged at her leg in an attempt to stop her, but the young healer simply dragged the telok along. Jerra had a faraway look in her eyes, and she raised her ring-laden hand.

"Jerra, no!" Kay cried.

The fire elemental turned his attention to the young girl who opposed him. A look of curiosity crossed its flamed face. It did not advance.

"Mmmm," the creature hummed. "What's this?" The fire elemental swayed hypnotically from side to side. "Like the waters of an entire ocean condensed into a single drop. Very powerful indeed."

The fire elemental slowly advanced toward the companions. "A power that once sealed me in this prison—this tomb. A power that could have thwarted the efforts of the goblins." Its face contorted into an evil smile. "If it had arrived in time."

The elemental grew in size until its head almost scraped the ceiling. Waves of heat blasted the companions, causing heavy beads of sweat to drip down their foreheads.

"It could have consumed us just as it did the goblins," Kay whispered to Felix. "I think the ring is buying us some time."

"Oh great," Felix snapped back. "We get an extra thirty seconds to live before we're fricasseed. Lucky us."

Without warning, the elemental suddenly lunged forward with blinding speed. There was no time to go for his sword. No time for a spell. No time for anything.

Chapter 59

A blinding beam of cool-blue light surged from the ring and struck the fire elemental full in the chest. The creature flew back with a furious roar, ebbing some of its tremendous heat. The other companions breathed a collective sigh of relief, while Jerra stood resolutely with her left hand clenched into a fist.

Kay ran to her side. "It's working. You're pushing it back!"

"Yeah, but now what?" Jerra asked. "I can't stay like this forever."

Kay looked into the chamber and saw that Jerra was all too right. The blue beam was still blasting the elemental, but the creature surged with power and pushed forward.

Closer and closer it moved. Waves of heat, fear, and desperation crashed into the companions. Soon it would be upon them, and they would share in the shamans' fate.

"We must fall back!" Deriah urged.

"You go," Jerra said. "I'll hold it off as long as I can."

"We're not leaving without you!" Kay protested.

"You don't understand," Jerra responded. "Something is holding me to the floor. I can't move my arm either."

"Bibo help," the telok said and attempted to lift one of Jerra's legs. Trying as boldly as he could, Bibo had to admit defeat. "Stuck to floor," he said sadly.

The heat and smell of sulfur were becoming unbearable.

"This is ridiculous!" Kay shouted. "You can't stay here alone!" He grabbed her outstretched arm forcefully, but it was like trying to bend an iron bar.

"Kay, go!" Jerra insisted.

"Take off the ring!" Kay said, reaching for her hand. As he tried to pry her fingers apart, the beam from the Ring of Carnac pulsed and grew brighter. Kay instinctively pulled his hand away in surprise, but saw that the fire elemental had halted its forward progress.

"It needs more power," Kay said in awe. "Power from us." He wrapped his hand around Jerra's. The beam intensified, but the fire elemental soon recovered and approached with a greater conviction.

Kay felt Deriah's soft, elven skin envelope his hand as she joined him and Jerra. Next came Bibo's furry paw. The elemental was slowed, but it still pressed on.

"It's not enough," Kay despaired. "Felix, add your hand. Felix?"

The sprite was nowhere to be seen.

"Felix! Felix!" Kay screamed, desperately turning his head in all directions but not daring to take his hand off Jerra's.

Kay was dumbfounded. Had Felix deserted them? They had been through so much together. Why would he leave now when their need was greatest?

"No more friends to help," the fire elemental said with burning, mocking words. Its eyes grew with the desire to consume. Tongues of flame spurted out from the fire elemental and landed all about. Soon they would be within its deadly reach.

Kay concentrated with all his might, trying to send as much of his energy into the ring as possible, but it was no use. He felt the tenseness of Jerra's hand beneath his. "Jerra, I'm sorry I gave you all that grief about Seamus," Kay blurted out.

"This is hardly the time to be worrying about that," Jerra responded through clenched teeth. Heavy beads of sweat rolled down her face, pasting her bangs to her forehead. She must have been going through an awful strain with her body acting as the conduit for the ring's power.

"Why do you fight me?" the fire elemental boomed. Its face twisted into an evil sneer. "Did you really think a little trinket like that could thwart my power?" It towered over the companions and let out a tremendous roar.

Kay braced himself for the inevitable.

Chapter 60

NOTHING but fire filled Kay's vision. This was not the end that he had imagined. They were supposed to seal the elemental's prison and save the day. Not this. The intense heat seared his flesh, causing the exposed skin on his hands and face to redden and blister. It was like being roasted alive.

"I didn't know there was going to be a barbeque," a familiar voice chirped.

Felix landed on the top of the companions' stacked hands. The beam from the ring intensified, but only a little.

"Felix...where...were you?" Kay choked out. "It's too late...You should go."

"Not when I've brought all these reinforcements," the sprite responded. "Come on in!" he shouted to someone over Kay's shoulder. "The party's just getting hot!"

An intense buzzing filled the air, and the tunnel grew bright with fairy light.

A brownie scuttled up Deriah's leg and hopped onto her outstretched arm. "Reporting for duty!" the fairy said with a miniature salute.

"The fairies," Deriah said in awe.

Breena added her hand to the stack, and it wasn't long before a teetering tower of tiny hands piled almost to the top of the archway.

"It's working!" Jerra cried in relief. "The elemental is shrinking!"

The fire elemental let forth a frustrated bellow. It tried to push back against the power of the ring, but it was no use. Smaller and smaller the elemental shrank, and its body began to lose its shape. The arms retreated into its torso, and its head wobbled and contorted like a bowl of mutant jelly. Soon, only a red orb floated above the floor, encased in the beam of watery light.

"Now what?" Kay asked. He wished that Alamin were there; he would know what to do.

"Jerra, can you move yet?" Deriah asked.

Jerra struggled and twisted. She shook her head, admitting defeat.

"Guide it over the hole in the center of the room," Deriah suggested. "That must be where its prison was."

"But the goblins have broken the seal," Kay said, noting the shattered circle of stone that lay next to the hole.

"We have to try something," Jerra said.

The orb moved to the center of the circular chamber and hovered over the elemental's former prison.

The hole began to glow with a green light. The ground vibrated, and dust and small pebbles fell from the ceiling.

"Lower it in," Deriah suggested.

Jerra guided the orb past the rim of the hole. As soon as it went below the rim, the floor immediately closed around it like a lizard snatching its prey.

The beam from the Ring of Carnac disappeared. Kay felt Jerra's body go slack, and he caught her just before she crumpled to the floor. The fairies' tower collapsed, and the tiny creatures scattered all about.

The broken seal still lay shattered next to where the elemental disappeared. No new seal took its place. The stones on the floor were plain and unadorned.

"What just happened?" Kay asked. "Is it imprisoned? How do we seal it off?"

The floor at the center of the chamber began to glow green again.

"Oh no!" Bibo cried. "It coming back!"

"Jerra, the ring!" Kay cried urgently.

Jerra raised her hand groggily and aimed the ring at the center of the chamber. No beam emitted from the ring this time; its stone was dull and lifeless.

"Could it be out of juice?" Felix suggested.

The companions stared helplessly as the opening in the floor grew wider. A shadowy hand crested the rim. Then another. A small, dark figure pulled itself up from the hole and stood at the edge, its stocky body haloed by the green glow. With slow but sure strides, it approached the companions. Heavy reverberations echoed throughout the chamber with each step it took.

"What is it?" Kay asked.

"I don't know," Deriah answered, readying her sword.

"Oh, put that down," a deep voice said dismissively. "I mean you no harm."

As the creature neared the companions, its features became more defined. The little man was made entirely of rock! Even its eyebrows, which moved up and down as it spoke, were made of stone.

"We usually don't intervene like this. But desperate times...well, you know the rest," the creature said with a rocky shrug of his shoulders.

"Who's the 'we' that you're talking about?" Felix asked.

The stone man looked taken aback. "Why, we earth elementals, of course," he replied with outstretched arms. "Guardians of life and all that."

The creature flicked his thumb over his shoulder. "That fire elemental was an especially bad one. He would have turned the whole surface to ash and cinder. Life would have been most unpleasant, and in many cases...nonexistent. Though we earth elementals can exist as molten lava, it's certainly not the guise we prefer."

"Did you seal the prison?" Kay asked.

The elemental's face scrunched up onto a stony grimace. "And risk having this happen again? Oh no. My brothers and I sent him back to the bowels of our world where the fires forever burn, and his hunger and thirst for them will always be satisfied. It is where his kind are supposed to live and dwell."

"Do we really need his kind?" Kay ventured to ask.

"Would you like to live on a cold, lifeless rock?" the elemental questioned.

"No," Kay answered.

"Then, yes, we need his kind," the elemental stated simply.

"Thank you for what you have done," Jerra said. "I guess this wasn't enough." She fingered the aquamarine ring and massaged her raw and cracked skin.

"Nothing is enough all by itself," the elemental replied. "But don't discount that ring yet. There's one more piece to the puzzle." He gestured to the center of the chamber. "Although no longer a prison, that is still a portal to the fire elementals' realm. Come with me, my dear."

"I'm going too," Kay said, stepping forward.

"As you wish," the elemental replied with a blink.

Was it Kay's imagination, or did he see a sudden flash of icy-blue in those stone-cold eyes?

He looked again, but it was gone.

"We're all coming," Deriah announced and beckoned the group to follow.

The stone man led Jerra and the others to the center of the room. Heat still radiated from the glowing green disc on the floor.

"Here. Hold the ring over this spot," the elemental directed, taking Jerra gently by the hand.

She extended her arm, and the gem began to glow again. This time, no beam shot out from it. Rather, the stone appeared to melt. It lost its definition until it resembled a tiny, sparkling drop of water held in place by the ring's prongs. The drop wobbled and, with a final glistening glow, cascaded over Jerra's finger.

The brilliant-blue drop landed in the center of the green disc. It glowed and swirled with the combination of colors and magic. Faster and faster they went, creating a tiny whirlpool on the floor. The faster the colors swirled, the smaller the disc became. It finally winked out, and the companions were left standing in a silent circle in the ruined tower.

The earth elemental clapped his hands together with a mighty thud and smiled at those around him. "Well, I'm done here," he said.

The sound of stone grating upon stone echoed through the chamber as he turned and walked away. With each step, the earth elemental sank into the floor of the chamber, as if wading into the ocean. When he was waist deep, he looked back.

"Oh, I almost forgot," the elemental rumbled. "I called in a favor to an air elemental friend of mine. She's whipping up a sandstorm to disperse the goblins. When the wind dies down, you should be free to go."

The elemental turned away once more. Deeper and deeper he went until his head disappeared underneath the stone tiles.

The wind began to howl outside the ancient stone tower while the companions and fairies slumped down to rest on the cool stones. Jerra was too weak after her experience with the ring to use her healing powers, so she applied a salve to ease the burns on everyone's skin. Kay used his knife to cut away the singed ends of fur that covered Bibo's body while trying to ignore the stench of burnt hair.

In contrast to the storm outside, the occupants of the tower remained silent, wrapped up in their own thoughts and reflections. Everyone, that is, except for Felix and Breena. The two fairies had been arguing steadily ever since the earth elemental departed.

"You're unbelievable," Breena said with folded arms. "I should have let the fire elemental singe your sorry behind."

Felix looked at her innocently. "I was giving you a compliment."

"A compliment?" she screeched. "By saying that you finally encountered a bigger hothead?"

"Sure. The fire elemental *is* a bigger hothead than you," the sprite replied. "Although that expression on your face is making me reconsider."

For his part, Kay's thoughts kept revolving back to Jerra. They had been at odds for most of the journey. Hopefully, things would go back to the way they were when they returned to Marco's Keep. They would resume their studies and...and what? Something was different. He looked at Jerra and fruitlessly attempted to sort out the barrage of feelings that flowed through him.

Chapter 61

A sweltering and agitated wind whisked across the Desert Waste. Small dust devils formed in its wake and then slid across the sand until they disappeared over the horizon or petered out in lifeless tendrils.

A crumbled tower grabbed the wind's attention. It had passed this spot many times, but something seemed different. An ancient power had always radiated from the ruins, but now…

Gone, thought the wind.

Kicking up grains of sand in the deserted encampment that surrounded the tower, the desert wind hastened on with renewed energy. Nothing usually changed in the Desert Waste. It was a place where time stood still; sand dunes might erode in one spot and form in another, but that was it.

Something is afoot, the wind mused.

The wind soared higher to take stock of the land. It set its course to the east; the creatures and inhabitants to the east were the only ones who could have caused this. Those far to the west kept to themselves; it did not make sense to cross the Jagged Mountains only to choke on the dry desert sand.

Swiftly, the wind flew, zigzagging so as not to miss a single clue.

Many tracks…goblins. Retreating?

The trail led northeast toward the cold, mountainous frontier. The wind followed this route for a while until the tracks disappeared into a rocky outcropping.

Ah, the caves. No place for me. The wind shunned going underground where it would quickly be snuffed out and lifeless.

The wind looped and twirled, setting a new course to the south. It spied a small group of wanderers where the desert met the grasslands. Two of them were gesturing wildly, apparently having some sort of argument.

Typical humans, the wind thought and continued on its journey.

The hot breeze was about to meander its way back to its desert home when it caught the scent of something a little farther to the south. Staying low to the ground, the wind brushed across the patches of gray grass that desperately clung to life in the arid, dusty soil.

A lone figure trudged along a crooked path. It resembled a goblin, but it did not have the essence of a goblin.

Strange, the wind thought and dove in for a closer look.

The goblin appeared as if it had been through a war or battle of some sort. Its clothes were ripped and tattered—like someone threw a bundle of rags at the creature, and the pieces landed haphazardly. Its filthy cloak fluttered in the breeze, and it fingered a battered dagger in its claws. Dark and treacherous thoughts radiated from the creature's innermost being while it muttered the same thing over and over again.

"Krellia...Krellia...Krellia..."

***

The journey out of the Desert Waste took longer than Kay had anticipated. The sand sucked at his feet, making each step arduous, and the heat was more merciless than he remembered. Maybe the urgency of the journey had taken away some of the sting of the desert when he and his companions were trying to reach the tower. Now there were no goblins to face, no burden on their shoulders—only the oppressive heat and never-ending sand.

"Wow!" Felix exclaimed. "An earth elemental and a fire elemental! You don't see those every day."

Kay hummed thoughtfully.

"What's up with you?" Felix asked.

"When was the last time you saw an earth elemental?" Kay demanded.

"Well...never. That's why it was so cool!" Felix responded excitedly. The fairies had a special affection for earth elementals. They revered the keepers and growers of life in the forest.

"So you don't know what an earth elemental really looks like," Kay pressed.

"Of course I do!" Felix answered with a confused expression carved on his tiny face. "We *all* do now. Or did you hit your head in there in addition to being roasted alive?"

"We saw what he wanted us to see," Kay responded.

"He who?"

"The earth elemental, or whoever was disguised as an earth elemental."

Felix was, for once, at a loss for words. He gave Kay a queer look and said, "You've been hanging around Alamin too much."

"Or not enough," Kay mused. "I've got so many questions for him."

After what seemed ages, a new scent drifted on the dry desert breeze. Kay took a deep breath. It spoke of life, coolness, and water. "Do you smell that?" Kay asked Felix.

The sprite sniffed the air. "Yep. Pollen...grass...and buffalo poop," he answered dryly. "Lovely."

"What's up with you? Why are you in such a bad mood?"

"I'm actually in a very good mood. This is just how I express myself," the sprite answered. He sighed and looked off to the sky.

Felix's gaze had kept straying to the horizon ever since the fairy squadron departed.

Kay understood. "You miss Breena don't you," he prodded.

Felix's face wrinkled up. "What? Who, me? Miss her? No way! No how!" He paused. "Well...okay...maybe just a little."

"I don't understand how you can miss her so much," Kay said. "All the two of you did was argue."

Felix sighed. "Yes, but she argued so exquisitely."

It wasn't long before tiny blades of grass began shooting through the cracked, parched soil. The air felt fresher and cooler, and the companions responded with renewed vigor; they took longer and more confident strides on the solid ground of the outer grasslands.

Jerra had been especially quiet during their trek through the desert, so Kay decided to open up the conversation. "I can't wait until we reach the prairie," Kay said good-naturedly.

"Why? So you can go visit your fish friend in Greenfern Lake?" Jerra asked pointedly.

"Huh?" Kay responded in confusion.

"Coral," Jerra answered with a singsong sneer and a mock giggle in imitation of the mermaid.

"You mean Laurel," Kay corrected. *Why is she so cranky?* he wondered.

"Whatever," Jerra responded in a huff and picked up her pace to walk beside Deriah.

"What about you and goblin boy?" Kay called after her.

"That went well," Felix whispered with a smirk.

Deriah came to an abrupt halt and signaled everyone to crouch down. "Someone or something is approaching," she said, gesturing to the open grasses ahead of them.

Kay squinted into the rising sun. His eyes drooped, and exhaustion filled his entire body. They had not slept in over a day, and he thought that the elf might be seeing things that just weren't there.

"I don't see...wait...yes!" Kay whispered. "Could it be a goblin?"

"No," Deriah said with a shake of her head. "The gait is definitely human. If I didn't know better, I'd say it was—"

"Alamin!" Bibo exclaimed, finishing her sentence. The telok sprang up from the cover of the tall grasses and bounded across the prairie.

Kay raced after Bibo. He quickly passed and outdistanced the telok. Waves of relief spread across his entire being as he clasped his master's hand.

"Am I glad to see you," Kay said with a smile. "But you're a little late."

Alamin attempted to answer but was interrupted by a wide yawn. "Couldn't be helped," he finally said. "I see you needed the sword and gauntlets," he added, motioning to the amulet around Kay's neck. "I told Deriah to give them to you only as a last resort."

"They came in handy," Kay said with a smile as he unclasped the amulet and handed it to Alamin. "How did Deriah get it anyway? I thought King Roland was keeping this in his armory."

Alamin took the amulet and placed it in his spell-component bag. "Well, yes, he did," Alamin admitted with an impish twinkle in his eye. "The night we left Carival, I took a page out of Felix's book and 'borrowed' it."

Once Bibo and the others had arrived and gathered around, Alamin asked, "So, what did I miss?" He then broke into a wide yawn. "Oh, excuse me. That always happens…" He stopped to yawn again. "…after a wizard's sleep."

The companions spoke excitedly about everything that had happened since Alamin's departure from the *Albatross*.

"Don't forget to tell him about our newest goblin," Kay chided Jerra.

Jerra gave him a seething look and snapped back, "How about your adventures with fish face?"

The two argued back and forth, continually talking over each other.

Alamin looked to Deriah and rolled his eyes. "How long has this been going on?"

"On and off since I joined them," the elf answered with a disapproving shake of her head.

Felix sighed. "It's going to be a long trip home."

***

"Next stop, Eaglewood," Alamin announced after breakfast one morning. He then yawned heavily.

Home. Jerra sighed inwardly. She thought of her parents—how they granted her the power to heal through her birthright and the way they taught her to nourish that power.

They were good parents, she thought happily. This time, she didn't think of the goblins and her parents' deaths, but rather their life and the love they gave her. The feelings were overwhelming, and a warmth spread over her like she hadn't known before. Her mother and father were there with her. They would always be there. It was not their death that she needed to dwell on, but rather the treasure of their lives.

Jerra closed her eyes and smiled.

A furry hand took hers and guided her as she walked. Jerra continued a long while in this manner, oblivious to the others and the conversations around her. By the time she opened her eyes and looked about, they were almost within sight of the lakeside village—the place she called, and would forever consider, *home*.

A stray thought nagged at Jerra. Thanking Bibo, she let go of his hand and sped up to walk alongside Alamin and Strapper.

The wizard smiled, acknowledging her presence.

Jerra took a deep breath and asked, "Can we talk?"

"Certainly, my dear," Alamin replied. "What can I do for you?"

She didn't know how else to ask, so she just blurted it out. "Why did you have me carry the ring? Why not Kay?"

"Why *not* you?" the wizard said, answering her question with a question.

"Well…" She honestly couldn't come up with a satisfactory answer.

Alamin smiled. "You have a destiny to fulfill, just as Kay does. You cannot simply ride on his coattails. You are meant for greatness, but whether your paths will continue to intertwine or be separate is yet to be seen."

"Separate?" Jerra asked with concern. As much as Kay aggravated her at times, she couldn't imagine life without her best friend.

"We never know what this life will bring us," the wizard said with a nonchalant shrug.

"You can say that again," Jerra agreed.

"Is there anything else that you would like to discuss? Any new spells that you have been experimenting with?" Alamin asked with a raised eyebrow.

Jerra felt her face flush with embarrassment.

"So you know…" she said hesitantly.

Alamin nodded. "Magic can be destructive in many ways. You have to be careful with your powers."

"I lost control. I shouldn't have done it," Jerra said.

"But you did."

"I can fix it. I'll change him back," Jerra asserted.

Alamin took a deep breath. "It's not that easy. You have set him on a new path."

"He created his own path," Jerra said defensively.

"That may be, but you altered it. Now we must face the consequences."

Clearing his throat, Alamin abruptly changed the subject. "Oh well, enough of this heavy talk for today. It's been quite a while since I've visited Eaglewood. Do the villagers still like fireworks?"

Strapper barked in protest.

"Don't worry, Strap," Alamin said with a reassuring pat on the dog's head. "There's a lake nearby."

Epilogue

"A N earth elemental? Really?" Asok asked incredulously in the shadow of the ruined tower. "Do you even know what an earth elemental looks like?"

"Nope." Zelok shrugged and grabbed a fistful of desert sand. He watched it flow out the bottom of his hand. "But neither do they," he added with a wink.

Asok sulked. "You didn't even give me credit for that sandstorm."

Zelok patted his friend on the shoulder and gave him a sympathetic smile. "There will come a time when we will reveal ourselves, but for now, we must remain silent observers."

"You mean blatant meddlers," Asok shot back. "We were not supposed to help. You know the rules."

"Rules were meant to be broken," Zelok responded.

"And you revealed yourself to them in that cave," Asok accused.

"Only to the boy," Zelok corrected.

"Still, he'll ask questions."

"Alamin will have to tell him of us someday."

"Yes, someday—but not now." Asok threw his hands up in exasperation. "This is all your fault!"

"Really? Am I the one who invaded Gallard's dreams?" Zelok asked pointedly.

"Oh, I didn't know you knew about that," Asok replied sheepishly. A concerned expression clouded his face. "What will the Grand Master say when we return?" he wondered with more than a little fear in his voice.

"Hopefully, he will thank us for helping save the world from certain destruction," Zelok said, standing proudly with his arm raised and his index finger pointed high.

Asok gave Zelok a wry look.

"You're right," Zelok admitted with slumped shoulders. "We're in trouble. I think we've got six months of monitoring polar bears in our future."

"Not the northern outpost again!" Asok cried.

"It's better than this desert," Zelok contested. He rubbed the granules of sand from his hands. "Well, time to go," he added briskly.

The wizard stepped forward and disappeared into a sand dune.

"Hey, wait for me!" Asok called after him.

He thought of his home that lay far to the west—the Charmed Lands—and was gone.

CPSIA information can be obtained at www.ICGtesting.com
Printed in the USA
BVOW08s0550280916

463525BV00029B/22/P